C7035

D1387699

THE INMATE

ALSO BY SEBASTIAN FITZEK

The Package
Passenger 23
Seat 7A
The Soul Breaker
Amok
Walk Me Home

SEBASTIAN FITZEK

THE INMATE

Translated from the German
by Jamie Bulloch

HEAD
of ZEUS

An Aries Book

First published in Germany as *Der Insasse* in 2018 by Droemer Knaur

First published in the UK in 2023 by Head of Zeus Ltd,
part of Bloomsbury Publishing Plc

9 7 5 3 1 2 4 6 8

A catalogue record for this book is available from the British Library.

ISBN (HB): 9781804542323
ISBN (XTPB): 9781804542330
ISBN (E): 9781804542316

Cover design: Ben Prior

Printed and bound in Great Britain by
CPI Group (UK) Ltd, Croydon CR0 4YY

I have been happy, tho' in a dream.
I have been happy.

Edgar Allan Poe, 'Dreams'

1

Why's it so chilly?

Given that Myriam was on the threshold of hell, it felt far too cold down here in the windowless cellar, with its damp brick walls to which black mould clung like cancer to the bronchia of a smoker's lungs.

'Watch out,' the policeman said, pointing to her head. She had to duck to avoid hitting a sewer pipe as she stepped into the boiler room, even though Myriam was only five foot five. Unlike Tramnitz, who looked far too attractive for this horrific occasion. Broad shoulders, high forehead, slim but muscular. Tailor-made for the front cover of the Berlin Police calendar, if such a thing existed. Down here, however, dust and spiderwebs got caught in his blond 'I haven't had a wink of sleep again' hair that brushed tightly against the cellar ceiling. The little house on the edge of the Grunewald was built in the 1920s. People here must have been shorter then.

And surely not as evil as the last resident of this place. Or were they?

Myriam swallowed and tried to recall the first name of the friendly officer who had picked her up and driven her out here.

Not that it mattered. She was just attempting to distract herself. But no benign thoughts would form in her mind. Not here in a cellar that reeked of blood, urine and fear.

And death.

Tramnitz took down the red-and-white police tape that Forensics had stuck in an 'X' over the open doorframe. It said POLICE LINE in black letters at regular intervals.

But Myriam read: 'DO NOT CROSS! DO NOT LOOK INSIDE!'

'Listen,' the inspector said, nervously rubbing his three-day stubble. In the light of the dusty cellar lamp he looked as if he were suffering from jaundice. 'We really shouldn't be here.'

Myriam tried to nod and shake her head at the same time (*No*, we shouldn't. But: *Yes*, I have to do this), with the result that her upper body gave a curious twitch.

'But I want to see *it*.'

She said *it* as if it were an object. She couldn't bring herself to call the horror by its real name, by *her* name.

'I'm exceeding my authority here. The crime scene is still sealed off, and what you're going to see...'

'It can't be worse than the images inside my head,' Myriam said, barely audibly. 'Please, I need to see this with my own eyes.'

'Okay, but watch out,' the policeman said a second time, now pointing at the steps in front of them. The small wooden staircase creaked beneath her trainers. Tramnitz pushed aside an opaque plastic tarpaulin, like a shower curtain. Behind lay a sort of antechamber that the person living here had probably used as a dressing room or cloakroom, and which led through a fire door into hell.

A delivery man's uniform hung neatly on a hanger from some copper piping. Beside it stood a trolley with packages.

'So it was...' Myriam began.

Tramnitz nodded. He blinked as if some of the dust mingling with the sticky air down here had caught in his eye. 'Your suspicion was correct.'

Good God.

Unable to breathe, Myriam grabbed her throat; her mouth was parched.

When, after several weeks, the police were still unable to find a single trace of Laura, Myriam had embarked on the search for her daughter herself. She questioned all the neighbours again; everyone who worked in the shops around the Schweizer Viertel playground where the girl had last been seen.

It was an elderly tenant with mild dementia, whose statement hadn't been taken seriously – or followed up – no doubt because she was very quick to lose the thread and start wallowing in memories. Anyway, on the day that Laura went missing this woman claimed to have seen a delivery man. She said she felt sorry watching him struggle on his own with all the packages he had to take back to his DHL van because nobody in the apartment block in Altdorfer Strasse was at home. Then her credibility faded as she digressed, going on about how the man reminded her of her nephew.

And yet she had offered up the most important clue of all!

'He was indeed disguised as a delivery man,' Tramnitz said, gently nudging with his foot a 1.5-metre-high pile of packages on a trolley by the wall. To her surprise, and then to her horror, the pile toppled to the floor, even though the policeman had barely touched it.

'Papier mâché,' Tramnitz said. 'Hollow.'

An empty box, just for show.

3

One metre fifty high.

Enough space for a seven-year-old.

'Laura,' Myriam groaned. 'My baby. What did he do to her?'

'He drugged Laura, hid her inside this dummy package and pushed her back to his van undetected. Come with me.'

Tramnitz's strong hands pushed open the fire door, which had an old Sound & Drumland sticker on it. Could this monster possibly be a music fan?

Like Laura?

Myriam couldn't help thinking of the piano she'd bought only last summer and which had stood unbearably silent in the sitting room for the past few weeks. Down here it was unbearably loud. Here, in the square cellar room she was just entering, Myriam thought she could hear her daughter screaming. An echo of the memory that resounded from the corpse-grey walls and tiled floor with the runoff in its centre. Above them dangled a bare bulb, speckled with white paint, which seemed to give off more shadows than light.

'What's that?' Myriam rasped, pointing to the crate by the wall in front of them.

Tramnitz scratched the back of his shaven neck and peered at the angular wooden box. It sat on a metal table that looked like a pathologist's mortuary slab. The crate was made from brown compressed wood, around a metre and a half long and thirty centimetres wide. In the side facing them, two circular holes, around twenty centimetres in diameter, were cut out about a hand's width from one another. They were covered with a non-transparent film, as was the top of the crate, which meant that Myriam couldn't see what was inside.

'It's an incubator,' Tramnitz said, turning the hell of the

cellar even colder. Myriam felt sick when she realised that the holes were for putting your hands in to touch whatever was concealed behind the walls of the 'incubator'.

'What did he do to her? What on earth did he do to my baby?' she asked Tramnitz without looking at him.

'For many years he worked in a neonatal unit before being fired for indecent behaviour. He never got over it and so set up his own baby unit down here.'

'To do what?'

Myriam took a step closer, put her hand out to tear off the film, but was shaking too badly. She couldn't do it. As if a magnetic field around the 'incubator' were repelling her fingers ever more forcefully the closer she came to it.

Tramnitz came up from behind, laid his hands gently on her shoulders and cleared his throat. 'Is this what you really want?'

Rather than running away, screaming, she nodded.

When the officer ripped off the plastic film from the 'incubator', Myriam couldn't close her eyes quickly enough. She had glimpsed it, and the horrifying image imprinted itself on her mind like a branding iron would an animal's skin.

'Laura,' she gasped, because there could not be any doubt. Although the body was covered with several layers of odour-absorbing cat litter, and maggots were already writhing beneath the wide-open eyes, Myriam had recognised her daughter by the dimple on her chin, the mole beside her right eyebrow and by the princess clasp taming her wayward fringe.

'He cared for her.'

'What?' Myriam's mind was miles away from all reality, adrift on an ocean of pain and mental agony. The policeman's words swept into her consciousness as if from another dimension… and they made no sense.

'He gave her food, medicine, warmth. And love.'

'Love?'

Myriam wondered if she'd lost her marbles.

She turned and looked up at Tramnitz. Blurred in the veil of her tears was the handsome, symmetrical face of the police officer, as if behind a wall of rain.

To her horror he began to chuckle. 'Oh, this is much better than I'd hoped for. The expression on your face!'

At a stroke Myriam felt certain that God no longer existed. Just her, Laura's body and the devil before her.

'You're not a policeman,' Myriam was going to scream. *'It was you! You abducted my baby, then tortured and murdered her!'*

But none of these words issued from her lips because an axe had been driven squarely between her eyes.

The last thing Myriam heard in this life was a painful, splintering sound, as if an entire forest of bone-dry branches were snapping in her very ears, intermingled with the nauseating laughter from Guido Tramnitz as he struck. Again and again. And again.

Until everything around him and Myriam was one red mist, then a final, violent pain. Then nothing. Not even black.

2

TILL BERKHOFF

The baby was suffocating, but the bald guy didn't care.

He raised his fist and slammed it down on Till's bonnet as if it were Thor's hammer. 'Move your fucking vehicle out of the way. This is a one-way street!'

'Keep pushing. Three times, like I said. You'll do it,' Till said, getting out of his ambulance.

He wasn't talking to the hulk before him on the road, whose tracksuit was three sizes too small for the muscles on his body, but to the mother on the phone who was about to hyperventilate with panic.

She'd made the emergency call five minutes ago. Ever since, Till had been trying to guide her remotely. 'Now try mouth-to-mouth again. We're almost there.'

Assuming Mr Boxing Boots finally lets us through.

They were about four hundred metres as the crow flies from the woman and they'd taken the shortcut via Eichkatzweg to avoid an accident on Eichkampfstrasse. But because this idiot with his SUV was refusing to move out of the way, they couldn't get the ambulance any further down the narrow one-way street. The lane didn't even have a pavement.

And evidently the oik was prepared to use force to get the ambulance to reverse out.

'I'm only going to say it once more, then I'll let my hands do the talking and it's not applause we're talking about – get me?' The powerhouse shot a brief glance back at his car in which a red-haired skeleton was making up her inflatable lips. 'I'm in a hurry and you're in the fucking way.'

Till breathed deeply and took the mobile briefly from his ear. 'Listen, what does this look like to you?' he said.

He pointed to the ambulance the idiot had just slapped and the flashing lights on the roof, rotating in silence.

'I need to get to Dauerwaldweg and I'm certainly not going to reverse through the eye of a needle just so you can make it to the gym on time.'

It was not uncommon for pedestrians to complain when emergency vehicles double-parked, but even by Berlin standards this was a whole new ball game. *Although.* Only yesterday there had been a note on the windscreen in Lankwitz: *'Just because you save people's lives doesn't give you the right to pollute our air with your emissions. Next time switch off the engine while you go and stretcher someone from a house!'*

Quite clearly it hadn't occurred to the irate individual that this would have also meant switching off the life-sustaining equipment for the stroke patient. Either that or they couldn't care less. Just like this meathead couldn't give a shit about the suffocating baby.

'Hello? Are you still there?' Till heard the mother call out anxiously as Baldy came closer.

He held the mobile more tightly to his ear. 'Yes, yes, I'm still here. Keep going with the mouth-to-mouth resuscitation!'

'She's turning blue. Christ. I think she's, she's...'

'Just leave it,' Till's partner called out from behind. Aram had already got out with the medical case. 'You reverse out and I'll run there.'

'That's it,' Baldy laughed, 'listen to your darkie mate. Now, reverse, sharpish!'

There it was again, that tingling in his fingers. The warning signal Till's brain sent out when he was on the verge of doing something wrong. Till couldn't tell whether it was because the oik had insulted his Kurdish partner, or whether he was wound up enough anyway. In any event, the life of a six-month-old was at stake. The last time he'd felt this pinprick-like sensation in his fingertips was when he'd gone to tackle a fire three weeks ago. The operation that had led to disciplinary proceedings against him.

Till was a firefighter, a member of the rescue team. A crew manager with paramedic training. Actually he ought not to be here in Westend playing the medic, but somewhere on the front line, hurrying into a burning building with breathing apparatus and pickaxe.

Actually.

'*Over-impulsive behaviour. Potential risk to colleagues,*' it said in the psychological report that had got him transferred. A demotion. Paramedic in south-west Berlin.

And all of it down to a stupid cat. But what should he have done? The old granny had cried bitterly, telling him that her dear pussy was all she had left in the world, so he'd gone back into the flames and up to her apartment. In the end a colleague had to come to his aid.

Just before Till had run into the fire, he'd felt the tingling in his fingers. The warning signal: don't screw up again. *This time*, he told himself now, *I'm going to heed it.*

Quite apart from the fact that Till had no time for this nonsense, Mr Boxing Boots was clearly a different class of fighter. It wasn't that Till was short and weedy, but he had an unerring eye for street fighters and martial artists. And the man opposite looked far superior in these disciplines.

Okay, discretion is the better part of valour, Till sighed in the face of the oik's scornful laughter.

He got back into the ambulance and started the engine with tingling hands. Put the vehicle into gear and tried to suppress his fury.

He waited until the idiot was back in his SUV.

Then he rammed his foot down.

Half a second later he'd hit the bonnet. Although the impact wasn't severe enough to trigger the airbags, the hulk hadn't yet fastened his belt and so crashed his head against the steering wheel.

The redhead screamed so loudly that Till could hear her even through two windscreens and against the scrunching of tyres on asphalt and the shattering of glass, plastic and chrome, as she was shoved backwards along with the car.

A driveway appeared soon afterwards on the left and Till wrenched the steering wheel while putting his foot down again to push the battered SUV to the side with spinning wheels, damaging another two parked cars in the process. But finally the way was clear and Till had to slam on the brakes to avoid shooting like an arrow into Alte Allee.

He stopped, opened the door and briefly turned around to Aram, who was standing in the road as if paralysed by shock beside the write-off of the SUV in the driveway. The hulk was attempting to clamber out, his nose broken and blood streaming down his face. He looked totally spaced out.

'The baby first,' Till called out to his partner. 'The nose can wait.'

3

Eight hours later

'I want to show you something,' he heard him stammer. Half whispering, half weeping.

Till got a fright because once again Max had crept up on him like an elite soldier. As always, he'd left the door to his attic study open. Till hated closed rooms as much as he adored his six-year-old son, who had the knack of being able to hover up these stairs in silence.

'What's wrong, little one?'

Till closed his laptop on which he'd drafted his statement, even though it wasn't worth the effort. The facts of the matter were clear; what was there for him to tell the investigation commission?

Yes, he'd flipped out once more. Yes, again his behaviour had been impulsive and unrestrained and this time there were even witnesses who would testify how he'd lost it and broken a man's nose, quite apart from the damage to four vehicles that would run to hundreds of thousands of euros. The fact that minutes later he'd saved a baby's life was beside the point. You didn't use your ambulance as a tank to get to your destination on time. Till would be fired as soon as the press cashed in on the story and depicted him as a paramedic on the rampage.

'I've finished the Millennium Falcon.'

His son carried the Lego spaceship into the study as if it were some holy relic.

'That looks brilliant,' Till said in admiration, although he wondered whether allowing Max, only six years old, to build a Star Wars space freighter armed with laser canons was responsible parenting. 'Incredible. On the box it says it's for nine years and upwards.' Even though he knew that these age guidelines were often sheer fantasy. 'If in doubt,' he'd once been told in confidence by a toy developer whose warehouse fire they'd put out, 'we say it's for older children and then the parents think they've got a little genius on their hands.'

'I can see Han Solo and… is that Chewbacca there? You've even got Luke Skywalker in the cockpit. Wow! It's all perfect. So why the tears?'

Max sniffled, then hummed and hawed. 'Mummy,' he said eventually.

'What about her?'

'She said I can't.'

'Can't what?'

'Show it to her.'

Till smiled and ruffled the thick, brown hair that Max had inherited from his mother, Ricarda. Just like the full lips and long eyelashes.

Most people, however, said that Max looked like him, which could only be down to the large, dark eyes that always appeared sad, even when the boy smiled.

'When you say "her", do you mean Anna?' Till glanced through the gallery window. Snow had fallen last night in Buckow and was now piled on the roofs of the neighbouring houses. The neighbour's daughter was Max's first love and Till had to admit that she was truly stunning. She was clever, nice and polite too; in fact the perfect daughter-in-law, were there not the slight age difference. Anna was seventeen and revising for her final school exams, while Max was still in his first year at school and wanted to be a fireman. Like his father.

Anna played along nonetheless. Max drooled over her and she allowed him to hug her now and again. She even answered his crude love letters. Whenever she saw Till she would give him a cheery 'Hello, father-in-law' and, to avoid breaking Max's little heart, she didn't tell him that the young man who occasionally came to pick her up on his motorbike was her boyfriend.

'Is Anna there then?' Till asked.

Max nodded.

'And Mummy said you shouldn't go over?'

'But I just want to show it to her.'

'Hmm, I understand. I'm sure she'd like it.'

Till wondered how he could sort this one out without getting it in the neck. His need for strife and tears had been satisfied for today. After everything that had happened, he was longing for a little harmony. In the end he settled for the middle way again, which in truth was just a lazy compromise.

'Okay, little one. This is the deal. If you clean out the litter tray I'll let you pop over to Anna's and show her the Millennium Falcon. How does that sound?'

Max nodded. Till wiped the last of the tears from his son's

cheeks and gave him a gentle pat on the bottom. 'And tell Mummy I'll be right down for a chat.'

Knowing Ricarda as he did, he wouldn't be able to talk to her for at least another hour, having once again undermined her authority with Max.

So much for wanting a little harmony.

She must have good reasons for not wanting him to go out again as it was about to get dark, even though Anna's house was just a block further up the road.

'He's playing us off against each other,' she would reproach him on a regular basis – and she was right. Till was unable to refuse his son anything, especially when he stood there crying and stared at his father like an abandoned puppy. He sometimes thought that the main reason for Ricarda's wanting another baby, their daughter Emilia, was so that Max didn't remain an only child who Till would keep spoiling excessively.

'Oh, and Max?'

His son turned around on the top step of the gallery stairs with concern in his eyes that his father might revoke the deal.

'Yes, Daddy?'

'What's the password?'

4

MAX

Ice cube, Max thought, clutching the model spacecraft.

He stepped out of the front door into a cold that perfectly suited the password he and Daddy had agreed on last summer. They'd got the idea from a policeman who had visited Max's nursery and given a warning about wicked people who wanted to hurt little children. The policeman had recommended that parents and children agree on a password that only the family knew.

Daddy had liked the idea.

They'd practised it again and again, on their walks through the forest, in the car or while they were waiting for the bus. They'd run through the scenario the policeman had talked about and which had made Max so terrified.

'What do you do if a stranger says you should go with them because they'll give you sweets or show you some little pets?'

'I say, "No!"'

'And if they say your parents said it was alright?'

'Then I ask them for the password.'

'And what is our password?'

'Ice cube.'

'Okay. So what happens if the person doesn't know the password?'

'Then I know you didn't say it was alright.'

'What do you do then?'

'Then I shout "Help!" as loudly as I can and I run away.'

'Ice cube,' Max mumbled and went carefully down the steps into the front garden.

Daddy had gritted the short path to the fence this morning, but it had snowed again since. Max mustn't slip and knock something out of place or even break the spaceship.

He was already looking forward to Anna's reaction when she saw it and the cuddle she'd give him. She always hugged him when they met. She smelled so good. Of peaches perhaps, but he couldn't be sure what she washed her hair with. At any rate it smelled different from the dinosaur jungle stuff that Mummy lathered his hair with.

Concentrating hard, switching his focus from the garden gate, which he nudged open cautiously with his foot, to the spaceship, he walked slowly, but then a voice startled him and he almost did drop the model.

'Hey, little boy!'

Max looked to the right and saw a man standing beneath a street lamp. As if obeying an order, the light came on at that very moment, as did all the others in the small, cobbled street.

'Yes?'

'Do you know where number 65 is?'

Max didn't want to be held up on his way to Anna's and, besides, it was getting colder by the second.

'What's the password?' The words just slipped out.

'Huh?'

The man looked at Max as if he'd been speaking the secret language he'd worked out with his best friend, Anton.

'Doesn't matter,' Max said after a while and decided to help the man. 'Number 65?'

The man came closer, but Max wasn't scared.

After all, the man hadn't suggested he come with him.

And the password rule could hardly apply to a delivery man trying to pull a trolley laden with packages through the snow.

5

TILL

One year later

Nothing. No sound. No footsteps. Not even a knock.

Till Berkhoff hadn't heard his brother-in-law come in the front door. And Oliver Skania wasn't exactly an elf who floated across the floor as light as a feather. Normally the criminal inspector's 120-kilogram frame stepping through a door was enough to turn heads, whether he was entering a crime scene, an interrogation room or, as here, a private house.

But right now another greying man was bellowing so loudly inside the sitting room that a helicopter could have landed in the garden without Till noticing.

'*At this very moment, ten months after his arrest, the serial killer Guido Tramnitz is being transferred to an intensive forensic psychiatry ward. The reasons for this are unknown.*'

Till had turned the volume on the television almost to maximum so as not to miss a single word of what the newsreader had to say to accompany the gruesome images. His voice had that insincere, narcissistic and dramatic tone that Till hated so much in TV presenters.

'*In January, Tramnitz was convicted of the murder of seven-year-old Laura and her mother, Myriam S. He then directed police officers to the location of another body, that of six-year-old Andreas K.*'

Crime scene pictures of a filthy cellar and a crudely made wooden crate, reminiscent of a child's coffin, alternated with school photographs of the two murdered children.

It then faded in to the photo that had turned Tramnitz into a horror superstar. Taken by a paparazzo right after the arrest: Tramnitz sitting in the police car, smiling straight into the camera.

An open, friendly face, like that of a model with the blue eyes of a newborn.

'*In court the so-called "incubator monster" was deemed to be not criminally responsible due to severe schizophrenic disorder. Tramnitz was convinced that evil powers had implanted an object inside his brain to direct his thoughts.*

'*After a trial lasting only three days, Tramnitz was taken with police escort to the Steinklinik, a high-security psychiatric hospital in the Tegel area of Berlin. At the moment it appears he is in a critical condition. So far we only have unconfirmed rumours suggesting that Tramnitz is to undergo surgery today.*'

'I hope his fellow inmates beat the crap out of him,' Skania muttered.

The television now showed the hospital and a man, who must be the doctor treating Tramnitz, responding to questions about his patient's condition with a mere shake of the head and hurrying past reporters. The caption read: *Dr V. Frieder, surgeon.*

The newsreader then said, '*The Steinklinik is equipped with an intensive care and trauma ward to deal with emergencies, as offenders with mental illnesses frequently resort to self-harm. In some patients the psychoses have physical causes and require brain surgery. Dr Volker Frieder refused to pass comment on whether this is the case with Guido Tramnitz.'*

Till recognised the name; he fancied he recalled having met the doctor once when bringing a casualty from a fire to Virchow Hospital. Later he'd heard rumours from the nurses. Supposedly Frieder had once lost a patient while under the influence of alcohol, but there had never been a trial. The relatives must have reached a settlement with the hospital, involving a large sum of money. Since then Frieder had been working as a GP and the Steinklinik must call him in for emergency operations.

'You shouldn't be watching that,' Skania said, taking off his coat.

Till glanced at the shoulder holster with pistol spanning his brother-in-law's vast chest, then he turned back to the television, but lowered the volume with the remote control.

'The Guido Tramnitz case has hit the headlines not just because of his indescribable brutality, but because criminal investigators and forensic scientists believe that the psychopathic serial killer is responsible for at least one further murder. But as Tramnitz, on the advice of his lawyer, is saying nothing, it is likely that any other crimes he may have committed will never be cleared up.'

Till flinched when the next image he saw on the screen was of a man who looked strangely familiar yet also completely unknown: himself.

The reporter had been lurking outside his apartment. Till could barely remember what state he'd been in when accosted by the press parasite who'd tortured him with tactless questions: *'Herr Berkoff, do you think that Guido Tramnitz is responsible for Max's disappearance? Is he going to confess to your son's murder? What would you do to the accused if you had the chance?'*

That last question was a blatant allusion to the reports of Till's 'impulsive, short-tempered disposition' which had cost him his job.

When Max disappeared, Till was the prime suspect to begin with. Not in the eyes of the police, but for the media, who very soon got hold of information relating to his personnel records and the disciplinary procedures in which Till was certified as capable of violent and reckless behaviour. When, for an appropriate fee, the bald hulk with the SUV gave interviews to the same rag, explaining how Till had tried to kill him with his ambulance, reporters started enquiring at Max's former kindergarten whether the little boy had ever turned up with any unusual injuries. Had the father ever been violent to his son, perhaps?

Livid, Till switched off the television set, but the images in his head refused to go away.

The street. The cobbles covered in snow. The Lego bricks. How fitting, Till thought, recalling the broken spaceship – the only thing of Max he still had in his life, now broken too.

After their son failed to come home and they discovered that he'd never got to Anna's house, they had only found individual pieces. Forensics had collected each single Lego brick and put the entire thing back together in the laboratory. To check whether the abductor had grabbed a trophy as well as Max. And indeed, one figure was missing.

Luke Skywalker.

Disappeared off the face of the earth, just like his son.

Now Ricarda had disappeared from his life too. She rightly blamed him for the tragedy even though she never uttered the words he'd been torturing himself with constantly over these past twelve months: *'If you hadn't let him go to Anna's, none of this would have happened.'*

Till got up and shook himself like a wet dog, but he couldn't rid himself of the memories. Nor of his uninvited guest who evidently wasn't bothered that Till had been ignoring him since he arrived.

'What do you want?' he hissed at last, but this didn't seem to faze Skania either. After many years in the police force, his brother-in-law was probably used to hearing bereaved persons vent their despair on criminal investigators. Either that or he considered it his familial duty to stand beside Till, even if it was only a matter of time before his sister filed for divorce. Ricarda had already moved out and taken Max's sister with her.

'Listen, there's been a development, but…'

Skania pulled on one of the folds of skin beneath his double chin, a tic of his whenever he was mulling over what to say next.

'What?'

'They've finally abandoned the search for Max.'

6

Till ran a hand through his greasy, unwashed hair. It was past one o'clock in the afternoon and he was still in his pyjamas.

'What? But my son's only been missing for a year!'

His brother-in-law nodded. 'That's true. But they're sure that Tramnitz is responsible. The modus operandi, the locality, all the details of his crimes are totally consistent with your son's case. You know how things are in the force. Do you think I like it? But there's no point in hunting for a criminal who's already serving a life sentence. We know it was him.'

Till felt as if all the air had been sucked from the room.

The finality of this news threatened to suffocate him.

'But you don't know where Max is. You *have* to keep on searching!' Till protested throatily.

Skania nodded. 'Believe me, things would be different if I were in charge. I'd leave no stone unturned in this city and keep searching till we found him. And I wouldn't care that we had neither the money nor the personnel to do it. But that's precisely the reason why I wasn't officially put in charge of the case.'

'I understand.'

As Till's wife's brother, Skania was biased. How could he

be objective in such an investigation? But not being part of the investigation team didn't mean that his colleagues cut him off from the stream of information.

'They *can't* abandon the search for Max. I need to know what happened to my son!'

'You know *what* happened to him,' Skania retorted.

Yes. He did.

Till rubbed the ten days of growth on his chin, which equally could have been a fortnight's. Ever since Max's disappearance, one day had very much been like another.

Get up. Think of Max. Get dressed. Think of Max. Despair. Think of Max. Get undressed. Think of Max. Lie down. Think of Max. Despair. Be unable to sleep. Think of Max. Get up.

And since Ricarda left him, he hadn't even had to get dressed or undressed either.

'You know what happened to the other children,' Skania said, gently trying to get through to him.

Yes. He did. A girl, a boy. Seven and six. Disguised as a delivery man, Tramnitz had abducted both children from their front gardens, drugged and taken them to his cellar where he tortured, abused and killed them in a homemade incubator. No child under his control had survived for longer than forty-eight hours. Max had disappeared well over a year ago now. Shortly after the neighbours had seen a DHL van and a delivery man in the street with a fully laden trolley.

Soon afterwards the bastard was arrested. They found the body of Myriam Schmidt, the mother of Laura who'd been abducted. Through her own detective work she'd got too close to Tramnitz, at a time when the killer had been keeping a close eye on the single mother in the wake of his crime, probably to revel in her suffering. When Tramnitz was arrested they found endless photographs and video recordings of Myriam – pinning flyers with pictures of her daughter's face to trees or wandering through the streets where her child had last been seen. She'd been right on the mark with her theory that the kidnapper had disguised himself as a postman or delivery man, which was why Tramnitz wanted to get her out of the way before she went to the police. It was only by chance that he was seen trying to dispose of her body in a boathouse on the Teltow canal, and so ultimately Myriam *was* responsible for the conviction of her daughter's killer and that of at least one other child. Under pressure Tramnitz had led the police to the bodies of Laura and a six-year-old boy from Pankow. He remained tight-lipped, however, about what had happened to Max.

'Come with me. I've got something to show you.'

Shuffling past Skania into the bathroom, Till opened the cupboard beneath the sink and took out an air-freshener spray.

'Febreze?' Skania said, confused.

'Anti-monster spray,' Till replied, and Skania was still none the wiser.

'It's a year and a half ago now. Back then I made a mistake and told Max a grisly bedtime story. He'd wanted one because he'd seen *Moana* at the cinema and was frightened by Te Kā, the volcanic demon. So he wanted me to tell him something equally terrifying. I know, I know, I shouldn't have mentioned the green-eyed monster in the wardrobe. After that he came into our bed every night until I told him I'd bought some anti-monster spray in the ghost shop.'

Till shook the can with the 'Goodnight Lavender' fragrance. 'I told him that if we sprayed it in the wardrobe and on the bed he'd sleep safe and sound. Nothing could happen to him. And he believed me.'

Tears surged in his eyes. 'Every night I sprayed it in his room and he never crept into our bed again. He slept through the night from then on. Max wasn't frightened any more.'

'Till!'

'Do you think he asked his abductor about the monster spray too?' His voice cracked. 'You know what? I lie there every night, my eyes wide open, staring at the ceiling, and hear Max calling for the monster spray because he's so frightened. But there's no one to bring it to him. There's no spray. Just the monster...'

'Max is dead!' Skania raised his voice.

'I know!' Till hurled the can at the mirror which by some miracle wasn't even scratched. 'I know he's dead,' he said, his voice growing louder with each word until he was yelling at his brother-in-law. 'But I have to see him, his body. I have to bury Max, don't you understand? *I need certainty!*'

He raced out of the bathroom and Skania hurried after him.

'Of course I understand. I want that just as much as you – or Ricarda.'

'Your sister has left me. And taken Emilia.'

Skania eyed Till sympathetically. 'I know. She told me. But be honest, are you surprised? Take a look at yourself. You're letting yourself go. You're going to seed. You're refusing to face the truth.'

'What is the truth?'

His brother-in-law raised both arms. Till saw sweat patches the size of beer mats beneath Skania's armpits.

'If that bastard doesn't tell us where we can find Max...'

Skania cleared his throat. 'I mean, you know how it was with the other children. You read the reports. Tramnitz did such a thorough job of burying those bodies that if he hadn't told us where they were, we'd never have found the poor souls. So deep beneath the old dump that there wasn't even the faintest bark from the cadaver dogs. But since he's been in prison...'

He's not talking any more. Saying nothing. Silence.

Till closed his eyes.

On his lawyer's advice Tramnitz hadn't said a word since his first confession. Which had left Till in the worst state of all: uncertainty. But as Germany observed the rule of law, the very threat of torture was punishable. Even against a monster. There was nothing they could do to make this beast talk.

Nothing except...

Till had an idea. It was absurd, verging on ridiculous, beggaring belief. And yet this was the first idea that had inspired him in a long time.

'What would you do to the accused if you had the chance?'

'How certain are we that Tramnitz killed my son?' he asked Skania.

'Our previous assumption was ninety-nine per cent. But in the last hour, we've reached one hundred per cent certainty.'

'How so?'

'They found something,' his brother-in-law said. 'Actually, that's why I came.'

Till felt sick. The world around him began to spin and he held on to the chair he'd placed in front of the television.

'What?' he asked, and just this one word required an immense outlay of energy.

What did they find?

Skania opened his large fist, but Till couldn't see anything to begin with. The dusty light slanting into the room through the Venetian blinds was at such an awkward angle that it blinded him. Especially as the object in Skania's hand was small and white... *and plastic!*

'Luke Skywalker,' Till whispered, recoiling as if the Lego figure in Skania's hand were contagious. 'Where was he found?'

'On Tramnitz's bedside table. When he was taken into the operating theatre. The bastard put his trophy on public show in the loony bin. There's something else too.'

'More proof?'

'Possibly.'

Skania pulled the fold of skin down further.

'There are rumours. Prison telegraph so to speak.'

'What?'

'Supposedly Tramnitz is bragging about a diary he's writing in the hospital, detailing all his crimes.'

7

FRIEDER

'Frieder?'

Confused by the unknown number on his private mobile the surgeon sat back down at his desk. He'd just been about to leave the office they'd given him at the Steinklinik to head down to the garden level where the operating theatre was.

'I'm sorry to disturb you,' Frieder heard a deep, sonorous voice say.

The man sounded slightly feeble and exhausted, however, and his words were almost drowned out by the thrashing of the rainstorm raging outside. Here on the first floor of the hospital, when the wind worked its way through the ventilation and lift shafts, it sounded like the whining of a frightened dog.

'Who is this?' Frieder asked impatiently.

'My name is Till Berkoff. I'm Max's father.'

Oh, God.

Frieder swallowed and nodded subconsciously.

Now he knew *who* was on the other end of the line. And because he had a rough idea of what the poor man wanted from him, his heart started beating faster. His pulse accelerated and he began to feel hot.

'How did you get my number?'

'As a former crew manager in the fire service I still have good contacts within the authorities.'

Frieder reached for his neck and unfastened the top button of his pink polo shirt. Pink was his favourite colour because he thought it went well with his solarium-tanned skin.

'Listen here,' he said. 'I'm not allowed to talk to you about my patients.'

'I don't want to talk. I want you to do something for me.'

The caller's voice was shot through with cold fury. Frieder understood at once what Berkhoff meant with his euphemism *do something*.

He could equally have said 'eliminate the problem' or 'give justice a helping hand' or 'save the taxpayer a pile of money'.

'Are you recording our conversation?' Frieder asked, switching off the desk lamp. He really had to leave for the operating theatre to start his preparations.

'My son isn't a story,' Berkhoff spat, and now his anger was directed squarely at Frieder.

'Forgive me, that's not what I was getting at. It's just that, I...' He hesitated. 'I can't even entertain the idea of what you want from me.'

Even though I can well understand. Me too – I'd also wish an agonising death on the man who'd abducted and killed my son.

'Oh, yes, you can.'

'No.' Frieder's hands started to tremble. 'I can't kill people and I don't want to either,' he said loudly. He'd deliberately made a clear and honest statement just in case Berkhoff was recording this after all.

But to his astonishment the father rebutted him: 'That's not what I'm asking you to do.'

'What, then?'

He heard a snuffle, Berkhoff blew his nose, gave a curt apology and then said, 'I'm asking you to do quite the opposite.'

'I don't understand.'

'I'm asking you, no, I'm begging you: do everything in your power to ensure that Guido Tramnitz pulls through. He must survive the operation, do you get me? He's the only one who knows what happened to my son. He mustn't take his secret to the grave.'

'Okay, okay,' Frieder said, rather touched. 'I'll do what I can.' The father's emotional, unexpected, but ultimately understandable request had profoundly moved him. When he hung up his fingers were trembling so badly that there was no other option.

The only way he could calm his digits was by opening his desk drawer and allowing himself a sip. Not much.

Just a shot.

8

TILL

'An undercover patient?'

'Yes.'

'What do you mean?'

'I want you to smuggle me into the Steinklinik.'

'To get to Tramnitz?'

'Exactly, as an inmate in the psychiatric ward.'

Till, who was becoming seriously irritated that their conversation was turning into an interrogation, turned his back to Skania and gazed out of the window.

The rainy autumn storm gusted a plastic bag across the pavement and into the branches of a weeping willow, from where it hung like the last remnant of a shredded sail. There wasn't a bird or squirrel to be seen in the garden, no sign of life. No wonder, given this deluge. All the same, Till would much rather be outside at the mercy of natural forces than waiting here in the warm, damned to inaction.

Behind him, his brother-in-law cleared his throat and even this got on Till's nerves. 'That's one of the most hare-brained ideas I've ever heard,' Skania blustered. 'Even if I were willing to do it – and I'm most certainly not – how do you imagine I'd get you in there? *Idiotical Island* isn't exactly an amusement park you can just wander into and look around as you please.'

He was quite right, of course.

The Steinklinik for forensic psychiatry was a high-level security institution in Reinickendorf. A single complex of buildings on a peninsula in the Tegeler See, it had acquired this nickname among Berliners – a nod to the Brandenburg water park called 'Tropical Island'. Originally, a wealthy investor had planned to build a grand hotel there. But after the inner-city airport failed to close on time thanks to the sheer chaos of Berlin politics, no guest was going to pay 650 euros a night to be lulled to sleep by deafening engine noise. Not even the fact that a star architect had modelled the building on the White House in Washington, with a magnificent columned entrance and three-storeyed east and west wings, could save the project.

A private hospital operator eventually bought the plot along with the shell of the building and today it housed not well-heeled guests, VIPs or politicians, but some of Germany's most dangerous psychopaths, though the odd critic claimed that the psychological make-up of the current guests didn't differ much from the ones originally hoped for: schizophrenic rapists, sadistic murderers, insane perverts. The inmates included the Blood Painter, a thirty-two-year-old man who looked like an adult education college lecturer. His hobby was to paint seascapes using the bodily fluids of his victims, who were forced to watch as they bled to death.

So Guido Tramnitz was in the very best company here, with other criminals who had been legally certified as not criminally responsible on account of their mental state, and thus would remain locked up in this psychiatric institution forever.

Till took a deep breath and spoke as he breathed out. 'I don't have a clue how you'll manage it, but I've got to get in there. To Tramnitz.'

'Why? So you can beat your son's killer to a pulp?'

Till shook his head. 'I need certainty, Oliver. I can't go on living like this. I need something to hold on to. To say goodbye. Do you understand?'

He could see the answer in his brother-in-law's eyes. Of course he understood. Skania was a policeman. He was well aware of the impact of a child's death on parents. Their lives came to an end. Their soul, their happiness, everything that constituted their very being, vanished forever. Even so, they had an advantage over those parents who could never be 100 per cent certain of what had happened to their children. For their struggle with death never came to a conclusion.

'I feel like a horse with broken legs in a ditch.'

'You think a meeting with Tramnitz would be something of a *coup de grâce* for you?'

'Precisely. He's refusing to talk to the police, the public prosecutor or the judge. So I have to go to him. I want to know where he's hidden Max's body.'

'Hmm, great idea. I'm sure Tramnitz will be only too happy to tell you.'

Till shook his head again. 'I might not have to talk to him if I can get my hands on his diary.'

Skania burst out laughing. 'How naive *are* you? That's just a rumour. And even if it does exist, which I doubt, Tramnitz is hardly going to leave it lying around, is he?'

Till could appreciate the logic in what Skania was saying, but he refused to accept the truth, as otherwise he'd be forced to admit to himself that he had no plan save for the courage of the desperate man.

'There can't be that many hiding places in the high-security wing,' he said almost defiantly.

'Exactly. You said it: high security! I haven't the faintest idea how you think you'd be able to move around in the loony bin, let alone creep up on Tramnitz. Even if I could achieve the impossible, at best they'd stick you in the normal, closed psychiatric section. Tramnitz, on the other hand, is level IV security.' Skania raised his hand and counted on his fingers. 'That means: body scanner in the security gate to his ward, fingerprints and iris checks at all the relevant doors and a double fence in the outside area monitored by drones, which is like the old Berlin Wall.'

'I'll worry about all that when I'm inside. I'll find a way.'

'Bollocks! Don't expect me to help you in this kamikaze mission.'

'No?' Till said, grabbing a clump of his hair by the roots. And tearing it out.

There was a popping in his ears as if he'd burst a whole section of bubble wrap.

Blood shot to his face quicker than Skania could yell, 'What the hell are you doing?'

'I'm preparing myself.'

Till tried to drop the hair he'd yanked out, but his hands were bathed in sweat. Then he grabbed another clump, this time in the middle of his head.

'Stop it, for God's sake. No!'

He pulled again. Harder. The pain was easier to bear than all the blood now dripping on the floor.

'Have you lost your mind, you fool?'

Till forced a smile. 'See how quickly I've convinced you? So?'

'What do you mean?'

Till showed him the clump of hair that used to adorn his head and which was now stuck to his hand smeared red like part of a scalp. 'When I'm done with the hair I'm going to drink some bleach from the bathroom. And while I'm waiting for the ambulance I'll find a way of extracting my teeth. Maybe I'll even find the courage to gouge an eye out.'

'You're insane.'

'Yes. I'm a danger to myself.' Till pointed to the place where Skania's pistol was bulging through his coat. 'And once I've nicked your gun I'll be a danger to others too. You'll see, I'll find a way to get in there. So?'

Till wrenched another, even larger clump of hair from his head.

'For fuck's sake, man,' Skania cursed, now practically shouting. 'Alright, stop! I'll see what I can do, okay?'

For a while he stood there, baffled, totally overwhelmed by the situation. Then Skania did what he always did when he'd had enough. He marched hotfoot out of the room and slammed the door behind him.

Till waited another minute and then began to cry. With relief that his brother-in-law was willing to help. With pain that surged with a vengeance only now that the stress hormones were no longer keeping his body on red alert.

And with fear.

Jesus Christ, I'm frightened.

Till didn't have a clue what he'd be letting himself in for should Skania be able to make the final wish of his life come true and have him admitted to the Steinklinik.

9

PATRICK WINTER

Death stood in the sitting room, one hundred metres from the kindergarten, and sweating.

Patrick Winter stared through the floor-to-ceiling window at his overgrown garden that bordered the back garden of the kindergarten. The two properties were separated only by a narrow alleyway.

Had anyone outside ventured to peer in, they would have seen on the ground floor a trembling man in his early forties on the verge of losing the battle with his inner demons. His curly hair, a touch too long, had been a real effort to tame, and his prominent chin was patchily shaven. There was cold fear in the tired eyes.

Outside on the streets of the villa-studded district of Ruhleben, near the Olympic Stadium, he wouldn't have merited a second glance. Not this evening, when far more sinister figures were up to mischief. Even though it was already gone eight o'clock. In this solidly middle-class area, people were usually watching the news at this time or having a family dinner. They wouldn't go out for a walk until later, when the children were in bed. Unless, just because it was a special occasion, the kids were allowed to stay up later, to roam the streets as witches, ghouls or ghosts.

Today was Halloween. And not even the incessant, cold-provoking rain of the last few days could stop the children and teenagers dressed as vampires, skeletons or zombies from adorning their neighbours' front gardens with loo paper if they failed to open the front door.

Trick or treat?

Patrick bit the web of skin between his thumb and forefinger to prevent himself from shouting his head off.

Over the past half hour his doorbell had rung four times. Boys with grotesque, made-up faces, girls in ghostly robes, children holding lit-up pumpkins.

Once Patrick even opened the door and gave a little boy with a skeleton costume and fake spiderwebs in his hair a chocolate bar, which was virtually all he'd been subsisting on for the past few days. The boy, who couldn't have been more than eight and whose parents were waiting in the street, bore no resemblance to Jonas; of course he didn't. And yet those large, questioning eyes did remind Patrick of his son.

Patrick was tempted to wave at the boy as he left. Perhaps, he thought, it would have changed everything.

If I'd waved and he had smiled.

But he'd merely watched him hurry back to his parents, before disappearing around the corner with them and the chocolate bar, and thus out of his life.

After that, Patrick ignored the doorbell in his empty house. An 'architect's villa', as the estate agent had pitched it to him and Linda, when his wife was six months pregnant with Jonas. Which explained why they could afford this place. In estate agent speak, 'architect's house' stood for quirkiness that made a property tricky to sell, and certainly the layout of the house needed some getting used to. It started in the sitting room, where the previous owner had installed a hexagonal jacuzzi in the middle of the floor. A bold idea even for single people – Who took a bath in front of the television? – but perilous for children, which was why he and Linda filled the tub with cushions and converted it into a sofa for 'adventures and cuddles'.

They lacked the money to renovate back then, when everything was still right with the world, their life not filled with unbearable pain. And so the ugly black-and-white chessboard tiles in the open-plan kitchen had also stayed put. Unlike Linda, who'd left him some time ago.

Quite rightly too.

Patrick looked beyond the chestnut tree, which had been hit by lightning two summers ago, over to the brightly lit common room of Waldkater kindergarten, where the parents' evening had already begun.

Today of all days!

For the past three-quarters of an hour the adults had been sitting in a circle in the newly renovated common room, on the tiny chairs of the two- to six-year-olds who were looked after here during the day. Children with names like Jasmin, Igor, Alexander, Jura, Thorben, Mehmet – *and Frieda.*

My Frieda.

At least she's still alive.

Patrick must be the only parent still unaccounted for. All the others who couldn't be there, such as Linda, had duly put their names on the list of apologies at the entrance or, if they'd forgotten to do this when picking up their children, had at least sent an email.

Order prevailed in Waldkater kindergarten; everything was proceeding as normal.

I wonder if they're even expecting me after everything that's happened?

I mean, fifty per cent of my children still go to the kindergarten.

The other fifty per cent were rotting somewhere in the earth.

Wiping the tears from his eyes, Patrick looked at the pistol in his hand.

He was a sporting marksman with a gun licence and trained regularly with the local shooting association. He knew how to position the pistol to ensure that you blew your brains out properly.

But the longer he stared at the kindergarten, past the devastated chestnut tree, in which he'd planned to build a treehouse for his children, the more inappropriate it felt to use his gun.

Wrong. Cowardly. Too harmless.

Patrick moved away from the window and crossed the sitting room to the hallway, where he opened the basement door. Although the space down below had been converted into a living area – with bright carpet, a shower room, and windows to let in daylight – as he went down the stairs, his nose was hit by the typical basement mustiness of damp dust and old books.

I'm going to miss this smell too.

Patrick went into the guest room, where the bed was still freshly made as if awaiting its next visitor. Only the layer of dust on the bedspread betrayed the fact that no cleaning lady had set foot in here in ages.

Reaching under the bed, he pulled out the sports bag he used to take to the gym. In the last three months (*ever since the worst of all possible days*) he hadn't needed to exercise to maintain his weight. His appetite had deserted him.

Patrick opened the bag and stared at the PET bottles without labels, which had once been filled with mineral water and now contained an amber-coloured liquid. Four 750-millilitre bottles.

He'd helped himself from the caretaker of the glass skyscraper in Potsdamer Platz that housed his employer, Xantia, one of the largest private health insurance companies in Germany. His shoebox of an office was on the twenty-second floor in the department of risk management, though it did look out over the Berlin Philharmonie.

I won't have any view soon.

'Let's get this show on the road,' Patrick said, opening the first bottle.

Time for my liquid Halloween costume.

He put the pistol in the bag and took out the first bottle. He closed his eyes as he tipped the contents over his head and hair, opening them only to unscrew the second bottle that he poured over his torso. He couldn't prevent the fumes from irritating his nose and throat, causing him to cough, but he continued undeterred.

The doorbell rang upstairs.

Trick or treat?

Patrick put the empty bottles down on the now-stained carpet and waited for the children or teenagers to give up. Then he climbed the stairs back into his sitting room with its redundant jacuzzi. Here he opened the garden door and, totally drenched, stepped out into the cold and damp autumn air.

It was raining again, but the few drops were not going to thwart his plan. He'd tipped far too much petrol over his body for that.

'Right then,' Patrick said by way of encouragement. Only when he was sure that his storm-proof Zippo was still in his jeans did he make for the kindergarten beyond the chestnut tree.

10

FRIEDER

'Come on, Dr Frieder, admit it!'

Guido Tramnitz sounded curiously cheerful for a patient lying on his side who was about to undergo an operation on his carotid artery without general anaesthetic.

'You'd love your hand to slip by accident, wouldn't you?'

Frieder tried to block out the arrogant, slightly nasal voice of the child- and woman-killer as he focused on the tiny golden clamp in his hand. Hopf, the senior doctor assisting him, had marked with a blue ribbon the right carotid artery beneath the Y-branch, the 'vascular dumping ground' as Frieder casually referred to this part of the body.

Here, where the *carotis communis* branched into the vessels for the face and brain, turbulent blood flow often led to calcium and fat deposits. It was something they were increasingly seeing in pensioners. But although the muscular, athletic twenty-eight-year-old had always paid careful attention to what he ate, the yellowy-orange residues that Frieder was now going to have to painstakingly remove were already shimmering through the delicate pink artery.

'Why not give the bastard his just desserts right here and now – that's what you're thinking, isn't it?'

No, I'm thinking about Till Berkhoff and his desperate plea to save you, you fucker.

Tramnitz smiled. For an operation like this, a general anaesthetic was out of the question. Only a local anaesthetic was possible to enable the patient's neurological functions to be monitored continually. Regrettably this also meant that Frieder couldn't shut the bastard up.

'Squeeze my hand!' ordered Dr Andrea Schilf, the anaesthetist, to check the patient's motor functions as well as his facial expressions whenever Frieder performed another intervention. A green drape hung between her and the surgeon, above which the two of them maintained eye contact. Schilf watched Tramnitz from the left-hand side while Frieder attended to the right carotid artery. Just as he was putting the golden clamp, similar to a paper clip, on the critical branch, his fingers actually started itching to make a mistake.

Frieder knew of course that thoughts such as these were unethical. *But hey*, he was just human after all. Before Berkoff's call, he'd briefly wondered how bad it would be if his 'hand slipped'. Nobody here would shed a tear for the fucker afterwards. On the contrary, if the operation succeeded, the 'incubator monster', as the press called the former paediatric nurse, would be a financial drain on the state for years to come. He'd also be a ticking timebomb for fellow inmates and even for other families if he were to escape.

Moreover, Tramnitz seemed to be out to provoke him.

'Forget your Hippocratic oath and think about what I did to those children, Frieder.'

'Quiet,' the anaesthetist snapped, but Tramnitz wouldn't be deterred.

'I always brought changes of clothes with me, you know. For boys and girls. A bag in the boot, full of different sizes, because I wanted to be prepared for every eventuality. As soon as they were in the car, I changed them. So they wouldn't be so easily recognisable if a search was launched promptly. Mostly the young things did it all on their own. They thought it was a game.' Tramnitz chortled. 'They didn't think that any more when they were in the incubator.'

Oh, God. He's talking as if there were more than two victims. Many more than two.

'I built the incubator myself. Much better than the small crates we had in Virchow.' Tramnitz sighed as if reminiscing about a lovely beach holiday. 'Fantastic, I could do everything with them. Stroke and feed them, change their nappies – goodness me. A dream.'

'I'm now going to cut off the blood supply,' Frieder said loudly, heralding the start of the twenty most critical minutes. Once he'd disconnected the right-hand fork of the Y-branch, nothing must go wrong. The brain was dependent on it.

The sick brain of a psychopath.

'It could have gone on like that forever. If only I hadn't lain a finger on the slapper. But the mother had done her own detective work. She was on the verge of exposing my package trick. The voices ordered me to kill her.'

The voices, of course.

It was inconceivable to Frieder that psychiatrists and judges could have been taken in by these lies. Tramnitz was possessed for sure, but not by invisible forces steering his thoughts. No, by a lust for killing. He belonged inside a prison, a Siberian labour camp if possible, not in a psychiatric hospital with all-round care.

Frieder closed his eyes briefly, opened them again and applied the scalpel.

'If only I'd disposed of her body more carefully, they'd never have got on my trail. Oh well. Shit happens, doesn't it?'

Frieder glanced at Hopf, who just shook his head as a warning, as if trying to say, *'Keep calm, take your time. Don't make any mistakes. This guy's not worth it.'*

But Frieder couldn't restrain himself.

'Look here. At this very moment I'm trying to save your life. Why can't you in return show at least a modicum of decency and admit all your crimes to those parents you've caused so much pain and suffering?'

'Am I mistaken or are you referring to my Luke Skywalker figure?' Tramnitz said.

'If you put your trophies on display, you could at least admit it too.'

'What sort of trophy?' Tramnitz giggled. 'The police wouldn't stop questioning me about this figure. I just bought one so I could see what it looked like.'

Frieder caught another glance from his senior doctor, accompanied by another head shake. *'Stop. This is not the right time.'*

But he had to let off steam. 'Okay, it's not worth it. Just keep your bloody trap shut while we're working,' he said, at which Tramnitz laughed out loud. His neck moved and it was impossible to make an accurate cut.

'Or what? Will you damage my recurrent laryngeal nerve like you did to Florian Broder?'

Frieder froze.

How the hell did Tramnitz know about that? The name had never made it into the press.

Of course. He worked in Virchow when I was there.

The gossip factory inside a hospital was even worse than Facebook.

'A harmless operation on the thyroid, but now Broder has double paralysis of the recurrent nerve and has to rely on an artificial respirator for the rest of his life. Correct? And all because yet again you were on the piss the night before.'

'Don't get distracted. I'm afraid we can't switch him off, Volker,' Hopf whispered, but Tramnitz had heard.

'Volker? I thought colleagues only called you by your nickname: *Vodka* Frieder.' Tramnitz giggled. 'You got that because you've always needed a bit of Dutch courage. What about today? Have you tanked up for me too?'

'You'll find out soon enough,' Frieder hissed angrily, slicing through his carotid artery.

11

PATRICK WINTER

It was too much for the adults. Some sat, mouths agape, on the kindergarten chairs, others at the parents' evening turned away. One mother in a flowery cardigan, whose son Emil was in the Sunshine group, even held her nose.

He couldn't smell the petrol any more, but the scented candles on the shelves by the colourful windows wouldn't be able to cover up the stench. Patrick must reek like a petrol station. Or worse.

'Please, why don't you take a seat?' Viktoria asked. The head nursery teacher was the first person to say a word to him.

Up until now only he had spoken. Like a waterfall, ever since he'd punched in the code for the kindergarten that all the parents knew.

'I'm sorry, I'm sorry,' he'd said upon entering the common room that was used for drama and singing groups and where the children all had lunch together. Today there was space for a discussion group of around fifteen people, all of whom had winced when they saw him.

'You weren't expecting a real ghost, were you? I mean, who wants to come face to face with someone like me on Halloween?' He gave a crazy laugh and ran a hand through his hair that was soaked by petrol and rain. 'What? What? I don't want to see any embarrassed faces. After all, *your* kids are still alive.'

He'd taken the Zippo out of his trouser pocket and now held his arm up like the Statue of Liberty. Nobody had stood up. Nobody had even moved a muscle. Apart from Viktoria, who had grabbed her mobile, presumably to call the police. But that was fine by him.

'I bet you all wish you'd stayed at home tonight, don't you? Or that you'd listened to your whingeing kids who wanted to get dressed up. But Mummy and Daddy had to go to the parents' evening. What crappy planning!' He flashed his eyes at Sonja, one of the teachers. 'I mean, how can you arrange this for 31 October? How stupid can you be?'

He tapped his wet brow. 'Because today is not about whether the brats can bring in their toys or how many sweets are allowed in their lunchboxes. Today the errant souls of the dead need to be driven away. Like Jonas's. Like my own.'

He swallowed some saliva and coughed.

'Tough shit, dear parents. You didn't get dressed up. And I've dared to come in. Now I'm here. Living proof of the fact that evil exists. That children can die. Not just on television or in the newspapers. But here in Berlin, right before our very eyes.'

At this point most did actually look away. Embarrassed, shocked. Very alarmed. Men and women.

'I'm very sorry to have to destroy this ideal world for you. Look at me!'

He had screamed at them. The gay couple with the foster child; the grandmother stepping in for the hardworking estate agent parents, who once again couldn't make it to the parents' evening; and of course the model helicopter parents who came as a couple to show how important their offspring was, both of them with notepad on thigh as if they were at school themselves, listening to something so important that it had to be jotted down.

Well, then, why don't you all write it in capital letters: 'YOU'VE ALL JUST BEEN VERY LUCKY!'

Patrick had screamed at them, with spittle at the corners of his mouth. Now, his right hand holding the Zippo still raised, he said, 'What happened to me could have just as easily happened to you. Do you think you're infallible? No. You're not. And that's why I don't see—'

'Herr Winter?'

That was the moment when Viktoria's soft voice threw him off track.

He turned to the sixty-two-year-old teacher who was wearing an orange batik dress as usual. Because of the weather she'd swapped her ballet pumps for wellies this evening.

'Wouldn't you like to sit down?' she asked, pointing to a free stool.

'No, no, I just want…'

He faltered when she offered him the mobile. Did she want him to speak to the police?

'Your wife's on the phone,' Viktoria said and Patrick had to admit that she was a smart woman. He'd always thought most highly of the teacher who was close to retirement and with all her experience had started dozens of generations on the right path. Calling Linda was a gambit he hadn't anticipated.

How clever.

How understanding.

He took the telephone and tried to swallow the lump in his throat. 'Linda?'

'What's wrong, darling?'

Darling.

When did she last call him that? She used to three times a day. In the morning, in the afternoon and in the evening. At least. But when his son was torn from their life together, so were the loving words and phrases.

'I can't really talk at the moment, love. I've written it all down. The letter's in the post.'

'I don't understand. What are you doing?'

'I'm at the parents' evening.'

'I know that. But what are you planning to do? They're saying, well, Viktoria says that... You're not going to do anything stupid, are you?'

He shook his head without taking his eye off the assembled company. Of all the idiots here, the muscly car dealer with the silly ear studs was the most likely to play the hero and bring a chair down on his head.

'I already did the most stupid thing in my life when I...'

'There's no point,' Linda interrupted him. Now she was in tears too. 'Darling, beating yourself up about it isn't going to bring our child back.'

'That's true. But you're not going to come back either, no matter what I do, are you? I've lost my entire family.'

'Darling...'

'I belong in hell.'

'No, wait. Please. Whatever you're planning, don't do it!'

'I have to burn, Linda, please understand. And not just me. I want all the parents here to find out what it's like to burn in hell.'

That's why I'm here.

With these words he hung up, sparked a flame and held the Zippo to his head.

A split second later, when the entire group of parents seemed as one to be screaming in horror, his hair was alight.

12

TILL

At 8:45 p.m., an ambulance shot along the wet tarmac and, with its blue lights and sirens, cleared its way through on the city motorway. Now and again the vehicle had to brake sharply, the driver honked his horn energetically and even skidded around a bend, but then regained control before racing at top speed through puddles and flooded sections of road.

The rain increased steadily. As did the anxiety of the sole occupant in the patient area.

After a ten-minute drive the ambulance slowed down. It was rocking gently, as if driving along an unsurfaced road. Then coarse gravel crunched beneath the tyres. Finally the vehicle came to a halt and the sirens fell silent. Briefly, for only about the thirty seconds it took the overweight man to emerge from the roof of a car park and climb into the ambulance.

Then they sped off again.

'You really want to go through with this, then?' Skania asked, having stared for a long while at Till, in both admiration and disgust. Because of his size he had to pull his head in slightly. With his hairy hand he held on tightly to the frame of the stretcher to which Till was strapped. Only for show, of course. Everything had to look genuine the moment they arrived.

'Have you got a file on the man?' Till asked. His brother-in-law nodded.

Skania's suit was drenched. The policeman must have been waiting quite a while outside the ambulance without adequate protection from the rain. He pulled a brown paper folder from his jacket and opened it.

'Your new name is Patrick Winter; you're forty-one years of age and you work at Xantia.'

'The health insurance company?'

'Exactly. You were working as an actuary in the head office on Potsdamer Platz.'

'What the hell is an actuary?'

'An insurance mathematician. They calculate premiums, compile risk prognoses, that sort of stuff.'

'You can't be serious.'

'Why are you looking so shocked?'

'Are you saying I've got to assume the identity of a maths genius? Oliver, I was a tough guy in the fire service, have you forgotten that? It's the only job I could get with my grades. I only just scraped through school and never got better than a D-minus in maths.'

'Who's saying Winter was a mathematical genius?'

'Anybody who can count is a genius in my eyes,' Till said.

'Besides,' Oliver said, 'may I remind you that this entire crackpot idea was yours in the first place? I can't order the identity you want to slip into on eBay. But hey, I don't have a problem if you want to call the whole thing off here and now.'

'No, no, it's fine,' Till said, hurrying to steal his thunder. They'd had this same discussion far too often over the past few days. 'I mean, they're not going to force me to do mental arithmetic in there, are they? And even if they do, I've learned how to bullshit my way out of pretty much everything. By the way, what has Patrick Winter done to be sent to the Steinklinik?'

'He doused himself in petrol at a kindergarten parents' evening, then set fire to himself,' Skania replied.

'Why on earth?'

Skania looked at Till as if he'd never heard such an idiotic question in his life. 'Why do I have high blood pressure and my sister an underactive thyroid? How the hell do I know? Patrick Winter is sick, fed up with life. He's probably been on antidepressants since his student days.'

Skania tapped his fat fingers on the folder as if to say: *'It's all in here.'*

'At any rate it's a stroke of luck that you combed yourself with your fists,' he said, pointing to Till's head bandage.

After his act of self-mutilation Till had shaven all his hair off and rubbed a viscous iodine ointment into the wounds. *A blessing in disguise.* If someone took the bandage off his head (and this would happen very soon) it would look halfway genuine and smell of treatment.

'Married? Children?' Till asked about Patrick Winter.

'Yes, twice. His current wife is called Linda and they have a daughter, Frieda, five years old.'

One year younger than Max.

'So where is Winter now?' Till said.

'In a fridge.'

Till lifted his head and raised his eyebrows, while Skania closed the file again. 'He died less than two hours after his self-inflicted burns. Just after a judge had approved his admission to the Steinklinik because the guy was quite clearly a danger, not just to himself but to the public at large.'

Till rested his head back down. So that's why everything had happened so quickly. Scarcely had Skania hung up than the promised ambulance had pulled up outside his house.

'There'll never be another chance like this, will there?' Till said.

'Maybe it's not a chance, but just madness,' Skania muttered, making a dismissive gesture as if to say: 'Do *what you want.*'

Till paused for a while, then asked the forbidden question: 'How did you arrange for me to get Winter's identity?'

Skania twisted his mouth as if he'd just bitten into a lemon. 'Do you seriously believe I'm going to spill the beans on how our undercover investigations work?' He gave a bitter laugh. 'I broke around twenty laws and double that number of regulations by pulling strings to get Patrick Winter's death certificate ripped up, his picture swapped for yours in the file and those two paramedics up front to chauffeur you to the Steinklinik. The official line is that, by some miracle, Winter escaped with just a burn on his scalp because the kindergarten staff had the presence of mind to grab the fire extinguisher and prevent the worst. In truth his skull looked like a prune. Mine will look even worse if any of this comes to light. And I don't want you implicating any of my colleagues if you start blabbing.'

Till accepted this answer with a brief 'Hmm'.

'Have you sorted out all those things in the hospital I asked you to?' he asked Skania as they stopped with the engine running, presumably at a traffic light. From his stretcher Till could only peer through a narrow side window, and even half of that was taped up. Through the wet pane of glass he could make out a curved street lamp and the windswept crown of a tree by the side of the road.

'I've done all I possibly can in the little time available.' Now Skania was looking through the window too. 'We're almost there.' Turning to Till on the stretcher, he said, 'I'm going to ask you one last time. Are you sure about this?'

Seeing as Till had already given a comprehensive answer to this question during their last discussion, he made do with a curt nod.

Yes. I have to get in there. To Tramnitz.

I need certainty.

Although his brother-in-law obviously hadn't been expecting a change of mind, with an angry shake of his head he made perfectly clear what he thought of this undertaking.

'Okay, fine. Now listen up,' the policeman said, finally beginning his briefing. 'What we've managed to organise for you there isn't much, but it's better than nothing. Upon admission to the high-security hospital, all your personal effects will be taken away. You'll be given a tracksuit until your clothes have been thoroughly searched. Obviously they'll take your mobile straight away, as well as any sharp objects, belt and much more. So you can't take Winter's file in with you either. But if everything goes according to plan, you'll have a contact.'

'Who?'

Skania, who hated being interrupted, pursed his lips. 'She's called Seda. It's enough for you to know her name. Now, this is important. She's not a friend, not even a confidante. We don't know how trustworthy she is, only that she'll do pretty much anything for money.'

'What's her job there?'

'She drives the bus,' Skania said impatiently.

'What sort of bus?'

'You'll find out soon enough.' Skania checked his watch. 'Let's not waste any time on trivialities. Much more important is how you can get in contact with us in case of an emergency.'

'How?'

'Via a mobile phone. It's in the library. Bookcase three, shelf two. There's a weighty volume hidden right behind the Bibles. *Ulysses* by James Joyce. The old tome is so big and dry that none of the inmates has ever borrowed it. Even if someone were to discover it by chance, it looks at first glance like a perfectly normal book. But in fact it's been hollowed out after page eighty-four. In the recess you'll find a small Nokia phone. You can use it to text and make calls, but not go online.'

'Sure,' Till said. Anything else would use up too much battery and the phone could hardly be plugged in all the time.

'What about the numbers?' he asked Skania.

'My contact is saved. Speed dial one is my office, two my private mobile. You can reach Hartz on three.'

Hartz was Till's lawyer and notary. He'd had him certify a sworn statement that he was in full possession of his mental faculties and was only being admitted to the hospital under pretence. Besides Skania, the notary was the only person who officially knew this and he was sworn to secrecy under attorney–client privilege. Till hadn't even told Ricarda, even though he hated the idea of his wife worrying about him when he vanished from the face of the earth.

'If there are any problems, all you need to do is call me and let it ring three times. Then I'll try to get you out of there.'

'Try?' Till said to his brother-in-law.

'This was what *you* wanted, Till. You wanted to be admitted as an inmate to this high-security hospital. So please hear me out. The moment you walk through that door you'll have nothing up your sleeve to help you. And of course no doctors are in on it. Not even Seda knows what's going on. If I'd discussed this with any of the official staff at the hospital, it would be *me* strapped to this stretcher and *I'd* be the one they would lock up. Nobody would agree to such an insane undertaking – no police authority, no doctor.'

'I—'

'Quiet, I'm not finished with my lecture yet. I want and need to tell you this one last time. If anything happens to you, in your cell, in the yard, in the shower or even in the treatment room, nobody there is going to be able to help you. As far as the doctors and nurses are concerned, you're a perfectly normal mental patient. And it's going to take me time to get you out of there too. Do you understand? I can't just ring the Steinklinik and say, "April Fool, my dear Professor Sänger. You know Patrick Winter in room 211? He's just pretending. He's a fireman, not a mathematician. Please let him out as quickly as you can."'

Skania paused as the ambulance slowed down. There was now empathy in his eyes. 'But hey, I swear I'll move heaven and earth if you make an emergency call.'

Till thanked him and said, 'How do I get into the library? I don't imagine everybody will have access.'

'That's just one of the thousand problems you'll have to deal with on your own. What you ought to be wondering is how to get transferred to Tramnitz's wing and win his trust. And how to restrain yourself so you don't smash his face in when you first meet him.'

The ambulance stopped and the driver knocked on the partition.

'I need to get out,' Skania said. 'I'm not coming on the ferry.'

Till swallowed nervously. 'What do you mean, ferry?'

I thought the hospital was accessible by road.

'The road is under water. The rain's getting worse and worse and they've already got an acute problem with flooding on the island. For that reason alone you shouldn't spend too long in there.'

Skania rubbed Till's arm sympathetically. 'Hey, old chap. I know it's not my place to say this and I really do admire your courage. But do you think it's worth it? All these dangers and the risk?'

Till swallowed heavily. He barely recognised his own voice when he said, 'I've already lost the most important thing in my life. What more can happen to me after that?'

The rain pelted the roof of the ambulance like gravel, and Skania said nothing until another knock urged him to hurry. This time it came from the door outside. He was about to turn around, but paused to fish a white pill from the flap pocket of his jeans. 'Here.'

'What am I supposed to do with that?'

'It'll get you off your trolley. At the moment I think you're too calm and rational. Your nutty charade will look more credible if you arrive under sedation. In any case, Till, officially you've still got slight burns to your scalp.'

'Patrick,' he corrected his brother-in-law and felt his head. 'From this moment on my name is Patrick Winter. And thanks, but no thanks. I don't need a tablet. I've got a much better plan for making an unforgettable first impression when I arrive.'

13

RICARDA BERKHOFF

Ricarda Berkhoff was so desperate that she didn't care about
the stench of cheap frying oil which seemed to have penetrated
every pore of her body.

A year ago she would have smiled at those naive souls who
got ripped off by shady con artists.

It's your own fault if you're that stupid.

And now she was sitting with a fortune teller.

Or, more accurately, she was standing with him. For
Gedeon Schultz had neither tables nor chairs in his 'practice',
chiefly because he held his seances in the storeroom of the fast
food chain where he worked.

'I don't really do this any more,' Gedeon said, repeating
what he'd already told her on the telephone. He looked
younger than his voice suggested. A teenager with red
pimples among the fluff above his lip. Except that he'd been
through puberty twenty years ago. 'It's only got me into
trouble.'

Gedeon took off the silly cardboard cap that every member
of staff at the fast food giant had to wear. A newspaper article
had put Ricarda onto him: McMystery, the chip-counter
worker, apparently with psychic powers that in his free

time he used to help relatives establish contact with missing persons.

Whether by chance or not, he had in fact helped the police find a missing girl.

Gedeon piled a box of burgers on top of another and invited Ricarda to sit, but she declined.

'I'm sorry I can't offer you anything else.'

For a while the fast food chain had enjoyed the free publicity and they'd even made part of the staffroom available for Gedeon's 'practice'. But when too many nutters started turning up at the drive-in counter, asking what the next winning lottery numbers would be or for other prophecies, they said he had to meet his clients in the storeroom, and only in exceptional cases.

'Have you got what I asked you to bring?'

She handed him a photo of Max. One that hadn't found its way into the press and which her son must have handled himself. Ricarda had removed the picture from the collage that Max had made in the first year for Harvest Festival. One of the few images that showed the thoughtful child smiling.

'You haven't just lost your son,' Gedeon said, examining the photo that still had a residue of glue on the back.

'What do you mean?'

'Your husband too, isn't that right? He's no longer by your side.'

'How...' She bit her lip. 'Excuse me. I suppose it's like with magicians. You're not going to tell me how you do it, are you?'

Gedeon gave a bashful smile. His voice was so soft that Ricarda had to concentrate hard to pick out his words from the clatter of the unrelenting rain on the tin roof of the storeroom.

'Yes, I will. And it's got nothing to do with magic,' he said, pointing to her hands. 'You're no longer wearing your wedding ring. The indent on your finger tells me that you took it off not long ago.'

'Oh,' Ricarda said. 'What else do you see?'

'You stopped breastfeeding recently.'

'My body can tell you that?'

Ricarda crossed her arms in front of her breasts as if she could somehow change his impression after the event.

'Actually, your bra. It's too loose at the moment because you're between two sizes.'

Ricarda nodded. She was used to being closely scrutinised and had spent a long time wondering what to wear for this occasion, even though in her situation nothing could be of less importance than her external appearance. Unfortunately, however, her external appearance was precisely what the public focused on.

- She looks smart and well-fed. Shouldn't she appear more stressed by her son's disappearance?
- She looks haggard, really exhausted. There's no maternal love in her face.
- Look, that dress she's wearing is plain, but new. How can she have the peace of mind to go shopping at a time like this?
- Why's she wearing such old clothes? She looks slovenly. Maybe a kid growing up in a household like that just ran away.

Whatever Ricarda wore, she faced criticism. Of course she could ignore the opinion of the masses, but they were the ones who had to keep their eyes and ears open for little Max, especially now when barely anybody was still looking.

Especially now.

And so she was certain that the outfit she had on today (baggy jeans, winter boots, no make-up apart from colourless lipstick, her thick hair in a plait) would meet with disapproval.

'I can see that you're completely overwhelmed by the situation you're in,' Gedeon said.

'It would be pretty strange if I weren't,' she said bitterly.

'But I can see that you're nervous not just because you don't trust me. It's also because you have a choice to make.'

'What?'

'You have to make a decision.'

'What decision?'

'About whether we should go on wasting our time here or whether it wouldn't be better to leave straight away, through the same door we came in.'

Ricarda stared at Gedeon and noticed that he had a slight squint.

'I don't understand.'

'We have two exits here. The one behind takes you to the big kitchen.'

He pointed to a cheap, laminated chipboard door at the other end of the storeroom. Beside it stood steel shelving units full of white buckets that looked as if they were full of chemicals, and perhaps the mayonnaise they contained could be categorised as such.

'I'd take that door. Not the roller shutter to the car park.'

'Why should I leave now? You haven't told me anything yet.'

'But you have. I've already learned too much and I think it's best we end the session now.'

Ricarda made a baffled sound that resembled a cough more than anything else. She had been expecting the meeting to take a strange course, but not this.

'Why?'

'Because I sense you're not being honest.'

'*What* do you sense?'

He ran his hand across his face, sweeping away a strand of hair that wasn't there, and said, 'Now we're going to talk about things that I can only feel rather than explain.'

'And what, may I ask, are you feeling?'

'That you haven't come alone. That someone else is waiting out there.'

'Who?'

'Someone who owes you money.'

She laughed incredulously. 'If I knew anyone who owed me money I would have clawed it back long ago, believe you me.'

He nodded. 'Yes, a separation like that costs a fortune. New apartment, new clothes.'

She felt herself turning red. Till had always teased her about this and said that you could read the emotions from her face like subtitles in a film.

'Even if you get maintenance, the transition can be really costly,' Gedeon said. 'And, if I'm not mistaken, the media pay handsomely for exclusives. Especially for a story along the lines of "Desperate Mother Consults Fortune Teller".'

'My child has disappeared, you arsehole!' The words slipped out of Ricarda's mouth and she yanked the photograph from his hand. 'You bloody idiot,' she said, more to herself than to the charlatan, as she tried with difficulty to open her handbag. 'You come here to see a nutcase and he just insults and humiliates you.'

Eventually she stuffed the photograph into her coat pocket and was about to leave. In the roller shutter she'd entered through was a door, and in the turmoil of the moment she had as much trouble working out how to open it as she had her handbag. She took a deep breath, then said, 'How dare you say something like that to my face?'

'I don't like being used,' Gedeon said coldly.

'What gives you the right to trample so disdainfully over the feelings of a mother?'

Finally she recalled that earlier Gedeon had pulled the handle upwards to open the door. But as hard as she tried, it wouldn't budge a centimetre.

'Have you locked me in?'

She whipped around.

As Ricarda grew more furious, so Gedeon seemed to become calmer. He stood up and gave her the same friendly look as when they'd met. 'Don't worry, I'll let you go in a minute. Just as soon as you've calmed down and listened to my apology.'

'Apology?' The whole thing was getting more and more bizarre.

'Yes, I'm sorry,' Gedeon said, completing his volte-face. 'But I had to do it.'

'Had to do what?'

'I needed to see your real feelings, your honest emotions. You had to get rid of the mask you'd come in with.'

Is he alright in the head?

'I'm not wearing a mask.'

'Oh, we all wear masks. Without such a shell we'd be defenceless, at the mercy of life's slings and arrows. For example, you made me notice your lack of wedding ring by subconsciously trying to shield that finger with your hand. You're embarrassed that your marriage is no longer intact.'

Ricarda made a disapproving hand gesture and demanded again to be let out.

Undeterred, Gedeon continued saying something she had no wish to hear.

'They say that people reveal their true selves when drunk. As we don't sell alcohol here I had to make you livid, because in my experience anger has a similar cleansing effect.'

She blew dismissively through her lips.

Enough crap for today. I want to get out of here.

'The whole thing was a mistake.'

He nodded. 'I completely understand that you see it that way. Most of my initial sessions end like this.'

I'm not surprised, if you begin all of them like that.

'Now that we've met, why don't you sleep on it? And if you want to go on... well, you know where you can find me.'

I most certainly do.

He pointed again to the second door and this time Ricarda opted for the exit beside the shelves of buckets, which at least opened without any resistance.

Out of here.

Directly behind the door she found herself in a corridor that led to a kitchen where three staff members in silly uniforms were loading reconstituted meat onto flat buns. They barely took any notice of her as she hurried past the deep-fat fryer and into the gaudy restaurant area.

69

Out. Let's get away from here.

Leaving the fast food joint, she hurried to where she had parked her car, stumbling through a puddle in the gutter. As she struggled to open her bloody handbag and find the key, her hair got wetter and wetter. By the time she finally located it, she felt as if she'd had a shower fully dressed.

Exhausted, she fell into the passenger seat.

The media pay handsomely for exclusives.

'What an arsehole!'

There was a knock at the window. She wound it down and found herself looking at the animated face of a man who appeared slightly too old for a hipster beard and nose ring. Given the weather, he was also wearing a completely unsuitable woolly hat which was soaked through like a sponge.

'What's wrong?' he asked.

'I'm sorry,' Ricarda said.

'We were waiting for you at the back entrance.'

She nodded. Full of self-loathing she said, 'I know. But I just couldn't do it.'

Then she closed the window, started the engine and left the TV crew's production manager just standing in the rain.

14

TILL

Inside the hospital

Death.

This was how it must feel to be in its clutches. Stifling, relentless and cold. Every memory of warmth, love and security obliterated; every attempt to escape it condemned to failure.

It was as if Till were buried beneath an avalanche. He tried to fight his way back to the raw surface of his consciousness. Tried to breathe, move his ribcage, then his arms and legs. It felt as if he were attempting to swim in a liquid the consistency of mercury.

One part of his mind told him that this was just a side effect of the drug they'd sedated him with when he arrived at the hospital.

Right after I flipped out.

The first thing he was able to remember was standing in the half-open tube of the glass body scanner when he arrived, his arms raised in a 'surrender' pose. His beltless trousers had slowly but surely slid down over his narrow hips and he'd felt woozy. The anxiety and journey strapped to a stretcher had taken their toll.

'You can move on,' a sonorous, faceless voice had told him over the loudspeaker in the ceiling once he'd undergone the digital scanning procedure.

Till had no idea where exactly he'd arrived in the complex, but he suspected that the ambulance had stopped in the underground garage. The basement that had originally been earmarked to house the hotel kitchen had been converted into a reception area.

Till had followed an arrow painted on the grey, antiseptic plastic floor until he came to a security gate that reminded him of the interior of a shipping container, with video cameras on the bare ceiling. As he walked he felt as if he were swaying. Like in the ambulance when it drove onto the ferry that brought him here.

Waiting for him beyond the gate were two orderlies who looked as if they could handle beefier patients than Till. They gave him a friendly smile, but he could read in their eyes that he'd better avoid doing anything silly.

'Good afternoon, Herr Winter,' the white older-looking of the two musclemen had said, older-looking, perhaps, on account of the grey hair that he kept cropped short with a severe military parting. Till recalled how he'd flinched internally. *Winter*. The new name sounded unfamiliar and negative somehow, like a subtle accusation.

'We must ask you to empty your pockets,' the other, black orderly had said, in the friendly tone you might hear at an airport, but without taking his eyes off Till for a second. Till obeyed the instructions and put a packet of chewing gum, a scrunched-up tissue and a shrink-wrapped Aspirin Plus C in the plastic dish provided. He looked around.

Down there looked like the supply tunnels you find beneath airports, hospitals and modern hotels. Large enough to get lost. Cramped enough to accelerate his heart rate.

On either side of him, brightly lit, whitewashed, reinforced concrete corridors seemed to stretch into the distance almost without end, but they were secured at regular intervals by floor-to-ceiling grille doors. No opportunity to escape, but that was not his plan. On the contrary.

Till pointed to the security gate he'd come through. 'Am I right in thinking that the body scanner works with terahertz technology?'

He'd garnered this nugget of knowledge from a Discovery Channel programme about security technology at Frankfurt Airport.

'Why do you want to know that?' the grey-haired orderly asked, now looking alarmed rather than friendly.

'So does that mean you can only see what I'm wearing on my body and not what's inside it?' Instead of giving an answer, the black orderly unclipped the walkie-talkie from his belt. Till hadn't seen a weapon on either of them, but staff in German psychiatric hospitals were not usually armed.

'So you've got no idea what's in my stomach?'

'What the hell are you talking about?'

'Two hours ago I swallowed an acid-sensitive capsule. According to my calculations the acid in my stomach will have dissolved the shell and then it'll all kick off.'

'What's going to kick off?' the two orderlies had asked in unison. Till's answer, in combination with his half-hearted attempt to run away, had ultimately earned him his goodnight jab.

Two ticks later he was on the floor.

Now he'd woken up again, wondering whether the orderlies had overdone the sedative dose and he was crossing the final threshold. In any event, the last moments of his life played out again in his mind like a poorly lit Super 8 film.

The one thing that didn't really correspond with dying was this light. It wasn't a light you moved towards, but rather one you wanted to run away from.

Pink. Bright, pastel pink and absolutely everywhere since his first blink. Everything in the room was completely pink. Walls, ceilings, floors, even the skirting boards and lamps – all except for the stainless steel toilet without a seat and accompanying washbasin. When Till saw the sink he knew he was still alive and where they'd taken him.

Okay, that's the first hurdle successfully overcome.

Till closed his eyes and opened them again two seconds later, but perhaps it was two hours or even days. At any rate he was no longer alone in the room.

This fact ought to have reassured him, because he was still alive and had completed stage one of his plan.

But when he saw the man beside his bed, who curiously looked both familiar and unfamiliar, Till felt a sinister confusion. It wasn't the facial features or poise that he recognised, but something else. Something that profoundly disturbed him, because it reminded Till of himself: the hatred in the man's eyes.

The familiar stranger stared at him just as Till would stare at his son's murderer if he ever managed to confront him.

15

'Herr Winter, how are you?' the man asked in a voice that sounded as if it wanted to burst out of its owner's body. An alien body you had to get used to, just like the name he'd addressed him with. The voice was croaky, almost brittle. Slightly too deep for a man who was slim, verging on gangly, with the face of a crow. Deep-set eyes, narrow cheeks and a nose as pointed as a clothes hook.

'Who are you?' Till asked, and the man introduced himself as Dr Marten Kasov, senior doctor on Ward III, without explaining what differentiated this ward from the other two, or anything else. Till had no idea of the hierarchical relationship the doctor had with Professor Thea Sänger, who according to Skania was the actual director of the hospital.

'What did you give me?' Till asked, feeling for his head as he tried to sit up on his narrow bed, also pink. He was wearing a mouse-grey tracksuit, slightly too short for him. Till felt washed and clean. His bandage was gone too; now there were just a few plasters on his bald head. His feet, however, were in stripy socks with rubber studs.

'Flunitrazepam,' Kasov said.

Till nodded cautiously. It felt as if his head had been filled with a hot liquid that burned uncomfortably and with the slightest jerk could slop like soup over the edge of a bowl. He felt dizzy and nauseous. He didn't know if this was a normal side effect of the medication that had incapacitated him.

'Why am I still alive?' he asked, recalling the role he was playing. He had claimed to have swallowed a bomb, after all.

'Why shouldn't you be alive?'

Kasov looked around as if there was something else to gaze at in the pink cell apart from missing windows, missing door handles and missing privacy. Till was surprised that the doctor was standing in the room rather than communicating with him via a camera in the ceiling or through the flap in the security door. And he was surprised by the small notepad that Kasov took from the breast pocket of his doctor's coat without taking his eyes off Till.

Kasov flipped open the notepad and turned it so that Till could read the message that had already been written for him.

'Do you know where you are?' the doctor asked, but Till was no longer able to give a sensible answer. The few words that Kasov had scrawled in capital letters on his notepad had put him in a state of shock.

DON'T LOOK AT THE CAMERA ON THE CEILING!

Immediately, of course, Till was tempted to do exactly what the doctor had just ordered him not to. But Kasov had already turned the page and was showing him a new message:

I KNOW WHO YOU ARE!

'This is our crisis intervention room,' the senior doctor said, answering his own question and continuing to smile incongruously.

'Modern psychiatric institutions have at least two isolation chambers in case several aggressive patients need to be locked away at the same time. We have three.'

The way he was standing in front of Till, with his back to the door and thus to the camera, nobody outside could see how the doctor was communicating with him. Anyone analysing the video later would assume they'd had a normal introductory conversation.

'The walls and ceilings are painted Camilla pink, because studies have shown that this colour has a relaxing effect on people.'

Kasov held the notepad to his chest once more. This time with a single word that the ward doctor had just now scribbled on the paper and which gave Till an unpleasant hot flush:

FAKER!!!

Till blinked and wiped sweat from his brow that he could feel but wasn't actually there. He resisted the urge to feel his head. The lack of burn injuries had probably aroused the doctor's suspicion.

Till wondered whether to get up and snatch the notepad from Kasov, but there was already a new message:

ONE FALSE WORD AND I'LL KILL YOU!

'Well, does it relax you?' he asked, adding another three exclamation marks.

'What?' Till swallowed nervously, barely able to cope with the doctor's bizarre behaviour.

'The pink?'

'I'd prefer black,' he uttered after a while.

He tried to catch the doctor's steel-blue, alert eyes. 'It goes with my attitude to life.'

'I understand.'

Kasov put his notepad away and told Till he had to be getting on, but was happy that the patient was feeling a little better.

'Can I... I mean... I don't know my way around here... How does it work? Can I make a phone call?'

With a feigned smile on his lips, Kasov gave him a 'nice try' look. He then turned his back, which Till found astonishingly courageous, seeing as the doctor had just threatened him.

He was even more surprised when the doctor didn't close the door behind him.

The detention cell was wide open.

Although every fibre of his body bristled against it and an inner voice screamed at him not to do it, Till couldn't resist the open cell door. If you gave a bottle to someone dying of thirst they would drink it no matter how brown the liquid sloshing inside. So he got going, shuffling slowly forwards, metre by metre. And then Till stepped out of the pink isolation cell into the unfamiliar and terrifying world of the Steinklinik.

16

TRAMNITZ

The little boy ran quicker than he ever had before, although that didn't mean very much seeing as he'd only been born into this wretched life seven and a half years ago. Besides, his not particularly long legs felt numbed. He had pins and needles, which wasn't surprising if you couldn't stretch them fully for days on end.

The tingling in his legs did have the advantage, however, of masking the pain whenever his bare feet stepped on a branch, stone or pine cone.

Luckily it had just been raining so the forest floor was softer. In high summer he'd have sustained many cuts during his aimless dash.

It was dark and the clouds hung as deeply as 'the runs in the morning', as his father used to say, without ever explaining what exactly he meant by that.

He turned right onto a not particularly firm path that in good weather mountain bikers used on their way up to the Teufelsberg. Tripping over a tree root, he lost his balance, heard a crack, and a pain shot up his leg as if he'd fallen into a trap. He toppled forwards and was just able to break his fall with his hand, though that brought a second wave of pain no less intense than the first. This time it sped from his wrist right up to his shoulder.

'Shit!' he shouted, but didn't cry, something he'd learned from his lessons down in the cellar. And those had been far more painful than this silly fall in the dark.

No, not even if it hurt really badly. Boys don't cry. Wasn't that his father's favourite song?

'Shit, shit, shit!'

'You don't use those words,' he suddenly heard a voice say, coming from the forest right behind him.

Followed by a resounding clip round the ear that send him crashing to the ground again.

Only when he realised that his attempt to run away had failed yet again and his father had caught him could he no longer hold back the tears.

Barely ten minutes later he was home again. They lived on the edge of the forest, in an area they would never have been able to afford if Daddy hadn't got the groundsman's job at the hockey club. As part of the package they were accommodated in the little house behind the pitches.

'We're going to do some more practice,' Daddy said when they came in, sweaty and filthy, but Mummy wasn't listening. She was rolling a joint and staring goggle-eyed at the television, which was showing a porn film. Mummy always got new ones from the video shop. Daddy didn't like it if he came home and had already seen the film.

'Come on, then,' his father said when they were in the cellar and standing beside 'Trixi'. He had no idea why his father had given the thing this name. It sounded far too nice for what it was in reality: a wooden box full of fear.

'Get in.'

The little boy didn't hesitate. The last time he'd refused to climb into the incubator, Daddy had broken his nose and he couldn't go to school for a month. This time the punishment would surely be worse, seeing as he'd tried to run away from home. So he clambered awkwardly (his damn leg still hurt like hell after his fall) up the wooden step onto the workbench where Trixi stood, the size of a child's coffin. Barely had he lain down on the tatty towel, the only 'mattress' in the crate, than Daddy closed the lid and bent his knees so he could talk to him through one of the plexiglass circles in the handholes on the side.

'Why did you run away?' he asked. His father had good intuition; he always knew when he was being lied to, which was why the boy would be better off telling the truth.

'Because I'm frightened, Daddy.'

A pause. For a long while his father said nothing, and then, 'I understand. Do you remember what I said you mustn't ever do if you feel frightened?'

'Run away.'

His father clicked his tongue approvingly. 'Precisely. You have to confront your greatest fear. Look it straight in the eye. It's what's called fear exposure.'

Closing his eyes and summoning all his courage, the boy in the incubator said, 'I–I don't think it's getting any better, Daddy. My fear. It's getting worse in here.'

'Oh, really? Is that what you think?'

'I'd rather...'

'What?'

'Play. With Thomas and Alex. My friends. Outside.'

'Hmm. I thought you wanted a pet.'

The boy opened his eyes again and tried to snatch a glance through one of the circular plexiglass holes in the side, but all he could see was the dusty cellar floor and a tin of varnish beside the garden tools.

'Yes!' he hurried to say keenly when his father asked again. Of course I want a pet. *'That too.'*

He heard his father laugh.

'That's what I thought, my boy. And that's why Daddy has got you one. It took me a long time to find it.'

With these words he opened one of the handholes.

'What is it, Daddy? A little cat? A puppy?'

Perhaps just a guinea pig, but that would be great too. Even though he'd heard at school that you should never keep one guinea pig on its own.

Hopefully Daddy had thought of that.

'Have fun with your new friend,' he heard him say before it turned dark at a stroke. His father had switched off the cellar light.

And the child was alone. Alone with himself. With his fear. And with the large, hairy spider that was trying determinedly to climb across his cheek as Guido Tramnitz screamed ever louder in distress.

17

'Bad dream?'

When Tramnitz opened his eyes his immediate worry was that his arsehole of a father had somehow managed to rise from the dead and catapult himself from the nightmare of his memories straight into the hospital room. Then he acclimatised to the harsh overhead light in the room and gradually realised that the nightmare with his father was over and actually it was another fucker standing beside his bed.

'Piss off, Frieder,' he hissed at the surgeon who had cleaned up his artery last week, thereby saving his life.

'Oh, you're welcome. My pleasure.' Frieder smiled back. For that alone Tramnitz really wanted to smash his face in, but still felt too weak.

It wasn't the first time he'd suddenly blacked out and collapsed. Fucking genes. He'd inherited the shitty carotid artery from his father.

But it was the first time that an MRI and operating theatre had been close by, first to diagnose and then treat at once the spontaneous blockage in his artery.

The Steinklinik was bloody well kitted out seeing as it only housed psychos. It was almost better than the Virchow, where

Tramnitz had worked on the neonatal ward until they nabbed him. But there had been complications with the dressing of the wound. The operation scar had become inflamed. On the day he was due to return to the closed ward he had a temperature, breathing difficulties and red blotches on his skin – all symptoms of substantial blood poisoning. Thanks to antibiotics he was on the mend, but the tablets were upsetting his stomach.

'The nurse has been to see me, the senior doctor came even though I didn't ask for him, so what do *you* want now?'

Frieder, who Tramnitz thought moved like a poof (softly, calmly and almost noiselessly on the lino), walked around the bed and said nothing. Guido hated everything about this man: the designer baby-pink polo shirt he wore with the collar up like a yuppie; the simple but elegant clothes which curved over his affluent belly. He wore deck shoes, of course, rather than orthopaedic slippers and all in all he looked as if he'd just arrived freshly tanned from the lake, where the airflow on his motorboat had given him a blond blow-dry, even though the guy was about as sporty as a potato.

Now Frieder was standing by the window in the single room, peering through the glass that not even a hammer could open. He let his eyes wander across the garden where usually at this time a group of patients would be having a stroll with the orderlies, puffing away by the hedges in the smokers' area or letting off steam on the basketball court. As the thick panes of glass were soundproof as well as impact-resistant, Tramnitz couldn't be sure so long as Frieder kept blocking his view. But given how heavily it was still raining, he suspected that there wouldn't be much activity out there.

'During the operation I got the impression that you're very

well acquainted with my private life,' the doctor said out of the blue and turned around. Although he wasn't wearing a ring, Tramnitz thought he'd heard that Frieder had been married in the past. *Maybe he's not a poof after all.* On the other hand, many queers got married as a front, didn't they?

'Losing a patient under the knife because of drunkenness – I don't call that private life,' he replied. Looking at the freshly showered pretty boy, Tramnitz felt even more unkempt. The bad food here had given him a small pimple on his nose and his hair hadn't been washed since the operation. He hated his unhygienic state and longed for the day when he could finally get back to the fitness bench.

'Been on the sauce already this morning, have you?' he said, trying to provoke the surgeon.

'No more than before your operation,' Frieder said, sounding strangely amused.

He pulled over a kick stool, which was meant for reaching the top cupboards beside the door, but which he used as a seat.

'Let me tell you a story.'

Tramnitz really did think he could smell schnapps on Frieder's breath.

'Can I press the alarm button in the meantime?' he asked the surgeon.

'Be my guest, but you'll never find out what's wrong with you.'

'What *is* wrong with me?'

Tramnitz was annoyed that the doctor was dictating the course of their conversation. Even if he called for a nurse, she would do an immediate about-turn as soon as she saw the boss.

'The thing is, my ex-wife hates dentists. She's absolutely terrified of injections and, well, as luck would have it, she of all people had to undergo root canal treatment.'

'And this is of interest to me because...?'

Undeterred, Frieder continued with his story and even crossed his legs as if making himself comfortable beside Tramnitz's bed.

'Two years later I wake up because I can hear her crying in the bathroom. I get up, feel my way across the dark bedroom and see her. I mean, I see my wife, but I barely recognise her. Her cheek has swollen to the size of a grapefruit, as if she's been in a fight.'

'Maybe she likes a good beating,' Tramnitz muttered, but Frieder seemed not to notice.

'So she goes to the dentist. A different one because the guy who did her root canal treatment has closed his practice.'

'Not a good sign.'

'You could say that. The new dentist, a woman, takes an X-ray of her lower jaw and guess what she finds?'

'A jerboa?'

'The tip of a needle. Right inside her jaw. It must have snapped off inside her root canal and the idiot didn't say a thing. Which meant they had to drill into my ex's jaw from below. A total nightmare, not just for someone with a phobia of dentists.'

Tramnitz grunted. 'It's a terrific story, but what's it got to do with me?'

He stuffed a pillow behind his back so he could sit up more comfortably in bed. When he stopped rustling, Frieder continued. 'I don't have children, but my best friend's got a son. Once, when he was eight, the boy disappeared in an adventure playground in Storkow. I'd gone along with them for the day. We lost sight of him and then spent two hours searching high and low. There was a cornfield they'd turned into a maze, and that's where he'd vanished. Not knowing where that boy was gave my friend the biggest fright of his life. Even today he breaks out into a sweat just thinking about it.'

'Unlike me – I'd get a stiffy.'

Frieder nodded. 'Indeed, and that's why I told you the dentist story.'

The surgeon's eyes glazed over. Frieder was so lost in his thoughts that all of a sudden Tramnitz felt as if the doctor were looking straight through him as he spoke.

'While I was in this adventure playground and we were calling out the boy's name over and over again, I swore that if he'd been abducted I'd help my friend kill the bastard who'd done it. Until the boy turned up again I had quite a good sense of what parents must feel whose children vanish without trace. And what perverted bastards like you do to the relatives.'

Tramnitz gave an exaggerated sigh. 'Why didn't you kill me when you had the chance on the operating table?' Gesturing inverted commas with his fingers, he said, 'Why didn't you make a "professional blunder", Doctor?'

'Oh, don't say that.' Frieder grinned, getting to his feet.

'What?'

Gradually Tramnitz began to guess what the doctor was hinting at.

'Didn't you con the assessor by claiming that a sinister power had implanted a chip inside you that made you hear voices ordering you to kill people?'

Tramnitz didn't respond.

'Well now there really *is* something inside you,' the surgeon said, pointing at Tramnitz's head. 'Why do you think you've got blood poisoning? I forgot something. Something which in all probability is going to cause you lasting and unbearable pain.'

'My lawyer will have your guts for garters,' Tramnitz threatened. 'Before, during and after the MRI scan I'm going to apply for right now.'

'Go ahead. But what I've left behind inside you isn't visible. Unlike the broken needle in my wife's jaw, it can't be detected by ultrasound, CT or X-ray.'

Tramnitz broke out into a sweat. 'What is it?' he said, instinctively feeling the dressing on his carotid artery.

Frieder's grin became more diabolical. 'Don't be so impatient. You'll find out soon enough when you're in sheer agony. Unless...'

Frieder made a vague hand movement, probably to suggest that he'd be prepared to remove the object from Tramnitz's body on certain conditions.

'Unless *what*?' Tramnitz asked.

'I had a very moving conversation recently. And I promised the father I'd do everything humanly possible to help him.'

'What the hell are you talking about?'

Frieder came closer and now there was no doubt that he'd resorted to Dutch courage for this conversation.

'Admit to the murder of Max Berkhoff and show the parents where his body is.'

18

TILL

Till stepped out of the isolation room and looked around, but the corridor was deserted; Dr Kasov nowhere to be seen. Only the oppressive feeling of menace that the man had left with Till was a reminder that he'd been there at all.

What does he want from me?

Till wondered whether he might have met the doctor at some point in the past. *No. I would have remembered that irritating voice. Or would I?*

And why was I greeted by such hatred?

Till looked left and right like a child trying to cross the road. The corridor outside the isolation cells was unusually wide for a hospital and it had a high, vaulted ceiling with spotlights that cast warm light on the cream-coloured walls.

He went left, in the direction from where he could hear faint classical music. The corridor ended in an area that made Till gulp.

No wonder there are so few pictures of the rooms inside the Steinklinik on the internet.

There were quite a number of people who regarded even a television set in a cell as soft justice. What would they say if they knew that mentally ill criminals were able to spend their free time in a lobby that could give that of the Ritz a run for its money?

Till was standing in an oval room whose domed ceiling, supported by columns, towered several storeys above him like a cathedral. The floor, set with heavy white-and-grey marble tiles, offered space for half a dozen sofas and twice as many armchairs, all of which looked as if you could sleep comfortably in them. And in fact this was precisely what an elderly, bearded man was doing. He was so small that the newspaper he'd laid on his stomach while he enjoyed forty winks looked like a blanket.

Instinctively Till looked out for liveried pageboys and waitresses, bustling among the guests with trays or menus, but he didn't see even a nurse or a doctor. Not even at the counter to his right, which must have once been constructed for the reception and above which a subtly printed sign advertised the 'DISPENSARY'.

So far as he could make out, it was only patients sitting here.

Two young-looking women were whispering to each other and gazing at the large fireplace, its flames behind a glass window, presumably for safety.

Right in front of the flickering fire a woman of indeterminable age was sitting on the floor, absentmindedly combing her ash-blond hair and humming softly to herself. A tall man, in a tracksuit like Till, stood apart from the others by the bow window of the domed hall, staring into the rain. The sun had already set and sulphurous-yellow park lamps were doing their best to prevent the outside world from being completely swallowed by a black hole. Beneath their shades the raindrops danced in beams of light like moths in a swarm.

Only now did Till realise that they were on the upper ground floor, for on the other side of the windows, which were no doubt locked, was a terrace from which broad, curved steps led into the hospital grounds.

But this was not the biggest surprise, nor was it the classical music (Chopin, if Till wasn't mistaken) gurgling from invisible speakers.

The really unusual thing, which had almost completely captured his attention as he entered the lobby, was the Christmas tree! It appeared to be growing out of the marble floor and almost reached up to the domed ceiling.

'I know what you're thinking,' Till heard a friendly voice behind him say.

Till, who'd been staring at the ceiling to work out where the tree stopped, turned around and was nonplussed once more when he read the name tag on the woman's white coat.

He'd expected Professor Thea Sänger to be a white woman in her early fifties, not an Asian woman who looked as if she were in her mid-thirties or even younger.

Professor Sänger wore a doctor's coat that was slightly too large for her five-foot-three height, and shapeless shoes, clearly chosen with the intent of concealing any sexual attraction. This was surely a smart move in an institution where twenty-five per cent of the inmates were sexual offenders, but it was a poor attempt all the same. As long as she failed to hide her dark, almond eyes and jet-black hair, she could go around in a sack and still arouse the illicit desires of some of those here present.

'What did you say?' Till asked when he found his voice again.

'Too early for a Christmas tree.' The director pointed at the undecorated fir. 'That's what you're thinking, isn't it?' But it's part of the occupational therapy. We're all going to decorate it together next week. Each patient can make a wish for the new year and hang it as a colourful note on the tree. The hospital management will read it and who knows? Maybe some of those wishes will come true.'

Till knew what would be on his note.

I want to know what happened to my son.

But he certainly wouldn't hang it on the tree to get an answer.

'Come with me,' the director said, gently stroking his arm and pointing at the corridor to their right. 'I'll show you the community.'

'The community?'

The doctor led the way and Till followed her. 'The domed hall separates the west wing from the east wing. If this really were the White House, we'd now be heading for the Oval Office. Officially, however, the west wing houses Ward III, the open part of the prison,' Sänger said without looking around. 'During the day you can hang out in the common areas, such as the lobby you just saw.'

They entered a tall, vaulted corridor that looked exactly like the one Till had come from, except here all the doors were open.

As they went past, Till caught a glimpse of the various rooms. In one stood an exercise bike and treadmill, in another three men were watching television and laughing. In the last room several benches stood in front of a plain altar. 'Gym, telly room and ecumenical prayer room,' Sänger explained with no let-up in her pace. 'Do you believe in God?'

'Not any more,' he muttered.

'This room here will be of far more interest to you, then.'

At the far end of the corridor the director opened a heavy, frosted glass door. In an instant, the air was filled with the clatter of crockery and cutlery, and the smell of schnitzel, roast potatoes and industrial vegetables.

'Our canteen and dining room. Fifty people fit in here comfortably, but, as you can see, everyone has their space.'

Till heard two women giggling, followed by the obscene throaty laugh of a man who he couldn't spot, as the seats were set at angles. Although it smelled of usual hospital fare in here, the way the place was kitted out, they could have easily wandered into a Starbucks or Marché by mistake. The interior was dominated by dark, hardwood furniture. Black, bulbous designer lamps hung from the ceiling and there were even some thickly padded lounge chairs by low coffee tables.

'I know again what you're thinking,' Sänger said with a smile. 'It's far more relaxed on Ward III than any of the others. But don't get the wrong impression. Of course there are fixed therapy sessions. And *open* imprisonment doesn't mean inmates can just go wandering off. The only doors open here are the ones we unlock for you. And so there's no access to the other wards, such as the one for multiple offenders in the east wing.'

She looked at him and for a moment Till was expecting her, like Kasov, to take a notepad from her coat. Instinctively he looked around for the ubiquitous cameras.

How the hell am I going to get to Tramnitz from here?

'Breakfast is from half past seven to half past eight, lunch between half past twelve and half past one. Supper is from six o'clock for an hour,' Sänger said. 'So you've still time to queue up now.'

SEBASTIAN FITZEK

A handful of people, predominantly men, were standing by the servery, waiting for a kind-looking, round-faced cook in a hairnet to shovel the dishes of their choice onto a plate.

'You're allowed outside from half past one to half past two every afternoon. And from ten at night until seven in the morning all patients are locked inside their rooms.'

'Why?' Till asked.

'Why do we lock you up?'

'No. Why is it so relaxed here on Ward III?'

She took him to a self-service island in the centre of the canteen where you could get sugar, milk and spices as well as drinks from taps. Till registered that all the crockery, glasses and cutlery were made of blunt Tupperware plastic like those given to little children to prevent them from hurting themselves.

Sänger took a glass and filled it with diet cola.

'Let me ask you a question: Why are you here?'

'You know my file.'

'I want to hear it from your own mouth.'

'Where should I begin?'

'With your name.'

'That's absurd.'

As Till looked around, it struck him that he hadn't encountered a single orderly or nurse since leaving the crisis intervention room.

'Here on Ward III we have twenty-three patients,' the doctor said. 'Three of them suffer from permanent amnesia. One can't even remember himself. How about you?'

He sighed.

Was this a test?

'My name is Patrick Winter, I'm forty-one years old and I'm an actuary. And I want to die.'

'Why?'

'Why should I go on living?'

'Good point.'

She took the first sip of her cola.

Then things went out of control. Till hadn't been anticipating this, and evidently neither had the director. They couldn't fend off the attack because it all happened far too quickly.

19

The patient had appeared from nowhere, even though he was carrying a fully laden tray in front of his sunken chest.

He looked ill, not just mentally, with his sunken cheeks and high, wrinkle-free forehead. *Like a skull covered with a layer of skin*, Till thought as the guy greeted him with a 'Hey, arsehole!' and barged into him. Then he felt the gunk in his eye. Warm, burning. And sweet, which was the most disgusting thing of all, because only when he smelled and tasted it did Till realise that the guy must have gobbed into his face and the spit run into his mouth.

'What the...?'

Till wiped his lips with his sleeve and was about to pursue the idiot to smash his face in, but Professor Sänger held him back with an astonishingly firm grip.

If she'd raised her voice, maybe even shouted, it would have only fanned the flames of the anger that had flared up abruptly inside him. But when she whispered, it confused Till, and in his confusion he missed the opportunity to assault the bastard from behind.

'Okay, let me give you three pieces of advice,' Thea Sänger said. She was so close to him now that he could smell her lavender shampoo. 'First: keep away from Kasov. He's an arsehole.'

While Till was wondering why the psychiatrist was using such language, she continued. 'Second: the idiot who just spat at you is called Armin Wolf. If you don't watch out, he'll kill you faster than you could kill yourself in here.'

'But why—'

'And last, but not least, the interfering old bag who's just appeared...'

Till turned around and saw the livid face of a very angry patient taking long, rapid strides across the canteen, her jaws tensed, both hands balled into fists.

'Not again!' she shouted, and Till wondered who or what the middle-aged woman with her greying updo could mean. It was only when she came so close that he could smell the peppermint on her breath that he realised the woman's 'I've had enough now!' was aimed at Thea rather than him.

'Give it back right now.'

'The old bag is quite right,' whispered Thea, who of course was neither called Thea nor the director of the hospital, unlike the person in the trouser suit who had planted herself in front of them and was barking at the patient beside Till. 'Give me back my coat and go to your room. This episode will have consequences, Frau Suharto.'

20

'Please let me apologise, Herr Winter.'

Professor Thea Sänger adjusted the turned-up collar of her coat, which she had taken off the patient and put on herself. She sat at the desk in front of which Till had already taken a seat.

The director's office was in the west wing, with a view of the grounds. The outside lighting by this part of the building was brighter, like floodlights, presumably for security reasons. Till marvelled at the Steinklinik's extensive parkland, which lay one storey beneath them and was reminiscent of a romantic, slightly hilly, moorland scene. With a little imagination you could picture the winding paths lined with fruit trees leading to the sea behind dune-like mounds – or at least a lake, but not a three-metre-high concrete fence reinforced by barbed wire, above which aeroplanes took off or came into land at regular intervals. The thick security windows kept out virtually all the aircraft noise, however.

'We are literally under water here at the moment,' Sänger said, turning to the window at her back and pointing at the treetops swaying in the wind. 'We've had problems with the pumping equipment and haven't been able to clear the access road of water. Our main entrance was flooded and I was there to get up to speed on the situation.'

She sighed.

'Clearly your fellow patient used the opportunity to pilfer my coat from the nurses' room. But I don't understand how you were able to leave the isolation room without supervision, Herr Winter.'

'It was Dr Kasov who—'

'Really?' Sänger briefly looked surprised, then said, 'Yes, actually that was agreed.'

She made a note on a pad bearing the logo of a pharmaceutical firm, tore off the sheet of paper and put it in her coat pocket.

'How are you?'

'Fine,' Till said, his answer as automatic as most people's when asked this question by a stranger. Then it struck him that he ought to be grabbing his head and grimacing.

But he didn't want to exaggerate; he was sure the director was well versed in sorting out the fakers from the genuine patients. Especially as her colleague Kasov seemed already to have seen through him, though Till couldn't begin to explain how his cover could have been blown so quickly.

FAKER!

He had to get to the emergency mobile in the library as quickly as possible and call Skania to find out if he knew anything about Kasov and his relationship with Patrick Winter.

'How are you coping with the medicine?' Sänger asked.

'The sedative?'

'I was actually thinking about the depot injection we gave you. The antipsychotic.'

'What the hell is that?'

Till bit his tongue because he'd responded spontaneously like an uncouth fireman rather than a mathematician who through his work at a health insurance firm might just know what the doctor was talking about.

'It controls your urge to self-harm,' explained Sänger, whose suspicion clearly hadn't been aroused. 'A depot injection is often effective for a month or more and obviates the need for a daily dose of medicine on the psychiatric ward.'

And makes it impossible to deceive people.

Bugger.

Till had hoped he'd be able to spit out the tablets they gave him, but now he could forget that. 'Is this forced medication legally authorised?'

The question appeared to catch Sänger off guard. For a long while she said nothing, just raised her eyebrows. She jotted down another note before finally giving him an answer. 'You can assume it is, yes.'

She got up and asked Till to follow her.

'How long am I going to be in here?'

Sänger paused and opted for the typical psychiatrist's trick of answering a question with a question: 'How long do *you* think you're going to have to stay here with us?'

As long as it takes to find out the truth from Tramnitz.

Talking of Tramnitz...

He couldn't, of course, reveal his true intentions to anybody in here, and certainly not to the director, but somehow he needed access to information about the perverted bastard as quickly as possible. Till decided that a perfectly naive question might not hold out any hope of success, but at least it was harmless.

'Is Tramnitz on this ward too?'

Sänger frowned. 'How extraordinary that you of all people should ask that. No comment.'

What did she mean by 'extraordinary' and 'you of all people'?

Till probed further. 'On the telly they said the child murderer was here.'

'Once more, I can't discuss other patients with you.'

'Is he near me?'

This follow-up question remained unanswered too. Till almost expressed his concern at having to breathe the same air as such a violent monster, but fortunately remembered just in time that this might not sound particularly credible coming from the mouth of someone who'd just tried to take their own life.

They passed a corridor window and Till paused. 'Is that a bus stop outside?' he asked, confused.

Sänger took two paces back and looked through the window too.

Here on the eastern side of the hospital grounds the tarmacked paths were wider than on the western side by Sänger's office. So far as Till could make out in the light of the lamps, they would be overshadowed during the day by large trees, some of which had already lost a proportion of their leaves that were now being scattered by the wind across a large lawn.

'Yes, that's a bus stop.'

'What for?'

Sänger shrugged and motioned to Till to keep going. 'I'm not a great fan of the idea, but I have to concede that it has worked.'

They turned right where the black orderly was waiting for them, the one Till had encountered yesterday at the security gate.

'Idea?'

'Occasionally we have patients who've got problems with their short-term memory. They forget why they've been locked up in here and become restless, nervous, sometimes violent. If we notice these patients getting particularly agitated, we allow them to sit out there and wait for the bus that's going to take them away from the hospital.' Her reply sounded as if she'd trotted it out hundreds of times before.

The orderly, who had gone ahead of them, opened an electronic double door with a switch in the wall and the three of them entered a windowless cell block.

'Thanks, Simon,' Sänger said, and now Till knew the name of the muscular black orderly with the friendly, relaxed face.

'A few minutes later the patients have forgotten why they're sitting there and where they want to go. They've calmed down and can go back inside.'

'And the bus never arrives, does it?'

Behind them, the double doors closed with a loud bang. Till was the only one who flinched.

'Not number 69 that goes to the station, as it says on the bus stop timetable. But our library bus stops there three times a week. The patients can board the bus and borrow books if they like.'

'She drives the bus.'

In his head Till heard his brother-in-law's voice and shuddered.

They passed a number of indestructible-looking security doors, in each of which were set two flaps that opened outwards. One was at eye level, the other one, lower down, was like a cat flap, through which a food tray could be pushed into the cell.

'You hired a bus driver specifically for that?' Till asked.

'No. A patient.'

Seda, Till thought. Skania had told him the name.

My only contact in here is a patient?

'It's what she used to do, you see. She drove the Steglitz mobile library. But I fear that after her performance today we're going to have to withdraw that privilege.'

'Performance?' Till said.

'Well, if the lady didn't introduce herself to you then I've already said too much.'

Till realised that the doctor could only be referring to the stolen coat and the charade in the canteen.

'Do you have any other questions?'

Yes, about a million.

Till shook his head. 'Not for the time being.'

'Good. Simon will now lock your room, then. We'll see each other on the early visit. Goodnight.'

For a while he watched the director go back the way they'd come, waddling slightly as she went. Then the orderly asked him to go on a bit further until they came to door number 1310.

Simon took a long-handled key from the depths of his trouser pockets and opened the lock.

A blend of odours of old socks, sweat and disinfectant assailed Till's nose. Even under normal circumstances he didn't like closed rooms, but here, as an invisible claw of claustrophobia clutched at his chest, the nightmare got worse with every step into the square room.

'Here we are,' Simon said, sounding rather subdued. Till couldn't be sure, but if he were correctly interpreting the expression on the orderly's face and the tone of his voice then the man seemed somewhat confused. Till too was surprised to see the sleeping man on the lower bunk, his face shadowed by the mattress above.

'Don't I get a cell of my own?'

Simon took out his mobile and pressed a button that obviously connected him to whichever superior he wanted to speak to.

'It's Simon here. Just a quick question,' he whispered. 'Patrick Winter in room 1310, is that right?'

After a curt 'Thanks' he hung up.

'Everything's in order. Your roommate is already asleep,' he said, turning back to Till. 'And you should get your head down as soon as you can as well. Tomorrow's going to be a long day, Herr Winter.'

'Hold on a sec. I want a single cell,' Till protested.

'Single room,' the orderly corrected him and shook his head. 'As you can see, that doesn't work. We're bursting at the seams here.'

The door closed astonishingly softly, but the metallic clicking of the various bolts that kept turning seemed endless. Eventually, though, it was quiet in what Till would never call the *room*, only *cell* or *prison*. The thick door muffled most of the sounds from the rest of the institution. At that moment all Till could hear was the patter of the rain that fell against the small porthole window in the top third of the wall facing outside. Then the room was filled by a smoky voice he was already acquainted with.

'Hey, arsehole.'

Till peered down. His cellmate had sat up. Till involuntarily felt his face and rubbed his eyelid. The memory burned almost more fiercely than the spit that had hit him earlier.

'*The idiot who just spat at you is called Armin Wolf. If you don't watch out he'll kill you faster than you could kill yourself in here.*' Seda's voice was still ringing in his ears when the guy punched him in the face with incredible force.

And when Till's head hit the hard concrete floor, the bars by the window cast a shadow on his opponent's face, which in the pallid light looked like a skull covered with a layer of skin.

21

It was as if a red paint bomb had burst behind his retina. When he hit the floor, the pain was first concentrated in a patch roughly in the middle of his field of vision, then spread to the periphery before Till saw the face floating above him as if through a blood-smeared filter.

'I've got to hand it to you,' Armin Wolf said, kicking him in the side. 'You've got balls. In your shoes I'd have begged for a different cell.'

But I didn't know who they were locking me up with.

I didn't even know that I'd have to share the cell with a lunatic.

Till wasn't in a state to voice his thoughts. He lacked both the air and the strength to utter a single word. The pain in his head, back and kidneys was accompanied by the realisation that he was locked up in the tightest of spaces with a murderous psychopath – and once again he was gripped by the vice-like claw of claustrophobia.

'What did you want with Sänger, that old tart? Did you tell her about me?'

That you spat at me earlier?

This absurd idea helped Till order his thoughts slightly.

Hoping that Armin wouldn't break his wrist, he stretched his arm out, coughed some phlegm on the floor and panted, 'No, no. We didn't speak about you at all.'

Armin took a step to the side, which in this small cell meant he was already at the door. He pressed his ear to the flap and his index finger to his lips.

Nothing.

Clearly satisfied, he returned to Till, who in the meantime had crawled to the window and was leaning with his back to the wall between the toilet and the sink. He'd briefly considered going for Armin from behind. But the guy wasn't just a head taller, he was also in much better physical shape. What Till had lost in body mass and muscle since the disappearance of his son was visible twice or three times over in the bicep and tricep mountains on Armin's arms and chest. With feline movements the man prowled like an experienced streetfighter as if hovering above the cell floor.

There was no doubt about it. In a direct confrontation he was hopelessly inferior.

Armin moved away from the door again and came back to Till. 'Okay, the black bastard's doing his rounds now,' he said, outing himself as a racist too. 'Simon only peeks through the flap every forty-five minutes. Which means we've got three quarters of an hour to have a nice chat.'

With that last word he rammed his fist into Till's stomach. Till wanted to scream but the pain was so great he couldn't make a sound.

A second blow hit him on the mouth. His head cracked against the wall behind and he felt at least one tooth coming loose.

This couldn't be real. How could something like this be

happening? You didn't put a new arrival in a cell with a murderous lunatic!

It was hardly likely that anyone here would hear his cries for help – assuming that he could draw sufficient breath – and on this cold floor Till was far from any objects he could knock over or hurl against the door to make his presence known.

To his horror he saw – now out of one eye only, the other having swollen fully – Armin remove a sock, presumably to gag him with.

'Stop,' he rasped, managing barely more than a grunt. Armin came closer, lunged, and among all the crazy ideas racing through Till's head was a television interview he'd watched with an underground inspector. When asked what advice he would give people who were attacked on public transport his answer was, *'Confuse the enemy!'*

'Your mother!' he wheezed as loudly as he could, which was only slightly louder than a whisper, but his pointless remark did seem to have an effect.

'What?'

Armin hesitated. His fist hovered in front of Till's face like a demolition ball halted in its trajectory.

'What about my mother?'

According to the inspector, now was the time to flee. But because of the lack of escape possibilities Till decided that rather than run for his life he would blather for it.

'Just tell me why?' he asked Armin.

'Why *what?*'

'What have you got against me?'

'You deserve to die just for asking that question.'

Grabbing Till's bandage, Armin wrenched his head back,

but before he could stuff the rolled-up sock into his mouth Till managed to ask, 'How do you know me, anyway?'

For a moment Armin seemed even more confused than after the mention of his mother.

'I know your type,' he said. 'All the scumbags in the world. You're all the same.'

'How?'

'How do I know you?'

Till nodded.

To his relief the question seemed to work and Armin lost his train of thought again. He let go of Till's head and even took a step back. Then he scratched the nape of his neck and frowned as if he were seriously pondering an answer. When he uttered it, now Till was the one who didn't understand.

'My father was a researcher.'

'What?' Till bit his tongue.

Why can't you stop gabbling, you idiot? Let him speak! Don't interrupt!

Armin laughed briefly. 'Are you saying you haven't got a clue what I'm talking about? Okay. Let me help.'

Armin kicked Till between the legs. The pain couldn't have been more excruciating if Armin had tipped petrol over him and lit a match. It felt like a caged wild animal, desperately trying to break out in all directions.

He panted, moaned, rasped and thrust his hands on his crotch, but he might as well have brushed his teeth; no body position or grip could relieve the barrage assaulting his entire abdominal area. Maybe a morphine injection straight into his balls...

Armin laughed again. 'Yes, that's right. Hold your gonads for one last time. You won't be needing them again anyway,

Winter. And while you're clutching your soft parts maybe you can just begin to comprehend what I have to suffer because of scumbags like you.'

The world, which for Till had transformed into a nine-square-metre cell of indescribable pain, was now spinning like a gondola on a Waltzer at the funfair. Till could taste bile, probably because he was throwing up. But he couldn't be sure.

His ego was only half present now. The remaining fifty per cent was swimming in an ocean of pain. And somewhere in the remote distance, the roar of the surf mingled with Armin Wolf's voice. 'As I was saying, my father was a researcher. And his chief area of research was pain. He was keen to know what his son could withstand. They chucked him out of university when he showed too great an interest in body parts in the pathology department. Even the army didn't want to take him on as a medical student so he had to study at home. And his favourite object of study was me.'

He bent down to Till and seemed to grin at him.

'Is the pain easing now?' he asked, patting his shoulder almost paternally. Till had assumed a stable position on his side and was panting as if in the throes of contractions.

'Well, he didn't do that to me. Because Daddy wanted to find out how long his boy could hold out not going to the loo. He took me down to his basement workshop, strapped me to a camp bed and tied up my little penis. With fucking parcel twine.'

Armin stood up again. Wandered up and down beside Till, who was convinced he'd never be able to take another step in his life.

'After a day the pain was driving me insane. I screamed

for my mother, but she didn't come. After thirty-six hours my bladder burst.'

Oh, God.

Despite his excruciating agony, Till realised that what he was being forced to endure here didn't come close to what Armin had suffered as a child. Assuming, of course, that the madman was telling the truth.

'Not a single day has passed since when I don't think of my dear father at least three times for three quarters of an hour. That's how long it takes for me to empty my ruined bladder, you see.'

Somehow Till managed to roll away from Armin towards the exterior wall. And he was even able to sit upright with his knees to his chest.

'I don't understand what any of this has to do with me,' he rattled, hoicking a lump of phlegm on the floor.

When was Simon coming back?

Till knew that the forty-five minutes were far from up, even though his body felt as if it had aged years.

'I hate all child abusers,' he heard Armin say.

'And?'

'And?' His cellmate, obviously a nutcase, gave him another kick in the side, although not quite as hard as before.

Hey, hey. I love children. I've got some myself. I'd never do anything to them, Till wanted to say, but then realised that he had to speak for Patrick Winter rather than himself. A man whose backstory he barely knew. So far he was only vaguely aware that the man had probably been a depressive.

Skania, whose identity did you get me?

What had the director said earlier when he asked about

Tramnitz? *'How extraordinary that you of all people should ask that.'*

'What did I do?' he asked Armin.

'Are you off your rocker?' Armin tapped his forehead, clearly missing the irony of asking such a question in a psychiatric hospital.

'I, I...' Till felt faint. 'Dr Sänger says I've got amnesia,' he lied.

'What?'

'The drugs. My body can't take the depot injection,' Till said, continuing to spin a yarn. 'I don't remember anything before I was admitted.'

'Are you telling me you don't know why you're here?'

Armin looked at him like a father might his child he has just caught lying.

'Yes. I tried to set myself on fire. I... I mean, I just can't remember what made me do it.'

'Hmm.'

Armin looked at the window, against which coin-sized raindrops were splatting like flies on a windscreen. For a good while the rain and the noise of Till's breathing were the only sounds to be heard inside the cell. Until Armin said, 'Okay, you've got five minutes.'

'For what?'

'To read this.'

Armin pulled down his tracksuit bottoms, then his pants, stood with his legs apart, bent forwards slightly and put his hand to his anus. Soon afterwards, he was holding a condom, which in the incoming light looked like a mouldy sausage casing. Armin removed the rubber band and pulled out a cigar-shaped roll of paper.

He handed the paper to Till, who overcame his reluctance and painstakingly unfolded it before he decided otherwise. The paper felt warm and moist.

'What the hell is this?' he asked.

'Don't piss me off,' Armin hissed at him. 'You've got five minutes. Read it! Then I'll show you what real pain is.'

22

It was a single sheet of paper, printed on both sides. In the upper left-hand corner was a series of characters that looked like a complicated password: PW12_7hjg+JusA. In reality it was a case file reference, as Till could clearly see from the title:

TRANSCRIPT OF PATRICK WINTER'S TRIAL

The protocol began in the middle of a sentence; a number of pages were missing. Strangely, the transcript contained the full testimony of the accused. Usually all that was published was a summary with indirect speech at most. But although it took a bit of effort in the insipid light coming from the lamps outside, here Till was able to read word for word what the accused Patrick Winter (PW) had replied to the probing questions of the Public Prosecutor (PP).

... asks for a glass of water. After a short interruption the testimony continues.

```
PW: Sorry.
PP: No problem, Herr Winter. Now, let's return
    to the afternoon of 20 July. How long in
    advance had you planned to do it?
```

PW: A long time. Since his birth, in fact.

PP: Why?

PW: I'm sorry?

PP: What was your motive. I mean, you've got a five-year-old daughter, Frieda. As the court has already heard, those close to you have described you as a loving father, Herr Winter. So why the change of heart?

PW: It was in the file.

PP: What file?

PW: My wife and I, we had an agreement. Linda would take the children to kindergarten in the mornings, allowing me to get an early start at the insurance company. Then I'd pick them up in the afternoons if there wasn't anything to detain me.

PP: Were you often detained?

PW: Unfortunately I was as time went on.

PP: You are an actuary. Could you briefly describe the nature of your work to the court?

PW: Briefly? Well, for my current employer, Xantia, I calculate insurance models and premiums. For example, I produce risk algorithms on the basis of demographic prognoses.

PP: Could you give us a concrete example?

PW: Of course. If q_x represents the probability of an x-year-old dying the following year, and ω_0 corresponds to the usual maximum age set in practice, then, as is known:

```
     qx = 0 f.a. x greater than or equal to ω0.
     Now if we take the random remaining years
     of life Tx… Sorry?
PP:  Thank you. What I actually meant was an
     example that all of us here can understand.
```

Till could almost hear the giggling in the public gallery, assuming that the public had been allowed in to watch this trial.

Good God, that Patrick Winter really had been a genius!

If I'm to survive the night in here, I'll have to pretend to be Rain Man!

```
PP:  Let me ask you another question. As a
     father, do you sometimes take work home
     too?
PW:  That's correct. I have a working from home
     clause in my contact.
PP:  And that's what you were doing on the day
     before 20 July?
PW:  Yes.
PP:  Could you tell the court what the file you
     took home that day has to do with our
     concrete example?
PW:  Yes, no. I don't know. It's complicated.
PP:  Take your time.
```

The piece of paper in Till's hands began to shake. He didn't dare look up for fear that Armin might misconstrue this as a sign that he'd already finished reading – and his cellmate had left no doubt as to what would happen afterwards. (*'Then I'll show you what real pain is.'*)

On the other hand, he didn't want to read any more, even though he couldn't understand what in those few lines had affected him so much that his heart was working away inside his chest like a drill.

Till was afraid of Patrick Winter's testimony. He knew it could only tell a story with the worst of all possible endings. Yet he had no other choice, and his eyes returned to the place where he had stopped.

PP: What was in the last file you'd taken home?

PW: I thought it contained the mortality tables, i.e. recalculations of the probability of death in a population in particularly risky areas of insurance.

PP: But that wasn't the information in the file?

PW: No.

PP: What was in it?

PW: Something about me.

PP: What precisely did it say about you, Herr Winter?

PW: It said what I'd done.

PP: Can you tell us more?

PW: Since his birth. Since Jonas's birth I'd had these desires. Terrible, unnatural desires.

PP: And these were in the file?

PW: My desires and my deeds. Dreadful deeds.

Oh, Christ, Skania. Tell me this isn't true! Patrick Winter has a second child!

Or had?

At this point the protocol noted a slight interruption because Winter was feeling ill. Eventually his testimony continued where it had left off.

PW: I have no idea how anyone at Xantia could
    know of my sins. I'd never told anyone
    about them and it was impossible that
    another employee at the insurance company
    could have compiled the document. I mean,
    I opened the file and it was as if I were
    looking inside my own head.

PP: Are you saying you were reading not only
    about what you'd done, but about your
    thoughts too?

PW: It was like a glimpse into the darkest
    depths of my soul.

PP: Could you please give the court some more
    details?

PW: I read about what had happened on one
    particular day in autumn. At half past two
    in the afternoon. Linda had taken Frieda
    swimming. Jonas was just one. I took him
    down into the basement. We've got a small
    sauna, you see. It was always troublesome
    because the door kept getting jammed. The
    previous owner of the house had never
    properly serviced it and it no longer met
    current safety standards.

So I went to the sauna. I'd lit the stove half an hour earlier, it was going at full blast and the temperature was almost ninety degrees. I waited until quarter to three, until the swimming lesson was over, because I knew that Linda always did a big family shop afterwards. So I had just under an hour.

PP: For what?

PW: To unscrew the inside handle. I took it off.

PP: Why?

PW: So that once I was inside with Jonas the sauna door couldn't be opened any more.

PP: You went in with him?

PW: Of course. It had to look genuine. Like an accident.

Till closed his eyes.

In his head he saw the father and son melting in the truest sense of the word. Desperately dehydrated as they became ever weaker. Did Patrick hesitate before closing the door? Did he change his mind at the very last minute, panic and hammer like mad against the door? Did he scream his deadly fear into the scalding hot air while his little son's face turned redder and redder?

PP: So, having tampered with the door, you entered the sauna with a thirteen-month-old child?

PW: Jonas had a slight cold and the heating in our house wasn't working properly that day. It was always problematic during the transitional periods. So I could have explained to Linda that I wanted to warm the two of us up and made a terrible mistake.

PP: Were you not worried about your own life?

PW: I knew that Linda would bring the shopping down to the basement first and find us. As an adult, I'd probably survive an hour of that heat. But Jonas? No way. He fell silent after a few minutes. After a quarter of an hour he was listless. It was just scorching hot and I'd also put him at the top of the sauna, close to the oven.

PP: But your plan went wrong?

For Till, who'd started sweating himself, these words came as a cooling relief.

Good God. He didn't kill the boy. Patrick Winter merely tried to. Skania didn't send me to this psycho prison with the identity of a crazed child killer.

PW: The cleaning lady was supposed to be going on holiday the following day. She always came on Wednesdays, but before the holidays she wanted to surprise us by putting on some washing and ironing my shorts. So just for once she came on a Tuesday.

PP: And found you in the sauna?

PW: Yes. After only twenty minutes. She thought she'd saved our lives. I gave her a very generous tip and begged her not to say a word to Linda. I mean, nothing had happened, the baby soon recovered and was already screaming blue murder again. So why bother fuelling nightmares for my wife? Of course I promised to change the sauna door, and I did. Now it just stays shut with a magnet.

PP: And all of this was in the file you took home and opened on the evening of 20 July?

PW: Yes, it contained a detailed description of my murder attempt.

PP: What did you think when you read it?

PW: I was shocked.

PP: As you were reading the file did you get the urge to eat it?

Till almost smiled at this rather crude attempt to condemn the accused as a fake. In the *Spiegel* magazine he'd once read an article about how psychiatrists expose imposters. People who feigned their delusions tended to admit to any form of bizarre behaviour. *'Yes, of course I wanted to eat the file. With a big dollop of ketchup.'* People who genuinely were mentally ill didn't invent any additional symptoms or modes of behaviour.

Either Patrick Winter had been familiar with this test or truly mad, because he responded to the public prosecutor with confusion:

PW: Why would I want to eat the file?

PP: So what did you want to do when you read the file?

PW: What it was ordering me to do.
PP: The file ordered you to do something?
PW: Yes, on the last page. There were detailed
    instructions.
PP: What did they tell you?

Till blinked and his mouth went dry when he read:

PW: How I could kill my son, Jonas. This time
    without anyone getting in the way. So that
    it worked properly.

23

'How much?' Till asked, without glancing up from the sheet of paper. Like a little boy with his hands in front of his face in the hope that this will make him invisible to other people.

His question seemed to buy a little time from Armin, who had sat on his bed while Till was reading. Instead of delivering another blow he asked, 'What do you mean?'

'How much are they paying you to torture me?' Till aimed these words in Armin's direction. 'You don't normally get hold of something like this in here. Someone must have given it to you. Who ordered you to hurt me?'

Armin stood up without saying anything.

Till, who still felt as if he'd been castrated by two bricks, pulled himself together and spoke so quickly that his words almost tripped up over each other: 'You're in here for life, right? You've got nothing to lose. Me neither.'

'So?'

He attempted another stab in the dark. 'How about your father? Is he still alive?'

'Why do you want to know?'

'If he's still alive I can do something about that.'

'You?' Now Armin gave a proper belly laugh and gripped

his sides with both hands like an old man with back pain. 'You'll never get out of this cell alive, let alone anywhere near the old people's home.'

Old people's home. Good. The old boy's still alive, then.

'I can kill him nonetheless,' Till said, putting all of his eggs into one basket. If Armin was no longer interested in revenge, if in the worst-case scenario the two psychopaths had managed a reconciliation, then that basket of eggs was ruined.

'How?' Armin asked, to Till's relief.

'I've got contacts. Contacts and money.'

Armin shook his head. 'Your contacts must be pretty crap if they can't even sort you out a single room in here.'

In a flash he grabbed Till's left hand and twisted his fingers so that Till had to turn ninety degrees and drop to his knees to avoid them being broken.

'Stop. Wait, I swear it's true. I've got a mobile phone.'

'Bollocks!'

'I do. When does the bus come?'

'Huh?'

'The library bus. When does it come?'

'Are you taking the piss?'

'No, my contacts have hidden a mobile there. I can show you. Then we can make a call together and your faaaaaaa...'

Till screamed. Two of his fingers were at an unnatural angle. One millimetre more and both of them would snap like toothpicks.

'A mobile? Here on the island?'

'Yeeeeeeees.'

'And it works?'

'I swear to you.'

'Seriously?'

Armin's grip loosened marginally. He grunted sceptically, but seemed to be pondering what had been said.

This was another period of grace for Till, who hardly dared breathe for fear of injuring himself with the slightest movement of his body. 'Yes, yes. Really. It works.'

'Hmm. Tonight I'll spare you, but tomorrow you're giving me the mobile.'

'It's a deal,' Till said.

'I'm still going to break your fingers though.'

Till's pulse accelerated and more sweat appeared on his forehead. 'No, no. Stop! Please. They'll transfer me. If I'm injured tomorrow they'll transfer me. Think about it, it makes no sense.'

But Armin just said, with an audible grin, 'I don't care. It's a risk worth taking. I'll get you outside of the cell, you child killer. And chill, I mean, it's only two out of ten.'

Till heard a dry cracking, followed by a short pause that was immediately filled by the pure, unfiltered voice of pain.

Born from the depths of his soul.

24

SEDA

Seda had a deep sleep, but not on account of the medicines she was administered. Even before her time at the hospital she'd been able to slip into the Land of Nod at the flick of a switch. It was something she'd had to train herself to do as a child to block out the smells, sounds and images she'd been exposed to when awake in the caravan. A toenail-yellow trailer which her mother used as a dining room, sitting room, bedroom and 'guest room', although the guests only stayed briefly, never longer than an hour, mostly less than that.

During the daytime Seda was able to play in the forest, although she had to take care she didn't slip on condoms or shit, because there was no proper lavatory here in the car park on the B213. Only a Portaloo that stank so badly even from a distance that drivers preferred to relieve themselves among the trees.

Some really did stop here for a bit of a rest, but most came because of the flashing red heart above the caravan door.

When it got late and Seda was fed up of freezing outside in the dark, she would go inside and sleep beneath the table while Mum entertained the 'guests' in the bunk. Some offered to pay more to have the eight-year-old watch, but Mum had always chucked out those sorts of guys, using her fists or a pepper spray if necessary. No 'guest' had ever touched or harassed Seda. At least, not that she knew.

Seda slept like a stone, which was why now, soon after waking in her single cell, she couldn't be certain how long Dr Kasov's hand had been inside her knickers.

'What the fuck do you want?' she gasped in horror, yanking the duvet back over her legs. Filled with disgust, she shifted up to the head of the bed.

The door to this shoebox prison, where she was forced to spend the night, was locked from the inside. It was as if the senior doctor had teleported himself into the room.

'I've got a new one for you,' Kasov said with his nauseatingly grating voice.

Her stomach tightened. They'd agreed on two per week, three tops. She knew she was in arrears. Which meant her period of respite was running out.

'Who?'

Unlike the men's cells in the next wing, those here on the women's corridor had individual bathrooms. Seda kept the mirror light above the sink switched on so she didn't feel frightened when she woke up. Occasionally she had problems with orientation and couldn't work out where she was in the first few seconds. The light that slanted through the gap in the door cast dark shadows on the walls, which made Dr Kasov appear even bigger than he already was.

'Guido Tramnitz,' he said in his cracking voice.

Seda hesitated. 'Why does that name sound so familiar?'

'He's been in the papers quite a lot recently.'

'Hold on, not the child killer?'

Kasov clicked his tongue and made the sort of face he

might if Seda were a child he had to reprimand for uttering a rude word.

'Every individual deserves a second chance. That's the goal of this institution, isn't it? To make people like you and him better and resocialise you.'

Seda felt a hot flush coming on and recalled her mother's words.

'Anger is like water, Seda. It wants to flow and always finds a way.'

At that moment her anger was finding its way like a torrential mountain river.

'Don't put me on a par with something like *that*,' she said.

Kasov just laughed and sat on the bed beside her. 'I don't think he means to play golf with you, my dear. He's got other special requests.'

She tapped the side of her head. 'I'm not going anywhere near him. You must be crazy.'

'You'll do exactly what I tell you, you little whore.'

Seda balled her hand into a fist, but before she could even lift her arm Kasov was gripping it so tightly that it cut off her blood flow.

'Don't go making any mistakes, sweetheart. You know the consequences,' he hissed. Seda could barely control her urge to hammer her head against his crow's nose.

Only the anger she felt at herself was greater. Three errors had put her in this dreadful position. The first, at the age of fourteen, was trusting the boy who assured her that you could only get hooked on heroin if you injected it. The second was choosing a Hell's Angel as her pimp when she had to give up her job with Steglitz library because she needed to sell her body to finance her addiction. But the third error, the biggest and most crucial one, was breaking the oldest rule of her profession: never trust a punter.

In the flat-rate brothel on the edge of Schönefeld Airport, Kasov had promised everything under the sun, and indeed much of what he'd said was true. Yes, he'd developed a 'secondary income stream' and he supplied most of Berlin's hospitals with 'private sexual-therapy services', as he called them. And yes, he had the money and influence to buy her freedom from her pimp and get her onto the closed ward of a withdrawal unit. But in here he also had the power to put her on medication, strap her down and have her rot in some isolation cell.

So Seda took a deep breath and abided by Kasov's order to obey her. At some point the day would come when she could pay back this squawking bird and take her revenge. At the moment, however, he held all the cards.

'If Tramnitz is into kids, what does he want from me?' Seda asked, a last, desperate attempt to avoid the whole thing.

'A bit of variety!' Kasov grinned, pinching Seda's right nipple through her nightie. His grip was so firm that the pain sent tears to her eyes and unleashed another memory of her mother.

There are things you never get used to, Seda. No matter how often people do them to you.

'Your appointment is at four p.m., the day after tomorrow. I'll take you to him in the infirmary.'

Seda looked up at Kasov and nodded.

He watched her for a while and she managed to hold his weaselly stare until eventually he exhaled and said, 'Great. Now I want you to tell me how it went with Patrick Winter. Did he tell you anything about me?'

25

TILL

Till was unfamiliar with both the office he was in and the car park he was staring at. He couldn't even remember his own name, but this often happened when he was dreaming.

Likewise when asleep he was frequently aware that he wasn't awake and that everything he saw, felt, tasted, smelled and heard was only taking place inside his head.

For example, the shimmering tarmac of the car park, which you shouldn't be able to see – let alone smell – from such a height. Actually it was rather a nice smell; it reminded him of summer and holidays.

And death.

Although Till couldn't say why. To his knowledge he'd never had a car accident, not even a bad fall from his bike. So why did the dusty car park make him think of waxy skin, the blue shimmer of a corpse and the sweet, rancid smell of meat rotting in the sun?

The only thing he could find an explanation for at that moment was why this unbelievable heat, which was gradually filling his body, had its origin in his right hand. He tried to avoid moving it, even though in his dream he was searching for a way to turn up the air-conditioning or somehow open the window, but it probably wasn't possible in this skyscraper.

Armin had broken two fingers on his right hand, and Till had taken this knowledge with him into the feverish, sweat-bathed sleep he'd finally managed to fall into after lying for ages in anguish.

His urge to escape the clutches of the madman was so great that on several occasions he'd been tempted to shout out for help or at least give Simon a sign on one of his periodic checks. Show him one of his purple, swollen, absurdly twisted fingers and say, *Hey! Take a look at this. This is what that nutter did to me. He must have mistaken me for someone else. You can't leave me alone with him!*

But what had Armin whispered? When Till (who, thank God, was left-handed) was just about to bash the cell door with his undamaged fist?

'*You know what they do with child abusers who get attacked by their fellow inmates, don't you? They never isolate the attackers, only the victims.*'

Armin had laughed and described in great detail how lonely and squalid life would be for Till in solitary confinement. Words that Armin had spat out had followed Till into his dream. '*Child abusers*' and '*solitary confinement*'.

Had Patrick Winter really abused a child?

A question he couldn't answer, especially not in a dream in which he was standing by a window as if rooted to the spot, people and cars like toys many storeys below. The only thing close to him was the resinous smell of tarmac filling his nose, even though people always said you couldn't smell anything in dreams. But the odour was as intense as Till's determination to avoid being isolated from the other inmates for even one single day. No matter what. He wouldn't be able to cope here for longer than was strictly necessary, and solitary confinement would prevent him from getting anywhere near Tramnitz.

So he didn't raise the alarm and didn't report Armin. He waited until the psychopath's breathing beneath him was calm and regular. Till had ignored the regular opening of the flap when Simon came to perform his checks, as well as Armin's flatulence, and despite the fact that his right hand felt as if it were swelling to the size of a pumpkin, he'd eventually fallen into this crazy dream in which nothing made sense apart from his pain.

And why, all of a sudden, could he see this name everywhere: 'JONAS'?

On the neon sign on the roof of the Ritz Carlton hotel. On the enormous tarpaulin covering the scaffolding opposite the shopping mall. It was even on the banner that a small aircraft flying towards the Red City Hall was trailing in its wake: Jonas.

What a nice name.

What dreadful fate had the poor boy met at the hands of his father?

What did Patrick do to acquire enemies like Armin in the hospital?

And who had provided his cellmate with the information from Patrick Winter's court file?

Who hates this man so much that he wants to see him die?

Even in his dream Till was sure that in real life he'd know the answers to all these questions. But in his sleep Till edged closer to the window, leaned on it and could hear this terrible cracking again. It was even louder than the moment when his fingers broke, because now something far larger than his bones was breaking. First he saw only a small crack, then the entire pane of glass his shoulder was leaning against shattered. The safety glass crumbled and was thrust into his face like confetti by the sauna-hot wind now blasting in.

Till shut his already-closed eyes, as a result of which he saw only more clearly how high up he was – hundreds of metres above Berlin – and how far down the depths that gaped open below him.

'Jump,' said the man responsible for all this, but whose name wouldn't come to mind right now. His fear of falling was so great that Till gripped on tightly to the window frame. And that was a mistake.

At once the pain shot from his injured hand into his brain, unleashing a fountain of sparks like a circular saw hitting metal.

'*Jump!*' the voice ordered again, and it felt as if the ground below were magically luring him down. Of course he was frightened of crashing onto the street. But something inside him was also looking forward to the last, conscious step. And the freefall which must be intoxicating. Until the moment his body exploded.

Down below. On the hot tarmac. Which he could already smell. Suddenly Till felt a shove. No, not a shove. Something was shaking him; now someone was pulling him forwards.

To the depths.

And it wasn't the man who'd hired Armin and wanted to ensure that Patrick Winter didn't survive the night. And this man wasn't shouting '*Jump!*' either, but the very opposite: '*Don't!*'

Opening his eyes, Till saw Simon's perturbed face, pushing him with all his strength back onto the higher bunk, from which he was just about to leap to the floor, having thrashed about in his sleep.

'Bloody hell!' the horrified orderly said when Till had calmed down and realised where he was. 'Bloody hell, what happened to your hand, Herr Winter?'

26

'An accident?'

Professor Sänger didn't even try to hide her scepticism. She made a 'Do I look that stupid?' face, which Till knew only too well from his mother. Whenever he came out with a poor excuse for bad marks, for having lost his wallet or for coming back home late from a party, she used to glare at him exactly like that: eyebrows raised, chin pressed to her chest and lips shrunken to a thin line.

'I tripped in the dark and fell awkwardly beside the loo,' Till said, repeating what he'd already told the assistant doctor before his middle and ring fingers were X-rayed and put in splints.

Till was sitting opposite Sänger at her desk. In spite of the open style of architecture and all the glass surfaces of the new building, the desk lamp and uplights were shining brightly as the storm clouds had turned the sky over Berlin dark.

'I hit my eye on the sink.'

'Oh, really?'

After waking Till, Simon had taken him straight to the infirmary, located on the top floor of the east wing. It could only be reached via a biometrically controlled lift, which wouldn't move unless you could prove you had authorised access by means of an electronic key and an iris scan.

'Are you telling me, Herr Winter, that your fractures and bruises have nothing to do with your roommate?'

Till shook his head, but didn't dare look the director of the hospital in the eye, keeping his gaze fixed on the crown of a weeping willow through the window behind her, which, shaken by the rain, seemed to be giving him a sign from outside: *'No! Don't say a word! Keep your mouth shut!'* This was similar to what Armin had said, and Till decided to listen to his intuition.

'No, not at all,' he said. 'It was just a silly accident.'

Sänger sighed, scribbled something in his file and said, 'Well, I'm going to transfer you all the same.'

Immediately Till had Armin's brittle voice in his head again, which, as Till recalled, sounded as if the thug was trying to cough muck from his lungs with every phrase. The last thing he'd said after climbing into his bunk was: *'You've bought yourself one night, Winter. If you get transferred to another cell tomorrow and don't give me the mobile, I'll wait till the first opportunity I get when you're having a shit, then I'll slice you up in such a way that you crap out your guts as well.'*

A barrage of rain hit the window as if someone had tipped a bucket of water against the glass. Till shuddered. For a moment he was tempted to protest against his transfer. On the other hand, Armin was going to torture him whether Till gave him the mobile or not, so putting a bit of time and space between himself and the nutter couldn't hurt.

The key thing was to avoid solitary confinement.

'If you say so,' Till therefore said.

Sänger took the X-ray out of Till's patient file again, which was of course labelled with the name of his alter ego, 'Patrick Winter', and sighed. 'It's fortunate that there aren't any complicated fractures and you don't need an operation.'

'Too few staff?' Till asked.

'Too few beds.'

Without looking, she gestured to the window behind her with her thumb. 'The garden level of the west wing is flooded as a result of this unremitting heavy rain. So we've had to evacuate and distribute the patients among other wards. This is also the reason why we made an exception with you yesterday.'

'I understand.'

So it hadn't been the original plan to put him together with Armin. Which explained Simon's reaction when he'd checked by phone that Till was in the correct room.

The question was: Who had Simon spoken to?

Till would have loved to ask Sänger who was responsible for the allocation of beds, but he suspected that this question would only arouse suspicion. If, however, a patient like Seda knew that Armin was his enemy, then it suggested that word had got around among the staff too. There seemed to be an adversary deliberately ensuring he remained in close proximity to that psychopath. And, if he wasn't very much mistaken, that adversary had already revealed himself to Till. He'd even openly threatened him during his visit to the intervention room. And, unlike in his dream, now Till remembered Dr Kasov's name perfectly well.

'Herr Winter?'

Till looked up at Professor Sänger and realised that, lost in his thoughts as he'd been, he'd failed to notice that the doctor had got to her feet behind her desk. She held out a note with a number on it.

'Please go to the dispensary; they've been notified and will give you something to help with the pain. Should you need anything stronger, contact me again.'

'Alright.'

He took the note with his undamaged left hand. The pain in his right still throbbed in rhythm with his pulse, although it was dulled by a local anaesthetic.

'I'd actually scheduled this time today for a one-on-one conversation, but we won't manage that before the group session at two.'

Till shrugged and stood up too. 'Okay. Where's that taking place?'

'Just this once, in the lobby. We need the large conference room for a staff meeting. And Dr Wozniak wants to make the end of our meeting so he won't be doing the whole hour.'

'I understand,' Till said, realising that time was too tight to make contact with Skania before the session. And yet he urgently had to ask him a question that was essential to his survival. What exactly had Winter done to his young son? And why, despite this, had he been able to wander into a kindergarten and set himself on fire like a human torch?

'Was there anything else?' Sänger asked after he'd been standing there for a while, hesitantly and in silence.

'Er... yesterday you mentioned the library bus,' he said.

Sänger shook her head. 'I'm sorry. It won't be coming for the time being. Too dangerous.'

Once again she pointed to the window and Till felt a hot flush rise inside him, similar to the one yesterday when he'd been unable to see a way out of the cell he was sharing with Armin. Slowly he was learning that his greatest fears were heralded by the sudden feeling of burning inside.

Without the library I won't be able to access my mobile. And without my mobile I'm cut off from the outside world.

Not to mention the violent reaction he could expect from Armin if he tried to fob the nutter off. For the first time Till seriously toyed with the idea of aborting the enterprise. What ill-considered madness had got him in here? Skania had warned him that he was underestimating the problem. Thanks to his daft idea he'd realised he was a sane individual, locked up with a bunch of mentally ill people, at least one of whom wanted him dead.

For whatever reason.

'In this weather there's no way out either for the time being,' Sänger added. 'Our advisory board told us this morning that the insurance will disclaim all liability if anyone is killed by a falling branch. That's why we've called the extraordinary meeting today. The storm is set to get worse.'

'So how do I get a book?' Till asked, sounding slightly too agitated for an apparently harmless question.

'Oh, that's not a problem. The bus is in a covered car park; we can still access it. If you tell me the title I'll have it brought to your room.' She smiled. 'Assuming we have it, of course.'

Oh, you most certainly do.

Bookcase three, shelf two. Right behind the Bibles.

Till swallowed and scratched the back of his head with his left hand, both of these unconsciously. Could he take the risk? What if the person delivering the book opened it? What if it made a noise as it was being carried or if the mobile fell out and clattered to the ground?

Then it struck him that he couldn't possibly explain how he knew of a book on the second shelf that had slipped to the back.

'I'd like to get the book from the bus myself if at all possible.'

'But why?'

'I love the smell of books; it calms me down,' he said, which wasn't in fact a lie. 'If, as you say, the bus is still accessible, couldn't you open it for me?'

Sänger's fingers played on Patrick Winter's file like an invisible piano. She didn't let on what she thought of his suggestion.

'Do you have any particular book in mind?' she asked.

'James Joyce,' Till heard himself say, because he didn't have another choice.

He needed to talk to Skania and find out whose identity he'd assumed here. And he had to win time with Armin and at least show him the mobile. Which was why he added, '*Ulysses*.' If Sänger was shocked by the choice of this classic of world literature, she didn't let it show.

'Okay, I'll check and let you know.'

Till thanked her. As he made for the door Sänger called out behind him, 'By the way, your chemo is scheduled for half past three this afternoon.'

Till stopped, unable to move. The inner heat had suddenly dissipated. His panic had reached another physical state. He felt feverish and cold at the same time, like before an outbreak of the shivers.

'What?'

Sänger smiled and answered him in a tone that suggested she was uncertain whether the patient was teasing her or not.

'Of course we'll continue the treatment from the stage you were at before the incident.'

Oh, God, no. Patrick Winter wasn't just a mental wreckage.

As if to confirm what he was thinking Sänger said, 'Let's just say that with everything else that happened you forgot your cancer, Herr Winter.'

27

TRAMNITZ

Tramnitz waited until the pot-bellied man in flip-flops called his deceitful wife a 'stupid whore' in the middle of the street, then he switched off the television set and with it the trash programme he'd been watching. He turned his head and gave his unexpected visitor a wolfish grin. 'Hello, Frau Wohlfeil,' he said to the slim woman with short blond hair, who tottered across the lino floor in her three-inch heels.

'Hello, Herr Tramnitz, how are you?'

'Fine. I hadn't anticipated seeing you so soon.'

'Given the circumstances, it was relatively easy to secure an appointment,' his defence lawyer said. She came over to the bed in which Tramnitz had been watching television since breakfast time in a half-lying, half-sitting position.

Shamelessly ogling her décolletage, he fantasised – not for the first time – about what it might be like to force her to slice off one of her nipples and eat it.

'You've just come through a serious operation,' said the woman who had given such an excellent performance in the courtroom. Without Pia Wohlfeil, he wouldn't have ended up here in the White House, but in Tegel prison, where they weren't quite as sympathetic to people harbouring his sexual preferences as the chatterboxes in the psychiatric unit. Among other things, she had advised him whenever under interrogation to mention the thing inside his head giving him orders. It was no surprise that her hourly rates were some of the highest in her profession, but Pia Wohlfeil was worth every cent.

'Naturally, I have to check up for myself on your state of health.' Pia bent down to him. 'And ensure that everything's in working order,' she whispered into Tramnitz's ear as she let her hand wander beneath the sheets.

He groaned when she took hold of his penis.

'Don't worry, handsome,' she said, putting two fingers on his chin and guiding his head back to face her when he tried to turn to the door. She gave him a kiss, opened her lips and slid her tongue into his mouth.

'Lawyer–client consultations are sacrosanct. Nobody is allowed to disturb our conversation.'

As she imitated the purring of a cat, it struck Tramnitz – not for the first time – that she far more urgently needed locking up than him. What sane woman fell in love with a serial killer? He'd heard, of course, of those disturbed women who believed that a man like him just needed a little of the love and affection he'd never had from his own mother and – bingo! – he'd be back on the straight and narrow, and would never flay another baby in his life. What nonsense.

Pia had saviour complex too. She'd told him how she'd fallen in love with him during their first meeting, *the stupid cow*.

In truth his lawyer was not the only woman who made advances. Every week he received letters from crazed sluts, some of whom didn't look half bad.

'Oh, Pia, you don't know how good you are for me. Without you, I'd never be able to cope with all of this,' he lied.

She smiled. 'You're so sweet. I realise how much we need each other.'

'Especially now,' he said, trying to pull her towards him. 'Come here, I have to be close to you. I'm out of practice.'

'You rascal!' She giggled like a shy schoolgirl, which from an age point of view Tramnitz would have preferred. It was crazy how strong, independent and successful women could mutate into submissive females in the presence of men like him.

'I'll tend to you very intimately again soon,' Pia whispered, gently squeezing his balls. 'But we need to use the time to discuss an important matter, darling.'

Tramnitz sighed; his penis was now fully erect.

Fortunately he'd ordered a prostitute from the corrupt ward doctor and she was due to visit tomorrow. He'd be able to last that long, especially as the infection had left him slightly feeble. In spite of the antibiotics, he sweated like a pig at the slightest exertion, which he absolutely loathed.

'I've been doing some research into Dr Volker Frieder.'

Tramnitz's eyes lit up. 'And?'

He'd immediately demanded to contact his lawyer following the surgeon's visit. Over the phone Tramnitz told her what the bastard had said about deliberately *leaving* a foreign object inside him during the operation.

'You don't have to confess anything. He's bluffing.'

'That's what I think, too,' Tramnitz said as his hand unconsciously moved up to the bandage on his neck. There was nothing inside him. *Although*. Was he mistaken or was the operation scar throbbing more intensely than yesterday?

'The guy's desperate,' Pia said. 'He's been skipping his Alcoholics Anonymous meetings for months now and is definitely drinking again. It's just a matter of time before another individual dies under his knife.'

'I'm sure that's true,' Tramnitz said, wiping a bead of sweat from his brow. Was it really so hot in here or was he feeling worse again? 'But the fact is, I did have blood poisoning after the operation. What if he really did infect me on purpose? If it's a virus or germ, he could do it over and over again.'

'Should I make an application to have you relocated?'

'What? To a fucked-up institution with 1970s flair?' Tramnitz shook his head. 'No way. Here I've got the ideal contact in Kasov. I'm not going to risk losing that.'

Pia sighed. 'You ought to have listened to me, honey, and not provoked anybody.' She pointed at the bedside table where the Luke Skywalker figure had stood before the operation. 'Did you really have to taunt everyone?'

'You never let me have any fun.' He grinned as she stroked his no longer quite so well-defined washboard stomach beneath the covers.

'Did you remember my book?'

'Of course.' The lawyer took a small, brown volume from her briefcase, which was fastened at the side by a ribbon.

'You're the best!'

Tramnitz ran his fingers affectionately across the smooth cover of the book without undoing the ribbon.

'Are you sure you want to keep it here?'

Until now Tramnitz had only written in her presence and Pia had taken the diary away again after her visits so it wouldn't be found in the hospital.

'I don't think they'll search my room. Here in the infirmary the checks aren't quite as rigorous as in the high-security wing. I could even move freely around here if I wanted to, almost like in the open part of the hospital.' Tramnitz pointed at the bars on the windows. 'But obviously the exits are as secure here as everywhere else.'

'Okay, I can't come back for another three days. Don't go doing anything stupid until then!' She swept her hair from her red face. 'Oh, there's something else too: our connection has just got closer.'

'What do you mean?' His stomach tightened in anticipation of bad news.

'I think you understand,' Pia said, giving him a long, intense kiss before pulling away again. 'Our romp in the meeting room was successful. I'm pregnant. And I swear, you'll be out of here at the latest by the time the baby's born!'

28

TILL

Till's new friends were called No Teeth, No Trousers and No Arm.

They were all sitting in the large domed hall of the lobby, not on the comfortable armchairs, unfortunately, but on functional folding chairs arranged in a semicircle facing the floor-to-ceiling windows that looked on to the park.

No Teeth was the only woman there, twenty-five years old at most, but she looked as if she'd just taken early retirement. Till had seen enough programmes on television about crack addicts to guess at the cause of this woman's physical decline. She was sitting diagonally behind No Trousers, a man who would be perfectly cast in the role of an unconventional aristocrat: angular chin, greying temples and furrowed brow. He even wore a pinstripe suit, which was just missing one tiny detail: the trousers. At least during the group therapy Till could spare himself the sight of No Trousers' scrawny, hairy legs by simply looking elsewhere. At Dr Wozniak, for example, the group leader who sat with his back to the park, in which the massive lanterns were the only things not flapping around like flags in the onslaught of the rain. The wind whipping in from the lake bent the bushes and trees as if they were made out of elastic rubber. Fat drops left their trace on the White House's curved, metre-high panes of glass like rain on a windscreen at high speed.

'If I may, I'll begin with myself. My name is Dr Krzysztof Wozniak. I'm a senior doctor at the Steinklinik and I lead the group therapy sessions.'

The therapy leader looked as if he'd just got out of bed. He had thinning, uncombed hair that straggled over his ears.

'Some of you know me from the music therapy in Room 5, where we've just been listening to Beethoven.'

The doctor spoke with the pleasantly melodic accent of a Pole who speaks German as if it's his mother tongue, but doesn't want to deny his roots. One by one he sought eye contact with each individual member of the group.

No Arm had sat to Till's left. He was continually feeling his stump with his right hand, as if trying to check whether his left forearm had recently grown back.

'Today we have a new face among us, and so I would suggest that we all introduce ourselves in turn.'

Wozniak nodded to the man beside him and No Arm had to start. Quietly, he said, 'My name is Tarek Bode. I used to manage a petrol station; maybe some of you remember it. It was on the corner of Mommsenstrasse and Bleibtreustrasse, but now there's an apartment block there. Oh yes, I suffer from BIID and xenomelia.'

Wozniak gave his patient a smile of encouragement and explained, 'For your information, BIID stands for Body Integrity Identity Disorder. Could you, in your own words, explain to the group what we mean by that, Herr Bode?'

'Yes, well, erm.' No Arm cleared his throat. 'Well, I get the feeling that certain bits of me don't belong to me. I regard them as foreign entities and have the urgent need to get rid of them.'

'Why don't you start with your head?' said the latecomer, whose arrival nobody in the group had noticed. Even Dr Wozniak had recoiled when the man suddenly appeared from behind the Christmas tree.

Till felt great trepidation when he saw who it was taking an empty chair and sitting behind him.

'Herr Wolf, would it for once be possible for you to be punctual?' Wozniak asked in irritation. 'In the open wing you enjoy a number of privileges, such as the fact that during the daytime you're permitted to move freely around the rooms made accessible to you. But these privileges can be withdrawn at any moment.'

'Understood,' Armin said, giving his death's-head smile and winking at Till, who had briefly turned around.

'Right then, who's going to continue with the introductions?'

Wozniak allowed his gaze to wander across the room until his eyes alighted on Till.

'You, perhaps?'

Till nodded, even though he wanted nothing more than to disappear into thin air right now. At least it wasn't like Alcoholics Anonymous, where you had to stand up.

'My name is Patrick Winter,' he began hesitantly, grabbing his swollen eye with his bandaged hand. 'I'm an actuary–'

'A what?' Armin asked from behind, even though he must have heard Till. Here in the lobby the acoustics were impeccable.

'An actuary is a mathematician who works in insurance,' Till explained. 'I calculate premiums and risk...'

'Mr Superbrain!' No Teeth, who had interrupted him, formed her lips into a whistle of admiration.

'No, no, I wouldn't say that,' Till stammered, wondering why a mathematician among the group should attract more interest than someone intent on cutting themselves up into small pieces.

Wozniak explained: 'We watched *Good Will Hunting* yesterday. Clearly the members of the group are still impressed by the story of the caretaker who turns out to be a mathematical genius.'

Great.

Till knew the classic film with Matt Damon and Robin Williams.

'Well, my abilities are not quite so spectacular,' he said, sounding dismissive, but Armin wouldn't let it lie.

'Hey, you're the only one of us here who's studied. For us thickos that alone puts you into the "genius" category. How about we have a little test?'

'Huh?' Once again Till turned around to Armin, but couldn't detect any evil in his eyes. The guy was a bloody good actor who even had Dr Wozniak wrapped around his little finger.

'Please, Dr Wozniak. You say yourself how important interaction is within the group. Could I get our mathematician to solve a little puzzle? With his IQ it should be child's play for him.'

'Yes, yes, a puzzle,' No Trousers said, and rest of the group seemed very keen too, shaking their stumps or giving toothless smiles.

Till wondered whether to feign a blackout or run away

screaming. In the present company the latter probably wouldn't be met by much surprise.

'Alright, then,' Wozniak said. 'I must say, I'm quite excited myself.'

Armin didn't need to be told twice. Playing the goody-goody, he said, 'Okay, Patrick – can I call you Patrick? – let's say you drive one hundred kilometres in your new car at exactly one hundred kilometres per hour. But on the way back you're not in such a hurry so you only drive at half the speed, fifty kilometres per hour. What's your average speed overall?'

'One hundred kph on the way there, fifty on the way back?' No Arm repeated.

'That's a piece of piss,' No Teeth moaned. 'One hundred plus fifty, divided by two, makes seventy-five.'

'Murhhh,' Armin grunted, imitating the wrong answer buzzer on a TV show. Till's initial guess had been incorrect too.

Then he had to smile with relief. In the tension of the moment it had almost slipped Till's mind that he'd seen this question on the internet before. 'The average speed is about sixty-six point six kilometres per hour,' Till replied and they all looked at him as if he really had obeyed his first impulse and leaped up screaming. 'As the length of the journey hasn't changed I need twice as long for the way back. This has an impact on the average speed,' he explained.

Armin began to applaud and kept clapping until Wozniak asked him to quieten down and the introductions continued with the next patient.

When No Teeth explained that her name was Dorothee and she used to work in a pharmacy, Till was no longer listening.

He was simply happy to have his head out of the noose – for now, anyway – and was thanking his lucky stars that he'd been set the only mathematical puzzle he knew. As he waited for his heart rate to return to normal he missed the fact that Wozniak was addressing him again.

'Isn't it, Herr Winter?'

'Erm… what, sorry?'

'I was just saying how wonderful it is that Frau Springer plays the piano as well as you do.'

As I do?

'Yes, yes, fantastic,' Till agreed.

'You're left-handed, aren't you?'

'Yes,' Till confirmed, without knowing what the doctor was getting at.

'Great, that means you can still use your good hand and both of you can play together tomorrow morning in music therapy.' Wozniak gave him an encouraging smile.

'Erm… I'm not sure. I fear I'm too handicapped.'

'Come, come, Herr Winter, let's not be so modest. In your file it even says that as a boy you won the Youth Symphonia Prize for your performances of Franz Liszt's B minor sonata. So you won't have any problems with the appassionata, especially with Frau Springer sitting beside you.'

Till felt sick. He looked to his right at the flickering flames in the fireplace and instinctively felt hotter.

'Of course,' he forced himself to say, even though he didn't even know which keys to strike for 'Three Blind Mice'.

Tomorrow morning?

On the one hand he had no idea how he was going to survive here that long with Armin breathing down his neck.

On the other that was far too little time to find his way to Tramnitz.

While he was still struggling for words, as well as a way to avoid the music therapy session, Simon appeared on the scene. With some good news for a change.

'Very sorry to disturb you, Dr Wozniak,' he said, handing the doctor a note. When the orderly had left Wozniak summarised the message for the group.

'The bibliophiles among us will be delighted to hear that Frau Professor Sänger has decided to open the library bus, for those interested, in the car park from five p.m. this afternoon.'

Not until five o'clock? For God's sake!

Why so late?

Till wondered whether the side effects of his first chemotherapy session would leave him in any fit state to look for the emergency mobile on the bus.

29

SÄNGER

'Did you want to speak to me?'

Kasov came into Sänger's office accompanied by the oppressively heavy scent of his aftershave, and the director wished she could have been spared both.

'Actually I just wanted to give you something,' she said, handing him a letter over the desk.

'What's this?'

'A written warning.'

'Sorry?' Kasov rubbed the tip of his nose and laughed as if she'd cracked a joke.

She'd have loved to give him another written warning straight away for his disdainful, arrogant behaviour.

'There must be some misunderstanding.'

Sänger waved her hand dismissively. 'Save your breath. You're not seriously going to deny that you defied my orders yesterday by letting Patrick Winter out of the crisis intervention room prematurely, are you?'

He shrugged and opened the letter.

'It was time and you were indisposed.'

'Just because the flooding meant I was needed elsewhere

doesn't give you the right to make decisions on your own. You know how important the first contact is after sedation.'

And how poorly you're qualified for it, she refrained from adding.

Otherwise it would have been her ultimately facing a disciplinary procedure rather than him.

'What's more, you seemed to have declared yesterday the day of open doors. The passage to our offices was open, which was why Seda was able to nick my coat and give Winter a tour undisturbed.'

'A slip-up.' Kasov grinned, but Sänger was far from finished.

'And what the hell got into you last night to put Winter in a room with Wolf?'

'You know how short we are on beds at the moment,' he said, trying to make excuses but not sounding especially credible. Or guilty in the slightest.

'Yes. But I also know the animosity among our patients.'

Kasov gave a crooked smile. 'Is that it?' he said smugly.

Sänger's right eyelid was twitching with anger.

She knew that at the moment she couldn't do anything about Kasov. Besides its role as a high-security state psychiatric hospital, the Steinklinik also accommodated seriously ill patients who had not been convicted of any crimes. Kasov was responsible for this privately financed area. Given his connections to hospital owners and the sponsorships he secured for the Steinklinik every year, he could pretty much do whatever he liked. But she wasn't going to allow this cocky bastard to keep walking all over her.

'No, that's not it. Just take a look at this,' she said, swivelling her laptop on the desk so that Kasov could see the screen.

'And?'

At first glance the images of the encounter between Kasov and Winter in the intervention room looked like nothing out of the ordinary. The ward doctor was standing with his back to the camera, almost blocking out Winter entirely.

'What are you doing there?' Sänger asked. She paused the tape. 'Your arms are at such a strange angle. As if you were holding something.'

'What?'

'I've no idea. That's why I'm asking you. If I were to hazard a guess I'd say you were holding a camera to your stomach and taking photos of the patient.'

'You have a vivid imagination, Frau Sänger.'

She tried to catch his eye. 'Possibly. But I'm also a good judge of character. I couldn't stand you the first time you walked in this door. And if your father weren't on our advisory board you'd have long been gone from here. As far as I'm concerned you're nothing more than a spoiled mummy's boy who's never accomplished anything himself and has always relied on the protective hand of his parents. But at some point, I swear, that's not going to be enough any more. You'll make a mistake which no one is going to be prepared to cover up, and then I'll have you by the balls.'

Without asking permission, Kasov picked up a biro and clipboard from Sänger's desk. 'Do you know what the difference is between us?' he asked calmly as he attached the disciplinary letter to the clipboard. 'You cost the hospital money. With your outdated methods, with your silly conversational therapy, creative therapy and music therapy. I, on the other hand, bring in the cash.' He gazed at her with pen and clipboard in hand like a painter examining the subject of a portrait. But in fact he just put a diagonal line straight through the text of the letter and started writing over it.

'Thanks to the series of drug trials I organise regularly, this place is running a profit. You'll never get rid of me. And, if you're being honest with yourself, you don't want to either. For if you discard me, you discard the hospital budget, and then ultimately yourself, Frau Sänger.'

With these words he passed the clipboard back to her and left her office without a goodbye.

'Cunt!' she whispered as soon as he'd closed the door.

'Arsehole!' she shouted out loud when she saw the message he'd scrawled on the disciplinary letter.

FUCK YOU!!! it said it capital letters right beside her signature. With three exclamation marks.

In any other business this would have been sufficient for summary dismissal. But Kasov was right. She could come up with as many disciplinary letters and complaints as she liked. Ultimately, however, he had the better hand, as evinced by the vulgar insult he'd left for her.

The only reason why Sänger wasn't thumping the desk in blind fury or swiping the vases on her shelves to the floor was that Kasov had left her something else along with the clipboard.

An answer.

His arrogance had unmasked him.

Sänger played the recording again, watching Kasov's arm movements for the hundredth time, and now she was certain: if Kasov had scribbled all over the clipboard with his back to her it would have looked just like that.

You communicated with Winter. You gave him something to read because you couldn't say it out loud.

Now Sänger knew. She even suspected that Kasov had threatened Winter. His secretiveness on camera made no sense otherwise.

Sänger just didn't know what he'd threatened Winter with. But she was sure she'd find out soon enough.

30

TILL

'I've had another think about it,' No Arm said out of the blue beside him. The adjustable leather lounger Till was lying on was so comfortable that he'd almost nodded off.

If there weren't a hypodermic needle sticking into the crook of his arm, through which his body was gradually being poisoned, he might have imagined he was dozing in the chill-out room of a sauna complex. The lights were dimmed, the cream slatted blinds were closed and a scented candle emitted incense aromas. Light classical music trickled as quietly and softly from the ceiling speakers as did the cytostatic drugs from the drip into his veins.

'I'd better not cut my foot off,' said No Arm, who had already been on a drip when Till was brought in by Simon twenty minutes ago.

'Okay,' Till said laconically, in the hope that No Arm would realise he wasn't interested in making conversation. Unless the patient with the quirky penchant for self-mutilation could tell him which form of cancer he was suffering from. Till could hardly enquire without running the risk of blowing his cover. Which was why he didn't yet know precisely what substance was being fed into him to destroy the cancer cells that were supposedly in his body.

'There's no point in amputating my foot.'

'You don't say!'

'I need to get rid of the whole leg.'

Till glanced to his right, where No Arm was fantasising to himself. His drip wasn't labelled either, and so Till couldn't tell whether he was undergoing a course of chemotherapy too or maybe just getting some vitamins. From the way he sounded, however, they could just as easily have been mind-altering drugs.

All of a sudden No Arm asked Till a totally senseless question.

'How about you? Have you had a think about it?'

'About what?'

'Were you able to clear it up?'

'I don't understand.'

'The hot topic. The illegal patients.'

Till glanced to his right again. No Arm still looked as if he were talking in his sleep.

'What are you talking about?' he said.

The answer unsettled him almost more than the question that had launched this meaningless dialogue.

'It's fine. It's fine. I'm sorry. I respect that.'

Till, who by now was convinced that No Arm was on drugs, couldn't bring himself to continue their bizarre conversation. Simon opened the door of the treatment room and came over to the two of them.

'Are you feeling alright?' he asked, removing the now-empty drip. Till felt a brief pain when the needle was pulled out and he was sure he'd have a bruise in the crook of his arm the following day.

'I'm afraid you have to keep going a bit longer, Herr Bode.'

Turning back to Till, Simon said, 'Your next infusion appointment is in three days, Herr Winter. But right now let's look for another appointment after that, erm... excuse me.'

He shot Till an apologetic glance and took the vibrating mobile from the pocket of his blue coat.

'Simon here. Yes. Sorry, what? Wait a sec, I can't hear you very well in here, Frau Sänger.'

Simon gestured to Till that he would be back in a minute and put the waste from the treatment on top of the appropriate dustbin beside the door before stepping into the corridor.

Till's heart inside his chest was like a bouncy ball on a trampoline. Although he didn't feel well, he didn't think it was the side effects of the chemo kicking in already, but the result of his agitation.

Should I? he wondered, already on his feet.

One glance at No Arm told him that the patient still had his eyes closed. And the feeling in his guts told him that this was a now-or-never moment, a chance he wouldn't soon come across again in here.

And so Till decided to execute the plan he'd conceived on impulse.

He hurried to the chest of drawers beside the door, on top of which stood a yellow plastic box right next to the sink. Because the needle bin was overflowing, the flap designed to protect the nurses and cleaners from cuts when emptying the sharp, spiky contents was half open.

Till thrust his hand inside, felt a stabbing pain, then stuffed his hand into the pocket of his tracksuit bottoms. Just in time, for Simon was already coming back through the door.

Although the orderly was surprised that his patient was already there, waiting and ready to go, he didn't notice that something crucial was missing in the room. Simon probably checked that the cannula, which he'd thoughtlessly placed on top of the brim-full plastic box before taking the phone call, was still there. What he missed was that the needle from the previous treatment was no longer sticking out of the bin.

Because now it was in Till's trouser pocket.

Which meant he had a weapon.

31

In the Steinklinik they observed the 'patient plus one' rule. This stipulated that a patient always needed an escort when outside and must never be allowed to walk in the park alone, even though it was probably easier to escape from a North Korean labour camp than negotiate the outer walls of the hospital.

Till too was led by a brawny orderly to the car park exit on the ground floor, and indeed a green bus was parked right there. It reminded him of the coaches he used to take on school trips as a child: a single-decker for around fifty passengers. The only difference was that here the windows were covered with a black film; you couldn't look in or out.

'You've got ten minutes,' the orderly said, fishing a packet of cigarettes from the raincoat he wore over his gown. They were standing in an area that looked as if it was set up for the delivery of medicines and instruments, but not for patients. Here they were protected from the rain, which was falling so heavily outside that it sounded as if the building were being sandblasted. The noise even drowned out the roar of aeroplanes taking off and landing nearby.

When the orderly unlocked the glass door with his

fingerprint, the noise became deafening. Till doubted that the man would be able to light a cigarette in this kind of storm.

Although there was a roof above the driveway, Till had to wade through puddles to the bus. The water couldn't seep away as quickly as it was emptying from the clouds and it was seeking other channels; the usual outlets must be blocked.

'Ten minutes,' the orderly called out into the wind, then he entered a code on the side of the bus and the driver's door opened with a hydraulic hiss.

No sooner was Till inside than the door closed behind him. He shuddered.

Alone.

For the first time in what felt like an eternity.

It was a pleasant sensation, a comforting shudder of the sort he remembered from his childhood when he'd escaped the foul weather and, back home in the cosy warmth of his bedroom, could look forward to an exciting novel.

The bus was well heated and the stimulating smell of old books certainly intensified these lovely memories. Hundreds of volumes filled the shelves, which stood on both sides of the aisle instead of seats.

Hardback works of non-fiction, penny dreadfuls, atlases, paperback thrillers. Till ran his finger along the spines while examining the titles in the light of the halogen spotlights.

Only ten minutes? He could spend hours here, preferably with a cup of hot coffee, in the row of seats at the back – the only one not to have been removed – his head resting against the window. The roar of the storm would be in his ear, which on the one hand was so close, and yet as far away as the worlds you could enter with all these books.

The only thing disturbing the snug atmosphere was the sobbing.

It was coming from the back of the bus, where you'd usually find the steps to the onboard toilet.

'Hello?' Till called out as he approached the sounds of a woman trying to hold back tears. He shuddered once more, but this time the feeling was the harbinger of burgeoning fear.

He slowly groped his way forwards, his hand grasping the needle in his pocket. Until he was close enough to make out who it was sitting on the steps of the rear exit.

'Seda?'

The patient who'd tricked him when he arrived turned around. Her dark eyes were swollen. She looked as if she'd just come in from the rain. Her face was wet; a few drops fell from her chin onto her chest.

'What's wrong?' he asked.

She shook her head. 'It's okay, it's okay.' Seda stood up.

'Did they lock you in here?'

'No, no,' Seda said, almost smiling. 'I'm allowed to be here on my own. When I'm working, at least.'

Till looked around. 'So, this is your work?'

'I used to be a sort of librarian, yes,' she said, confirming what he'd heard from Sänger.

'So why are you here?'

'Come on, you know us patients don't like talking about that.'

'Not even about why you were crying?'

To his astonishment Seda raised her hand and stroked his head. At first Till wanted to stop her, but the caress was so tender and affectionate that it triggered another pleasant yet painful memory inside him.

Ricarda.

How long was it since he'd been touched like this?

'Bookcase three, shelf two?' Seda asked all of a sudden, severing the cord of intimacy that had briefly tied the two of them.

'What? Yes, that's right.'

Till recalled that Seda was on Skania's payroll and privy to his intentions and goals. If anybody could have tipped off Kasov that he was faking it, it was her.

Moving away from Seda, he looked for the bookcase and, as promised, found the book on the second shelf, right behind the Bibles.

James Joyce, *Ulysses.*

It felt far too light. And when he shook the weighty tome, nothing moved inside.

Till opened the book and leafed through the pages.

Until he found the mobile after page eighty-four.

After making sure that Seda wasn't looking in his direction he took it from the book and pressed the speed dial button.

32

'Thank God.'

'Till?'

'Who else do you think has got this phone?'

He sat on the back row, as far as possible from Seda, who was now in the driver's seat, skimming through a magazine while listening to music through headphones. Even though he didn't think she could hear him back here, he was whispering.

'What's wrong? How are you?' Skania asked.

'Crap. For fuck's sake, whose identity did you get me? Who am I?'

'You don't sound great, Till.'

'I don't feel great either. To be honest, I feel even worse than before, and I didn't think that was possible after Max was kidnapped.'

'Calm down. Nice and slow. Tell me exactly what's wrong.'

Till's heavy breath fogged up the window stuck with film. He drew with his finger a question mark in the condensation and sighed.

'I don't know where to begin.'

'One thing at a time.'

A violent gust of wind shook the bus and Till recalled the first few moments after he'd been admitted.

'I thought I'd have to give them something to make them think I really was out of my mind. So I told them I'd swallowed a bomb.'

'Okay,' Skania said, sounding not in the least horrified or even surprised.

'The problem is, I was only able to convince some of the staff that I was potentially dangerous. They gave me a sedative, but as soon as I woke up in an isolation cell a doctor called Kasov paid me a visit and said to my face he thought I was faking it.'

'Interesting.'

'I actually think it's fucking dangerous,' Till ranted. 'Because for some reason this Kasov wants to silence me. I was locked up with a violent psychopath by the name of Armin Wolf.'

'You didn't get a cell to yourself? That's unusual.'

'Yes. The official line is that one wing is flooded and there's a shortage of beds. But I swear you it's this Kasov's fault that Armin broke two fingers of mine.'

'He did *what*?' Now Skania did sound slightly shocked.

'He wanted to break lots more besides. Seda says that the guy even wants to kill me.'

'So you've met Seda? Good.'

Till shook his head vehemently and felt the bruise beneath his eye begin to throb.

'Nothing is good. She's completely nutty too; she's a patient, you idiot. And she doesn't drive the library bus any more, because the grounds are under water.'

He glanced at Seda, who hadn't looked up even at the mention of her name.

'So how did you get hold of the mobile?'

'It's a long story. I'd rather you told me whose skin I'm in here. You see, it seems as if you got me the worst cover possible.'

Skania sounded irritated as he answered. 'I'm sorry. If you want to get a patient locked up quickly in the Steinklinik I'm afraid there's not much choice.'

'I know that. But did it have to be a piano-playing, mathematically gifted child abuser with a brain tumour?'

'Say that again.'

'You heard.'

There was a pause. Till heard atmospheric noise on the line, as if the wind were now gusting in the ether too, then an incensed Skania said, 'That's... that's rubbish. Patrick Winter isn't a child abuser. And I know nothing about a tumour.'

'You're poorly informed then.' Till got louder. 'I've just had to undergo my first chemo session. I'm poisoning myself here, mate.'

At that moment Seda looked back at Till, gave him a nod and tapped at an imaginary watch on her wrist.

Yes. The ten minutes must soon be up. Skania wanted to bring the conversation to an end too. And not just that.

'Okay, we're going to stop this. I'm going to get you out of there.'

'Stop, wait!'

'No! No waiting. This is over here and now. Right away. Shit. How can I let you lie next door to Tramnitz in the infirmary with a broken hand and cancer poison in your blood?'

Till, who'd been getting to his feet, sat down again.

'What did you just say?'

Skania obliged Till and reiterated what he'd said. Upon hearing the word 'infirmary', Till interrupted him.

'How do you know that?'

'You told me yourself about the broken fingers and the chemo. Where else would you be?'

Till twisted his upper body to one side like a schoolboy who wants to stop his neighbour from copying. Then, cupping his left hand as he held the mobile in his injured right one, he whispered, 'My question is how you know that Tramnitz is in the infirmary. He ought to have been back in his cell a good while ago.'

'They mentioned it on the radio this morning,' Skania explained. 'Apparently he's got postoperative blood poisoning. They're worried about the security requirements until he's transferred back. It seems as if you can move around pretty freely in the infirmary.'

'Give me a little more time, Oliver,' Till said, almost in supplication.

'So they can kill you in there? I'm not going to allow you to come to any more harm. You're really becoming a pain in the arse.'

'It won't get that far, I promise you.' He was speaking more quickly now. 'Tonight I'm on my own in a new cell. Nothing can happen to me there. And during the daytime I can look after myself. Give me two more days. If I haven't found out anything by then we'll call it off.'

Again a swooshing filled the gap in the conversation, but this time the wind came from outside through the driver's door, which had been opened.

'Twenty-four hours, Till. You've got one day,' his brother-in-law said eventually.

'Thanks. I won't need any longer to discover the truth.'

'Hmm,' Skania grunted. 'But please don't hang up yet. Your wife wants to speak to you.'

Only at that moment, far too late, did Till realise that someone else was on the bus, someone who had been listening – for how long? – and now was approaching him with a scowl on his face.

33

'*Ulysses*,' Kasov scoffed and assumed a tone which was probably meant to be a parody of a gay man. 'So, our Herr Winter is a bit of bookworm, and he reads highbrow literature to boot. James Joyce. Who'd have thought? May I see?'

He grabbed the leather-bound special edition and almost ripped it from Till's hands.

While Kasov, his head ducked, forced his way to the seats at the back, Till slipped the mobile into his trouser pocket, although he couldn't be sure that the mistrustful-looking doctor hadn't already spotted it.

At any rate he'd had no time to put the book back on the shelf.

'Are you enjoying the content?' Kasov asked, and both the ironic glint in his eye as well as the ambiguity of his question strengthened Till's suspicion that the doctor was playing a game of cat-and-mouse with him.

What does this arsehole know about me?

He looked up ahead at Seda who, like Kasov, was standing in the aisle and shaking her head silently as if trying to say to Till, *'I've no idea what he's up to either.'*

'I haven't read the book yet,' Till said in answer to Kasov's question.

A deep humming came from the bowels of the bus. The heating system must have started up.

'I assume you're intending to take it back to your cell?' Kasov asked, shaking the tome with both hands like a child trying to guess the contents of a Christmas present.

'I'm still thinking about it,' Till said, praying that Ricarda hadn't hung up yet.

And that it wouldn't occur to Kasov to open the book.

'What do you want from me?' he asked in the hope of distracting the doctor.

'I wanted to find out how your hand is,' Kasov replied with a mocking grin, not making the slightest attempt to conceal his lie.

He pointed at the light-blue finger bandage then at Till's swollen eye. 'I heard you were rather unlucky last night.'

'Yes. Someone made a mistake,' Till retorted provocatively.

Both of us know full well that you deliberately locked me up with Armin.

The question was: Why?

Till tried his best to avoid looking at the book, the cover of which the doctor kept fiddling with, but thankfully without peering inside. Otherwise he might discover the cavity between the pages. The secret compartment.

And then he'd frisk me.

'Someone?' Kasov asked. The expression on his face froze. 'I fear a certain someone could injure himself far more seriously if he doesn't keep his trap shut.' He smiled again. 'Is that understood?'

No. But I fear the real Patrick Winter would be aware of the circumstances and know why you're his enemy in here. That's why I'm going to keep my trap shut.

Till nodded and tried to look as subordinate as possible, which he only managed until first his breathing then his reason abandoned him.

For Kasov opened the book.

With a sadistic sideways glance, he opened the cover agonisingly slowly, as if it were as heavy as lead.

Till's heart pounded against his ribcage, threatening to burst it.

And just in case the doctor had been surprised by how light this monumental book seemed, he now discovered the reason for it.

He stroked the pages before skimming his way through the book.

On and on he went.

Until he found the mobile's empty hiding place.

34

Kasov didn't even bat an eyelid.

He didn't turn angry or loud.

He didn't even grab Till by the arm and take him outside, which was why, briefly, the 'patient' expected to be frisked here in the bus. Not only would the doctor find the mobile phone, but the syringe too.

The doctor remained calm. Apparently relaxed. But even though he merely stood there – *Ulysses* in his hands, open, the hiding place discovered – his presence radiated an icy coldness.

It was as if Kasov weren't exhaling carbon dioxide, but a coolant that was reducing the temperature inside the bus.

Good God, NO! Till screamed in his thoughts.

His only connection with the outside world would be cut if he had to hand over the mobile.

Till momentarily considered using the needle as a weapon against Kasov, but what would that achieve, apart from getting him locked up in an isolation cell? In the *best-case* scenario.

He'd more likely be thrown out of the hospital and presumably Sänger would call the police. Till didn't know which laws he'd already broken even without attempting to overpower Kasov. There must be several.

He then wondered whether Seda, who was still standing as stiffly as a statue in the aisle, would be disciplined too, as it surely couldn't have escaped her notice that Till had been speaking on the phone in her presence.

When Kasov looked up and for the first time Till noticed that his eyebrows curled over to his temples like moustaches, he felt sick.

Was it going to end like this?

Shit. He hadn't got particularly far, but he had made it into the hospital. Survived the night, albeit bruised. He had surmounted several major obstacles and he felt sure he would have found his way to Tramnitz.

If only I'd had more time.

Would he never now be able to say goodbye to his son just because of an arsehole like this?

Had it all been in vain?

'I can explain,' Till began, without knowing what he wanted to say. He didn't have a plan B in case he was unmasked.

Basically he didn't have a plan at all apart from getting hold of Tramnitz's diary, which, on reflection, was a desperate if not hopeless undertaking.

'I'm not interested,' Kasov said, and Till felt even sicker.

Now he'd probably find out what score the doctor had to settle with Patrick Winter.

Or with me, if for some reason he's found out who I really am.

I was wondering too why the book was so damaged, Till wanted to say, but before he could even open his lips, Kasov's words left him reeling. Because what the doctor said – and what could be inferred from what he said – was totally incomprehensible and thus extremely unnerving.

'You've got five more minutes.'

Kasov grinned and flipped the book shut.

Then he said, 'Have fun,' handed Till the book and got off the bus without turning around again or saying goodbye to Seda.

35

'Ricarda?'

There was no reply, but he could recognise her by the breathing. Or at least he fancied he was that familiar with her. After all these years.

Still.

So she was on the line. What luck she hadn't hung up. Maybe she'd heard the exchange between him and Kasov. Understood the predicament he was in. A predicament Till had escaped from without knowing why the doctor had let him off the leash.

He had no explanation for why Kasov hadn't searched him for smuggled goods. The doctor's behaviour scared him precisely because it was so inexplicable, absurd even. He was even more frightened, however, by what Ricarda had to say.

'I'm sorry, darling,' he whispered, by which he meant everything. For not having told her what he was doing. For undertaking something so insane. For having allowed Max to go to the neighbours' house.

'Your brother's told you where I am, then?'

'Yes.'

A single word, choked with tears. Too short. Three letters were far too little. Till couldn't predict from this what was going to follow. Understanding or rejection? Approval or criticism? Love or... *hatred*?

'He shouldn't have. I didn't want you to worry.'

'He's my brother,' Ricarda said. That was a little more – a whole sentence at least – and yet Till still couldn't gauge his wife's emotional state. Until she finally put him out of his misery by saying, 'I'm so proud of you!'

He looked up at the ceiling of the bus covered in grey material and wiped the tears from his eyes. And then began to weep more heavily.

Fear and relief surged through his body and it was a while before he was able to speak again.

'I'm sorry,' he repeated.

'No, *I'm* sorry. I know I shouted at you. I called you a loser because you let yourself go and didn't do anything. But, you see, I didn't know what could be done.'

'I understand.'

He leaned his head against the window, grateful for every one of his wife's words.

Even if she'd yelled insults at him it would have been okay. For that was still better than having taken the child away and left him alone. Her talking to him so affectionately and trying to explain her own behaviour was more than he had dared to dream.

'I was furious,' Ricarda said. 'Full of hatred. At the fiend who took everything away from us. He wasn't tangible, but my fury needed a channel. I couldn't be like you and sit at home, read all the newspapers and trawl through all the internet reports about Max, rotting on the inside in the process. I had to do something. Actively. Do something, go somewhere. But what? Where?'

Till left her question unanswered. It had been far too long since he'd last heard that warmth and love in Ricarda's voice. He didn't want to ruin the resonance of her words with a comment.

'So I took it out on you. Buggered off, bringing Emilia with me. I took it out on you, I'm sorry.'

'I'm going to make it all okay again,' he now whispered.

'No,' Ricarda retorted, energetically but without reproach. 'You won't. You can't. It'll never be okay again, because nothing can bring our Max back.'

'I know.'

'But you can redress the balance.'

Till nodded. He knew what she meant.

Evil had visited them, taking the form of Tramnitz in their front garden and robbing them of much of the meaning of their life. Emilia was the very best of reasons not to stick a pistol into their own mouths, but the balance had been destroyed.

In the pan of death lay a sorrow-filled weight of pain of blood and lead. In the pan of life merely a snapped feather of happiness.

'I'm going to kill him,' Till promised, and when Ricarda said how much she loved and missed him, he knew she didn't mean that unadulterated, pure love which had led them to the altar, and that things would never be as they had been before.

But he also knew that something between them had changed for the better.

'Make him suffer,' Ricarda said, and for the first time in ages he could imagine holding her in his arms again.

Just hold, nothing more.

At some point in the distant future.

As soon as he'd managed to find his way to Tramnitz.

His hand felt for the needle in his tracksuit bottoms.

For whatever reason, Kasov, his baffling enemy, had given him a chance.

He would be able to use it.

And no matter how painful his course of action proved to be, after this phone call Till was in no doubt that he would withstand the agonies awaiting him.

36

Barely had Till entered the canteen than the chitter-chatter and clatter of cutlery fell silent. As if everyone present, drinking their coffee, possessed an inner antenna for the menacing oscillations he was emitting.

There were six patients in the room, but no orderlies, no nurses and no doctors either. It was almost six p.m., there was no sign of supper yet, and the filter coffee from the thermos flasks didn't taste so good that the inmates were scrambling over each other to get some.

Till didn't have to look hard, therefore, to spot Armin Wolf. With that slight hunch that tall people often have, he was sitting with a bulbous mug and reading one of those newspapers that consisted of little more than headlines and photographs.

Armin seemed to be the only one taking no notice of Till. He behaved as if he hadn't noticed him come in until the very last moment.

'Hi there,' Till said, looking down at him. Armin lifted his head, grimaced and put his hand above his eyes as if blinded by the sun.

'Where's the mobile?' he asked.

'There isn't one,' Till replied. In fact he'd left it on the bus. It was probably much safer inside the book than in a cell devoid of hiding places.

'Then you're a dead man.'

'Or you are,' Till said, stabbing him.

Armin leaped up and screamed, although the jab in his upper arm must have surprised more than hurt him.

'What the fuck...?' Armin lunged with his fist but then, probably remembering the cameras on the ceiling, just grabbed Till by his sweatshirt. 'What was that?'

'A needle.'

Grabbing Till's hand, he prised his fingers apart and took the syringe. As if unable to believe what had just happened, he said, 'You've just signed your own death warrant, Winter.'

Armin, a head taller than Till, turned so that the camera could only view him from behind; he must have had lessons from Kasov. At any rate he held the needle right in front of Till's eyes.

'The first chance I get I'm going to ram this thing through your eye and into your brain, you fuckwit.'

Armin pushed him aside and was about to sit back down when Till said softly, 'I've got Aids.'

'What?' The colour drained from Armin's face.

'And you've got it now too.'

Till waited for Armin to jump up again and take hold of his chair before turning and counting down from ten as he made his way out.

When he got to eight he'd taken two steps to the exit.

At seven he felt breathing on his neck.

At about six and a half the chair smashed his skull.

37

SÄNGER

'Otobasal fracture with a crack in the temporal bone,' Professor Sänger said, looking at the MRI scan on her monitor.

'It was a battlefield,' said Simon, who she'd summoned to her office at this late hour and who was still visibly upset.

'I slipped on Winter's blood. Was that brain fluid coming out of his nose?'

Sänger shook her head. 'From what I can see here he hasn't suffered any secondary internal bleeding. No tears in his hard cerebral membrane. Frieder just had to repair the damage with bone adhesive.'

Simon's expression turned sad. He breathed out and looked shocked.

'Would it be better for you if I resigned?'

Sänger, who was massaging the back of her neck to relieve the tension, stared at him as if he'd enquired about the weather on Mars.

'What gives you that idea?'

He sighed. 'It's my fault that Winter got hold of the needle. It wouldn't have happened if I hadn't been so careless.'

Sänger watched Simon nervously scratch the cuticle of his thumb with his index finger.

As so often in the past, she was surprised by his sense of responsibility and his sensitivity. When she employed the Senegalese refugee he could barely speak a word of German. But this hadn't prevented him from developing an emotional connection with the patients more rapidly than many of his German colleagues simply because he paid attention to the slightest gesture and change in expression, and his strong empathy allowed him to register the faintest feeling. This time, however, his instinct was wrong when he thought her worried face and breathy voice were signs she was about to announce his dismissal.

'We all make mistakes and I'm afraid I will have to write a report on this. But the last thing I want to do is sack you. On the contrary, you have always offered very good advice and now I need it more than ever.'

Simon first looked at her cautiously then, when he realised that she was being serious, smiled so broadly that Sänger was worried the corners of his mouth might meet at the back of his head.

This was something else typical of her best orderly's behaviour. After making a mistake he didn't spend days wallowing in self-doubt, but soon bounced back when he heard good news.

'How can I help you?'

Sänger shut her laptop. 'Do you see that mountain?' she said, pointing to two heaps of files beside her desk. One of them was half a metre high, the other not much smaller. 'These are all the documents that have been gathered about Winter.'

'So many?' Simon said and whistled in acknowledgement.

'Over the last few days and nights I've read everything

we have on Winter. Medical reports, trial records, witness statements.' She sighed and looked Simon straight in the eye. 'But I still can't figure him out.'

'That's what I find with most patients here.'

Sänger returned Simon's smile. 'Yes, I know. I didn't put that particularly well. But what is he up to?'

'You're asking me?'

She got up and went over to the window. For days now she hadn't needed to close the Venetian blinds. At the moment, the weak November sun that Berlin was usually blessed with had to be substituted by artificial light soon after lunch.

Now, just before midnight, not even the lamps in the park were on any more and she stared at a dark, rainy hole that merely reflected her and the interior of her office.

'I'd love to know what he's planning,' she said, one palm pressed on the glass.

The coldness of the window spread to her entire arm. She really felt like opening it, untying her hair and sticking her head out into the rain that was lashing the building. *But not even that will calm the storm raging in my head.*

'Winter asked me about Tramnitz. Can you make any sense of that?' She turned back to Simon, who was staring anxiously at his large hands in his lap.

'I–I don't know.'

'But you have a suspicion, don't you?'

He looked up at her. 'Well, you saw for yourself the footage from the canteen. And heard the eyewitness statements. It really does look as if Winter provoked the attack.'

Sänger nodded. 'Not only that. He turned his back to Wolf. I examined his lip movements in close-up and it looks as if he was counting down.'

'Counting down?' Simon said, more to himself. 'He knew what was going to happen.'

In the distance Sänger heard the rumble of thunder. She waited until it was over then said, 'At the very least Winter was anticipating the attack.'

He knowingly sustained those injuries.

'And now he's in the infirmary. Just like Tramnitz, who he'd been asking about shortly before.'

'What does that mean?'

She exchanged conspiratorial glances with Simon. 'I've no idea. But I fear that this time we have to be much more careful than on previous occasions. Otherwise we're going to be in real difficulty, all of us together.'

38

TILL

Once more it was the smell of hot tar that reminded him of hell on earth, the gatekeepers of which had long known him by name. He'd entered it often enough. And once more it was a car park in the scorching summer sun, which he was looking down upon from a supposedly safe distance, floating many floors above the Berlin tarmac. The car was a new element in his dream, however. A black SUV with a shining roof reflecting the horizon of glass skyscrapers. It was the only vehicle in the huge, otherwise deserted car park.

Till thought he could feel a deep pain rising towards him with the shimmering air, then in his dream he tried to step away from the window and must have moved his shoulder in bed, perhaps his head too. At any rate the screwdriver boring through his skull drove him back to sleep.

It went on like this for a while.

Black. Pain. Heat. Tar. Pain. Black.

Till hovered in a loop between an agonising waking-up and a sleep numbed by painkillers until he was so terrified of remaining in this liminal state for ever that he summoned all his strength to wrench his eyes open.

A mistake.

A big mistake.

The dull light from a ceiling lamp was enough to bring a torrent of tears to his eyes. He shut his lids again immediately, but then committed his next mistake. When he tried to wipe the remaining tears from the corners of his eyes he first felt a slight stabbing in his broken fingers, followed by something akin to the blow from a baseball bat when he touched the bandage on his head.

This time it wasn't just a prop.

This time he was seriously injured. And the pain was so great that he was certain his skull would fall into two broken parts if he unfastened the bandage, which seemed to be the only thing holding his head together.

This thought made Till feel sick.

He would have loved to throw up with pain if it weren't for the certainty that he'd only feel even worse afterwards. So he tried to suppress the gagging.

Help, he called out in his thoughts and recalled that in hospital there was usually a red button beside the bed you could press to call the nurse and hopefully order a lorryload of painkillers, morphine if at all possible.

Assuming he was in the infirmary!

As he continued to keep his eyes closed he couldn't be sure. But where else would they have taken him? He was unable to recall all the details, only that he'd provoked Armin in the canteen in the certainty of ending up either dead or in intensive care. And because he was still blessed with every possible earthly suffering, he assumed he wasn't yet floating in the life hereafter.

Although – he couldn't be sure of this either.

Perhaps suicide was pointless...

What if we're all wrong and pain doesn't end with death?

This bloodcurdling thought made Till undertake a second attempt. This time, however, he opened his eyelids slowly, almost as if in slow motion.

His caution failed to spare him another fright, which made him shudder again. Despite the flashes of pain, he managed to register a number of things at once. He was in a white room, lying beneath a starched sheet in a hospital bed with a handle above his head. And he could see the shadow, which had shocked him beside his bed, pass the built-in wardrobe and quietly scurry out of the open door.

'Hey,' Till croaked to the shadow with female curves, in the hope that the nurse would come back and give him some painkillers.

Rather than make the mistake of trying to sit up he just turned his head slightly towards the door.

Till's view was interrupted by a metal rim in his blurred field of vision and it took him a while to identify it as the swivel-mounted tray of a bedside cabinet.

It took him even longer to identify the package-shaped object on it. And when he finally saw that it was the leather-bound copy of James Joyce's *Ulysses* on his bedside table, he also realised who the shadow was he had seen sneaking out of his room.

'Seda,' he croaked, slightly louder this time, but still fruitlessly. He extended his left hand out towards the book, which surprisingly he managed with relative ease, and flipped open the cover; he had to close his eyes again because of the pain. His sense of touch was functioning impeccably, however, which was why he could reassure himself that the mobile phone was still in its rightful place.

Seda brought me my phone! he thought, at once thankful and unsettled.

Did she know what was inside the book? Or had she wanted to give him the reading material he'd spent so long browsing on the bus?

No, coincidences that big don't exist.

Till's first impulse was to surrender to his exhaustion and fall straight back asleep again.

His second was to call Skania. But both were too risky.

What if somebody came into the room and discovered the mobile? Either while he was asleep or while he was using it?

No, he had to wait until he had a clear head in the truest sense of the word. Until he knew where, when and for how long he would be undisturbed.

He had to hide the mobile at once, the book too if possible, but how was he going to manage that?

Where can I put it?

Maybe it would be better to get Seda to return it to the bus.

If she were still in the infirmary it couldn't hurt to at least have a chat with her. After all, she was his only contact here, even though Skania had warned him that she couldn't be trusted.

But she seems to have access to all the wards and departments.

So maybe she knows where Tramnitz is?

The excitement had sharpened Till's senses. Although he still felt as if he'd tried to stop an oncoming train with his head, at least the adrenaline boost had quelled the sickness, which meant he no longer felt the need to throw up on the spot when he pulled back the sheet.

For the moment he thought it would be best not to leave
the book with the mobile lying around, so he put it in the top
drawer of his bedside cabinet.

Then, gritting his teeth, he grabbed the handle above the
bed and pulled himself up. Something inside his head seemed
to slop from one side of his skull to the other and his mouse-
grey nightshirt slid over his knees when he pushed his legs out
of the bed.

No sooner had his bare toes touched the floor than he felt
cold. He tried in vain to stop the shivering. With every step
he ventured towards the door, the feverish chill became more
acute.

Fortunately it was a small room and Till was able to support
himself first on the bed, then against a chair and finally on the
handles of the cupboard.

He noticed to his astonishment that the hospital room even
had its own bathroom.

Hadn't Sänger said something about a shortage of beds?

And now he was lying here in a comfortable single room.

He looked back towards the window in a hopeless attempt
to gauge the time of day. It wasn't night, at any rate, but that
was all he could glean from examining the rain-spattered
glass. Judging by the subdued, dirty light outside, it could
be any time between daybreak and dusk. A typical autumn–
winter day in Berlin. With torrential rain. Was he imagining
it, or did it already smell damp and mouldy in here?

The door handle felt clammy too. He pressed it, but
couldn't open the door.

It's locked, of course.

But hold on a sec.

He vaguely remembered that the regulations in the

infirmary were more relaxed than on the closed wards. Perhaps the stupid door was just too heavy, or he too feeble. Utterly exhausted and shivering, he leaned back against it.

And almost fell into the corridor.

Idiot.

He'd pulled the door, whereas obviously it opened outwards. This allowed the staff to open the door even if a patient collapsed right beside it.

There wasn't a soul in the corridor and Till struggled to keep on his feet, almost collapsing on the hard linoleum despite the handholds at wheelchair height along the walls.

Nothing, however, could save him from the flashes of pain behind his eyes that struck with every step. The effects of the painkillers had drastically declined. His head felt like a cooking pot whose lid was buckling because the pain had no way to escape.

But no matter how severe the pain, it was nothing compared to the emotional torture that Till had suffered since Max's disappearance and was still causing him agony now.

Max!

The thought alone of his son helped him to avoid screaming out loud and alerting the hospital staff. Till bit his uninjured fist and managed to restrict himself to a gentle whimper. He waited until the worst flashes of pain were just shadows flickering across his retinas, then he put one foot in front of the other again and headed down the small side passage where his room was. Past another closed door towards the main corridor that ran perpendicular.

And at the end of which was something that made Till's heart beat faster.

A shelf trolley.

The sort you see in hospitals for serving food. Only this one was narrow, waist-high and full of books.

Seda! Till was tempted to call out.

His fellow patient was still in the infirmary, seemingly delivering library books directly to patients.

He was sweating profusely by the time he finally got to the trolley at the corner where the corridors met.

Till was standing only a metre and a half away from a partly open door, which was marked with the number 217 and beneath it a small sign that said: 'MAXIMUM OCCUPANCY ONE PATIENT'.

Unable to see Seda, Till suspected that she had gone into the single room. He wondered whether he was being watched, and checked for cameras on the ceiling, but couldn't see any. He did, however, notice two figures at the far end of the corridor, standing beside the biometrically secured lifts.

To begin with, Till couldn't work out who was in conversation over there. But when he eventually managed to focus his streaming eyes a little better, he just wanted to run away.

There was the man who he'd tortured and killed a hundred times already in his head.

In the end he managed to stop himself from instantly wrecking the one chance he had. He needed superhuman willpower to avoid screaming out loud and releasing all the despair bottled up inside him.

He remained silent and as still as a statue, and so it was Kasov who moved first. He turned towards Till, as did Tramnitz soon afterwards.

As if the two of them had suspected they had a secret observer.

39

TRAMNITZ

'What's up?' Tramnitz said, bemused by the fact that Kasov had broken off mid-sentence and turned around.

'I don't know,' the doctor replied rather vaguely. Tramnitz followed his gaze down the corridor, but couldn't make out anything. It was empty save for the library trolley.

'I thought I saw someone.'

'Seda?' Tramnitz presumed and touched himself between his legs with a wolfish smile.

Kasov shook his head. 'No. The whore hasn't left your room. I just got the feeling that someone went in.'

'To my room?' Tramnitz asked crossly. The idiot had promised him that he could enjoy the tart undisturbed. 'I thought everyone was at the meeting.'

'They are.'

Kasov had called a second general meeting on the subject of 'high water and flooding' after a sewer pipe in the south wing had almost burst overnight. Apart from one orderly, who was on call in the nurses' room, all the staff were at that moment meeting in the lobby. And most of the patients were already in other buildings, which was why Tramnitz essentially had the floor to himself.

Apart from the guy with the mushed head, but according to Kasov he was in no state to leave his bed.

'Didn't you arrange for us to be undisturbed and make sure that the orderly would only leave the nurses' room in an emergency?'

'Yes, of course. Would I be wandering around with you so freely otherwise?' Kasov answered. 'But to be on the safe side, have your way with her in the bathroom. Nobody can burst in on you in there.'

The doctor smiled again, appropriately enough for a man who Tramnitz had made 2,500 euros better off.

Pia had personally taken the corrupt doctor's 'additional earnings' to his house, although she assumed she was paying Kasov for improved prison conditions, better food and longer stretches out in the open air. Pia might be a very tolerant woman, but she certainly wouldn't supply Tramnitz with prostitutes.

'Anything else you want to tell me?' Tramnitz said, resuming their conversation.

'That you'll be enjoying my services free for a month.'

Tramnitz frowned. 'I don't get you.'

'I'll supply you with everything you need. Coke, whores, porn.'

'And I don't have to pay anything?'

'No.'

'What, then?' Tramnitz asked.

Where's the catch?

'Look in your hiding place.'

Kasov had shown him where best to hide the diary from prying eyes.

'I put something there.'

'What?' Tramnitz asked suspiciously.

'You'll see. Use it.'

'For what?'

Kasov lowered his voice to a whisper, which made the whole thing highly suspicious as far as Tramnitz was concerned. If anyone happened to bump into them, how could he pass off this murmuring as a normal doctor–patient conversation?

'To solve a problem for me.'

Aha. Now we're getting closer.

'Does this problem have a name?'

'Patrick Winter.'

'The guy two doors down?'

'I've heard on the grapevine that he let his head be bashed in just so he could get close to you,' Kasov said.

'I've also heard on the grapevine that you gave fake documents to his cellmate detailing how Winter killed his own son.'

'Why would I do a thing like that?' Kasov grinned.

'To make the guy so mad that he would get the child killer out of the way for you. But that can't have worked, which is why now you're turning to me. Am I right?'

'No comment.'

'That in itself is an answer. So I know what you're up to, Doctor. But what does this Patrick Winter want from me?'

Kasov's smile froze. 'I wouldn't waste too much time on that question if I were you. Just solve the problem in the way you best see fit.'

You want me to stick him in an incubator and impale him with garden shears?

Tramnitz smiled and rubbed his now stiff penis through his trousers.

'Okay, I'll have a think about it. But first I've got to attend to the slitty-eyed tart. I hope Seda's robust.'

'No visible injuries!' Kasov warned him, but Tramnitz had already left him standing there as if he no longer understood the doctor's whispers.

40

TILL

Seda stared goggle-eyed, her jaw dropped; the expression on her face screamed, '*What the hell are* you *doing here?*'

Till would have liked to ask her the same question had he not been distracted by the red-hot needles trying to stab his pupils from inside his eyes ever since he'd entered the room.

'Get out, now!' she hissed.

Till made two mistakes. He nodded and then tried to turn back to the door he'd just slunk through. He suddenly felt dizzy and lost his balance. Stumbling forwards, he steadied himself on Seda, who had rushed over to him and whose collarbone felt so unbelievably thin that he was worried he might break it. But Seda managed to support him as far as the bed, where he sat down.

'You've got to get out of here right now!' she exclaimed through gritted teeth. The trembling in her voice left no room for doubt that her fear was as great as his pain.

What was she so afraid of? Why did her haunted eyes keep darting towards the door?

'I can't,' he said barely audibly. Not while Tramnitz was still out there.

I've got to hide here until he's gone again. I'm not in a state yet to interrogate him. I need to get my strength back and my head right first so that...

With this unfinished fragment of a thought, time seemed to freeze.

Till blinked, or at least he imagined he was doing so, then actually managed to move his lips. He asked the only question that was necessary to confirm the hunch he had just felt. 'Whose room is this?' he muttered.

And why are you here?

Wearing red lipstick and a half-open blouse?

'You've got to go *now*!'

'*Who?*' Till demanded an answer.

Seda rolled her eyes in such a way that had Till done it he would have passed out at once.

'Tramnitz, and now—'

Oh, God.

'—get out!'

He'd taken refuge in the psychopath's lair.

'What if he saw me in the corridor?' he thought without realising that he'd said the words out loud, but incomprehensibly.

I'm in a trap.

He'd achieved the objective he'd no longer believed was achievable. Just not at the right time.

He wouldn't be able to win Tramnitz's confidence if the latter found him as an intruder in his room. Nor could he beat the truth out of him. *Shit*, just walking almost brought him to the verge of fainting.

So what now?

He heard footsteps approaching from outside. Rubber soles squeaking on the lino.

'Fuck,' Seda cursed. She ordered Till to get off the bed, pushing him towards the window. Down from the mattress. Till gritted his teeth and rolled over rather than getting up. Holding on to the metal frame, he slid to the floor, wanting to scream the entire ward down like a wounded animal.

His nightshirt, which was tied loosely at the back, opened when his bottom hit the floor. 'Get away from there,' he heard Seda hiss, so he crawled over to the cabinet beside the bed. The coldness of the wall he leaned against between the bed and cabinet crept up his spine like a paralysing toxin.

Till began shivering again and Seda whispered, 'Don't move a muscle!'

Just in time, for Tramnitz came crashing into the room with the words, 'Why aren't you naked yet?'

41

Everything Till heard from that point on sounded as if a pair of noise-cancelling headphones had been put over his ears. Tramnitz ordered Seda into the bathroom and the thick, plastic-coated bathroom door seemed to close flush with the floor, allowing through only particularly low or extraordinarily high sounds. And these were further muffled by the deep-ocean pressure in Till's ears that now accompanied his headache. He could only guess, therefore, at what was going on between Seda and Tramnitz in the bathroom. What Seda was wearing combined with Tramnitz's shameless, vulgar greeting – uttered with the confidence of someone who had nothing to fear – made it clear why the patient was waiting in his room. What she had come here for.

But was it really possible that Seda was going to give herself to this monster?

Of her own free will?

From a documentary he'd seen Till knew that sex in exchange for money (what else could it be?) was available in almost every area of the state prison system. So probably here in the Steinklinik too.

Was that why Skania had warned him about Seda? Because he thought that, as a prostitute, she wasn't trustworthy?

And how was Kasov involved?

Till's stomach grumbled.

Ironically his body was demanding to go to the only place he couldn't visit now. He was desperate to throw up.

I've got to get out of here.

But if he stood up now (*God knows how I'm going to manage that*) he was worried he'd vomit on the floor.

Till glanced up at the bedside table and cursed the smooth, edgeless surface. The tray was too high. Nothing he could pull himself up on. Apart from...

The drawers!

The cabinet on wheels had three drawers. He opened the bottom one: empty.

All he needed was something to support himself with. Unfortunately the drawer turned out to be unsuitable. Hardly had he put his left hand on it than the table started rolling to the side. Worse than that, he was in danger of falling over. A magazine and two bottles of water tumbled to the floor. Luckily the bottles were plastic and barely made a noise.

All the same, Till held his breath, terrified that Tramnitz would come storming out of the bathroom and find him cowering here behind his bed.

But all he heard was a deep animal grunting.

And... was he imagining it, or was Seda moaning now?

Till pushed the bedside table to the wall so it couldn't roll any further and tried again. His hand inside the drawer for support, he tried to push himself up. With the opposite outcome.

First he heard the bottom of the drawer bend, then he felt himself push right through the thin layer of wood.

Shit!

Biting his lip, he took out his left hand, which fortunately wasn't injured, checked all his fingers... and then saw it:

The paper.

The binding.

The brown book with a ribbon, which through his clumsiness he'd just exposed in its hiding place beneath the false bottom of the drawer.

It wasn't the devil who had all the luck.

But the insane.

Till knew instantly what it was. An overestimation of his abilities had made him a fake patient. A fracture of his skull had brought him closer to the beast. And luck had delivered the diary to him.

He cut himself on an edge of chipboard as he tore open the false bottom further, which was hard going with one hand. He didn't care about the blood on his fingers.

Till took out the book and untied the black ribbon so he could open the diary.

It looked different from how he had imagined. Less used, somehow.

And in fact not even ten per cent of the pages had been written on, as Till discovered when he opened it.

If Tramnitz had kept a diary for each of his victims, then Till was now holding the final volume by this sadistic, sick psychopath. Which was confirmed by the very first sentence in nice, graceful handwriting that matched Tramnitz's attractive outward appearance.

The words written in black ink destroyed the last vestige of Till's belief in a benevolent God.

Today the boy in the incubator told me his name. He had so much blood in his mouth I could barely understand him. But I'm almost certain he said it was Max.

42

A scream. Not from him. He would have yelled out his emotional anguish far louder than Seda did her physical pain in the bathroom.

His scream flew inwards; he was imploding with despair.

Till's hands were shaking; tears of sorrow and suffering streamed down his face.

He had reached his goal. In his hands he had not only the proof of Tramnitz's crime, but possibly a detailed description of his son's final few hours. Something he'd never hand back until he knew for certain what had happened to Max. And where his body was.

Did he have to suffer for long?

Did Tramnitz kill him for fun and according to a plan?

Or on impulse because in the end he'd simply had enough of his 'whining', like that serial killer Till had once heard about on a podcast.

Good God!

Ricarda would perhaps take flight from the truth. Close her ears, leave the room, not wanting to hear, to know how Max's life ended.

But Till?

He shook his head, willing to face the pain that this would evoke. He needed the worst of all certainties, even if it smothered every last flicker of hope.

Because Till needed to say goodbye to Max, there was no way he could put the diary back now.

But he couldn't read it here either.

How long has Seda been busy with him?

When he looked towards the bathroom he felt that time, which had stood still the moment he read his son's name, was now shooting onwards like an arrow.

His first objective was to push the table back and close the drawer so that Tramnitz wouldn't immediately notice something was missing when he got back into bed. As he was doing this, Till spotted a small, shiny, metallic object in the drawer, which certainly had no place in a psychopath's hospital room.

Without a second thought, Till picked up the razor blade that had been hidden in the secret compartment beneath the diary.

Then he did what only a few seconds earlier he'd thought was impossible, but the discovery of the diary had revitalised him. His fury towards Tramnitz was so overwhelming that his instinct was to burst into the bathroom and smash the monster's head against the sink. Over and over again until his white teeth swam in a soup of bones and blood in the basin and the grey matter of his brain was visible through cracks in his skull.

But his miraculous boost of strength was just enough to crawl to the door on all fours. He blocked out the rusty mill of pain inside his head as he got to his feet and eventually fell out with the door into the corridor.

Empty.

Not a soul about.

What luck!

His undamaged hand gripped the diary more tightly, into which he'd slipped the razor blade. If his luck held out, he might even make it back to his room before collapsing with exhaustion and choking on his own vomit after blacking out.

Till didn't even get around the corner.

As he was about to pass Seda's book trolley, he heard a door open behind him and someone say his cover name.

43

'Patrick Winter? What's going on here?'

Till shoved the diary beneath his nightshirt and turned around, keeping his arms crossed around his stomach to hold on to the book.

'I... I just got lost,' he whispered, his torso bent forwards in pain.

'I can see that,' the orderly said, moving swiftly towards him. He was a head taller than Till, with dark hair and feminine eyebrows that arched upwards, which lent him a friendly expression, but one of permanent surprise.

He also talked like a waterfall. 'But why? Why aren't you in bed where you belong? Goodness me! I'm on my own here on the ward and I ought to be in the nurses' room, you know, in case there's an emergency. If I hadn't needed the loo I wouldn't have seen you, Herr Winter.'

He offered him his hand.

'Please, I need something to combat the pain,' Till said truthfully.

'I can imagine. I would too in your state. Why on earth didn't you press the button by the bed? Things like this can end badly. I once had a patient who got the wrong door and suddenly found himself standing outside. In the middle of the night, in January; it was minus twelve. Not here, of course, it was in the Johannesstift, but he wasn't wearing much more than you are now. Will you be able to make it or should I get a stretcher?'

Till avoided any reaction. He gritted his teeth and went stoically onwards, step by step, back to his room.

'Wait, I'll be right back with an injection to send you to sleep,' the orderly promised as soon as Till was in bed. 'Something wonderful to sweep the pain away and send you wherever your dreams want to go. Maybe the Playboy Mansion, although I imagine it's a bit desolate since Hugh Hefner died.'

Even as he left the room, the orderly didn't stop talking, his words getting ever quieter.

Unlike the jackhammer beneath Till's skull.

With the last of his strength, Till made use of the opportunity to put the diary and razor blade alongside the hollowed-out book in the drawer of his bedside table. Then his sweat-bathed head sank onto the pillow and his teeth started to chatter.

His acute fatigue response escalated into a full-scale epileptic fit, which not even the injection the orderly gave him could immediately bring under control. It was quite a while after the jab before Till's trembling subsided and his heart rate and breathing calmed down. The cold took leave of his body at the same rate that the pain monster withdrew the claws it had sunk into his brain.

Till would have cried for joy at the relief from his pain had he not fallen straight asleep.

Although he felt wretched when he regained consciousness, it was nowhere near as bad as the last time he'd awoken.

Christ! Whatever the orderly had administered, it was good stuff. It was still working.

Whereas Till's headache had masked all his sensory perception before, now he could feel his injured hand throbbing again and smell his bad breath, and he was glad.

Finally he no longer felt like someone with seasickness having to contest the twelfth round of a cage fight. He didn't, however, altogether trust this peaceful state so, after some blinking, he opted to keep his eyes closed even though the room was pleasantly dim, with just a nightlight illuminating the early morning or evening, depending on how long he'd been asleep.

The next time he dared open his eyes fully, he saw the book on his bedside table.

Ulysses.

His mind worked slowly, but clearly. He had a sinister inkling of what it meant that the book was no longer in the drawer.

At once Till pulled it open and felt for the diary. His hand grasped into thin air.

At the same time he heard the voice. To his right.

'Are you looking for this?'

Till turned to the side, only to see that it was indeed Tramnitz sitting on the visitor's chair beside the bed, a friendly smile on his lips.

And the open diary in his lap.

44

'I must say, I find you rather impolite. You come into my room unannounced while I'm occupied. I mean, I've nothing against visitors, but we haven't even been introduced yet, have we?'

Till swallowed heavily and wondered how evil could appear so harmless. Facing him sat a young man with a pleasant smile who looked friendly and level-headed. Nothing, not even a flash in his eyes, betrayed his dark thoughts.

How could you warn your children about such a degenerate? A perverted sadist with innocent eyes and cheerful laugh lines. Even the post-op plaster on his neck looked like a fashion accessory. Apart from a slight hospital pallor, there was nothing about Tramnitz to suggest that only a few days ago he'd been dangerously ill.

'Who *are* you?' Tramnitz asked, bending forwards with interest. The muffled engine drone of a plane coming into land filtered through the window.

Till glanced at the door, unsure whether he wanted an orderly to come to his assistance and get rid of Tramnitz, for he might never get a better opportunity to learn the truth. Torn inside between a hatred more intense than he'd ever felt and the fear of being unable to moderate this and ruining everything, he remained silent. The child killer smiled. 'Don't worry. We won't be disturbed. Kasov has won us some time. So, what is your name?'

'Patrick Winter.'

'And you are…'

'I am…' Till thought about this quickly and went with a flash of inspiration. 'I'm a fan.'

Tramnitz gave a hearty laugh. 'Yes, of course you are.'

'No, really. I've read so much about you. Seen you on television. I wanted to meet you in person.'

If there were a life after death and Max could follow this conversation as a ghost, Till hoped that his boy could read his thoughts and knew how hard it was for him to tell this lie. And just how much of an effort it was to stop himself from leaping out of the bed with a scream and demolishing Tramnitz's pretty face. Or at least to try.

'I admire you. Your crimes. I want to be like you.'

'And you think it helps to get a chair smashed over your head?' Tramnitz said with a giggle, sweeping a blond hair from his brow.

'It was my only chance to get to see you. We're not on the same ward. I'm not in your league. So I had to get transferred to the infirmary.'

'You *had* to.'

'Yes. We can move around more freely here. Chat. Like now. It wouldn't be possible otherwise.'

'Chat,' Tramnitz repeated. 'Stealing someone's diary is a strange form of *chatting*.'

Till raised a hand in apology. 'I came across it by chance.'

'You broke into my cabinet by *chance*?'

'I swear, I tripped. And then I read the first sentence. Wow, it's fascinating. The whole world wants to know what you did to Max. I'm sorry, I couldn't resist.'

In the pause that followed Tramnitz stood up and went to the window, where he pressed a switch on the wall. With a gentle whirr, the electric blind rose and the room got slightly brighter.

'Do you know what I think?' Tramnitz asked, gazing into the morning mist stuck between the trees in the park. Although it had clearly stopped raining, the low-hanging clouds were sure to bring more flooding.

'I think you're telling me a pile of crap,' he said, turning to Till. 'And do you know why I think that? Because I can smell it. Your fear. It smells worse than an old person's diarrhoea in a burst adult nappy. But don't worry.'

Tramnitz returned to the visitor's chair, sat back down and smiled. 'I like that.'

He gave Till a searching look and added, 'I love fear and its smell. It's one of the very few things that turns me on.'

Till clenched his left fist. 'Look, you're my idol,' he pretended and felt sick. 'Of course I'm going to be all excited in your presence.'

Tramnitz cocked his head. Looked at him sceptically with the hint of a mischievous smile. 'So you're telling the truth?'

'Yes.'

Till managed a nod without feeling pain inside his head. Either the drugs were still working or his fear of Tramnitz was effacing any other negative feeling from his consciousness.

'Hmm,' Tramnitz said, rubbing his chin thoughtfully. 'That would mean Kasov is lying.'

Till shrugged. 'I don't know what the senior doctor's told you.'

'He says you're faking it. You're just playing a role. You're not who you claim to be.'

'That's not true.'

'Why should I believe you rather than the doctor? You haven't exactly made yourself look trustworthy by breaking into my room.'

'I know,' Till said, trying to assume a guilty expression.

'Perhaps you're not a fan at all, but an informer?'

'What? No, I'm not spying on you.'

'Who were you talking to on the bus then?'

'Sorry?' Till pretended not to have understood the meaning of Tramnitz's question.

'Kasov overheard you talking on the library bus. Apparently you said, *"I won't need any longer to find out the truth"*.'

'That's…'

'Another lie? So you weren't talking to yourself on the bus then?'

No. I was on the phone.

'Well, if you *are* telling the truth then I'm really starting to get worried about our dear Dr Kasov. Clearly his brain isn't working much better than those of his patients. What do you think?'

Till gulped.

'He thinks you're after him.'

'What?'

'He reckons you've uncovered his prostitute racket, his nice little earner on the side. Are you planning to grass him up to Professor Sänger?'

'What? No. I don't care about Kasov.'

'Well, he sees it very differently. Maybe he's just being paranoid; after all there's a lot at stake as far as he's concerned. His income on the side.' .

'I haven't got a clue what you're talking about.'

'Really?'

The longer this interrogation went on, the more Tramnitz seemed to enjoy it. 'Well, now that we're such good acquaintances, I can tell you.' He laughed. 'We're talking millions of euros of research money which the EU lavishes on the pharmaceutical firms. That's assuming the drug manufacturers can prove that their expensive new medicines are somehow useful. And this is where our senior doctor comes in.'

'How?'

'Kasov makes sure the medicines work. He gets the drug boffins the human guinea pigs they need.'

Where does he find people who voluntarily allow themselves to be locked up in a psychiatric unit? The question was on Till's tongue, but in his excitement he couldn't see the irony of it. Then Tramnitz answered the question before Till could ask it.

'Kasov smuggles prostitutes into the hospital and invents suitable tales of mental illness for them. That saucy minx Seda, for example, takes pills for a bipolar disorder she doesn't actually suffer from. The only thing wrong with her is that she's so sensitive when you give it to her hard.'

Feeling a hot flush coming on, Till threw back the covers.

'Kasov smuggles in healthy patients for illegal drug tests?' A brilliant idea, essentially. When the tests are over, the patients are free of the symptoms they've never suffered from. And the pharmaceutical industry has the proof that the research money they've applied for has been put to good use. 'And then he also lets them turn tricks to maximise his profit?'

'Very convincing,' Tramnitz praised him. 'One really might believe you were hearing all this for the first time.'

'How do you know about it?'

'My lawyer. She represented Kasov over a similar business with his previous employer.'

'She's not too bothered about client confidentiality then?'

'Not during sex.'

After all the bizarre things he'd heard, this comment didn't especially surprise Till. But something else perplexed him. 'Why are you telling me this?'

'To find out which of the two of you is taking me for a ride.'

'I'm not, I swear,' Till said, placing a hand on his chest.

'Hmm.'

Tramnitz felt in the pocket of his tracksuit trousers and when he opened his fingers, there was the razor blade that Till had found in the secret compartment.

'Kasov gave me this for you.'

'To do what?'

Tramnitz rolled his eyes. 'Just because we're in a loony bin, it doesn't mean you have to go over the top with your daft questions. Now, surely Kasov didn't ask me to trim your bumfluff.'

Till instinctively put his hand to his chin, then swung his legs out of the bed, which he regretted at once. The movement triggered a flash of pain that shot between his eyes.

'Listen, you're making a mistake. Kasov's making a mistake. I don't know what makes him think that and why he's got it in for me. But you don't have to do anything to me. Look at me. I'm only here to be close to you.'

He stood up and hadn't felt so vulnerable in a long time. Half-naked, barefoot, dressed only in a nightshirt.

'Hmm,' Tramnitz said, thinking, and got out of his chair too. 'I don't know. Kasov hasn't bullshitted me before. But you? You've watched me, listened in on me and stolen from me. How can I be sure that in spite of all this you're who you claim to be: Patrick Winter, my biggest fan?' Tramnitz tapped his chin in a mock thinker's pose. 'Ah. I've got an idea. Here.'

He came so close that Till could smell Tramnitz's tart lemon shampoo. He held his diary under Till's nose.

Till began to stammer. 'What, what do you want me to do?'

'Read.'

'Why?'

Tramnitz opened the slim book.

The small, handwritten letters on the unlined pages swam before Till's eyes.

'Well, fans like to know everything about their idol, don't they? If you really worship me as much as you claim, then here's a tasty autobiographical morsel for you, Patrick. For sane people, i.e., those who rightfully detest me, the descriptions in there ought to be unbearable.'

Tramnitz tapped his finger on the section where Till was to begin and placed the diary in both his hands.

'You said yourself you couldn't resist the story of Max Berkhoff. So, read. I'm keen to learn what you think about the last few hours I was able to spend with the little rascal.'

45

Diary, p. 9

It was cold, cold, cold. So cold that the piss in your todger would have frozen, Dad might have said. And it was getting dark. I've no idea what the little boy was doing out there in the road. After all, we were in Buckow rather than on the Thermometer estate, where parents are happy if one of their brats is missing as they count them up in the evenings.

So my job was easy, even though this little boy was no idiot. 'What's the password?' he asked me in all seriousness. So his helicopter parents had taught him what to say if a man at the school gate asked him if he wants to go and see his puppies. Fortunately there is a universal password and it's called Rohypnol. It works on all children, especially if you administer it with a syringe.

Till nodded without looking up. He was worried that Tramnitz would already notice his disgust.

'How do you like my style? I just wrote it straight down for later publication as a book. My lawyer's handling the rights at the moment.'

That's perverted, Till thought.

'That's great,' he said.

Tramnitz laughed smugly. 'Okay, let's spare ourselves the blah, blah, blah and jump right into the meaty bits.'

The psychopath rubbed his hands, deadly serious now. Strong, well-formed hands of the sort you'd like your masseur to have.

'Go on a page to the second section.'

'Here?' Till said, showing him the book and corresponding place.

'Exactly. That's where I recall our first conversation. When Max woke up for the first time.'

'Where am I?'

'In your new home.'

'I–I'm frightened.'

The little monkey didn't know how much pleasure those words gave me. Yes, the snot around his nose, the little chest quaking whenever he spoke – those were sure signs. But it's always something different when my patients admit it openly.

'What, what is that thing?'

'An incubator. My father always called it Trixi. To this day I don't know why. I didn't give the incubator a name.'

'What is an incubator?'

'It gives you security, warmth, comfort. I can take care of you well in there.'

'What do you mean?'

Once again Tramnitz interrupted Till's hesitant reading.

'I'm not sure if Max was sobbing so loudly at this point that I could hardly understand him, or whether it was later, when the treatment started. Writing a record from memory is more difficult than I thought.'

Till had to clench his jaws to prevent himself from screaming. He gulped and hoped that Tramnitz didn't notice his eyelids quivering. His carotid artery throbbing beneath his skin.

On the killer's orders Till kept reading.

> 'Do you want to get out of there?'
>
> 'Yes.'
>
> 'Fine, no problem. Have you ever heard of kangaroo care?'
>
> 'A kangaroo?'
>
> 'Yes, that's where it comes from. It's a term from neonatal medicine and the treatment of premature babies. Premature babies are very special. They need huge amounts of attention. Just like you, my little friend.'
>
> 'Are you taking me to the zoo?'
>
> 'No, you silly billy. Kangaroo care means that the parents sometimes take their children out of the incubator and lay them on their bare chest. So they feel like kangaroo babies in the pouch. This warmth is very important.'
>
> As I said this, I dimmed the light. It was almost as dark as in a porn cinema. Like in the neonatal unit in Virchow. Just the right mood.
>
> I slowly got undressed and when I was naked I opened the holes in the side of the incubator so I could secure Max's hands and feet with cable ties.
>
> 'Shall we try it?' I asked him. No answer was necessary. All children love cuddles. At least at that age they do. Only later do they become obstinate.
>
> Sure, some of them are slightly uncertain and awkward, they

feel frightened in their new surroundings. They're not used to getting all this love at once. I mean, they've got parents who let them out alone in the street even when it's dark. I use the cable ties so they can't hurt themselves.

I took Max out of the incubator. He was really heavy for his age, but he had the mild smell of the baby shampoo I'd washed him with earlier while he was still asleep.

Baby shampoo and fear produce a wonderfully fragrant blend, I find. It ought to be bottled and sold in every health and beauty store.

I can recall how Max was trembling. The cold outside the incubator was always a shock.

But eventually he stopped whimpering and his tenseness relaxed. And while the two of us lay in the lounger beside the incubator, his body on mine, both of us naked, just as God created us, and the blood between my legs pulsated, I began to sing for joy:

'Dance to your daddy / My bonny laddy…'

At this point the text came to an end. Till turned a few more pages, but they were all empty.

'Well, what do you think?'

Till looked up and, with a superhuman effort, composed himself and said, 'What a beautiful text, so poetic. I wish I'd been there.'

Eleven words with which he once again spat on his son's unknown grave.

He'd have rather put his hand over his mouth or bitten his lip until it bled to avoid saying these words. Like No Arm, he wanted to cut off his tongue, which suddenly felt alien inside his mouth, slice by slice until he could no longer make a sound apart from incomprehensible cries of pain. But that wasn't necessary. Till couldn't deny his feelings. His body was already telling the truth. He was shaking, quivering, blinking and yet was unable to prevent the one single tear from emerging.

'Well, well,' Tramnitz said, gently taking hold of his head to wipe the tear away. 'I suspected as much.'

Till lowered the diary, cried and knew:

I failed. I didn't pass the test.

'Who are you really?'

Although he knew too that physically he was no match for Tramnitz, he ripped the sheet from the mattress and dragged it over the head of the surprised killer. He twisted it once, then again, like a rope around a bollard in a harbour, while pulling the head downwards. Then he hit Tramnitz right in the middle of his ghostlike veiled face. Hearing a crack he thought he must have broken the monster's nose.

Was that blood turning the sheet red?

He continued hitting him.

But...

Why was the guy not defending himself?

Why was he laughing so heartily beneath the sheet with each blow that struck him?

46

Till stopped, partly because he could barely use his right hand any more, which was holding on tight to the sheet. The bandage had become untied and it felt as if Armin had broken his fingers again. But most of all Till felt that it was pointless to keep hitting Tramnitz. He could sense it and when he took the sheet off he could see it too: you couldn't beat the evil out of someone. Viscous blood dripped from Tramnitz's nose, colouring his lips, teeth and the bottom of his neck red, but this didn't seem to bother the madman one bit. On the contrary, he was still laughing, shaking his head like a father expressing his amusement at his son's awkward slip-up.

'So Kasov was right. You're playing games with us.'

Till moved away from him, the bloody sheet at his feet.

Yes, I am. But not in the way you think.

'Your name isn't Patrick Winter,' Tramnitz asserted, snuffling. He spat out a bloody wad of mucus then asked, 'Who are you really?'

Now that Till had exposed himself with his unrestrained behaviour, he didn't see any point in continuing to lie.

'Till,' he croaked. 'My name is Till Berkhoff.'

A pause. For a moment the child killer seemed to have lost the power of speech.

'Hang on a sec, you're...?'

There was another moment of shock, but then Tramnitz couldn't hold himself back any longer. 'Are you telling me you're Max's father?'

Throwing his head back, the psychopath gave a belly laugh, sat on the mattress and slapped his thigh with some force.

'Well, I never. Oh, how brilliant!'

His laughter sounded odiously hearty, pure joy. 'Respect. I've got to give you that. Are you saying you smuggled yourself in here? To kill me?'

Till shook his head then had to hold the sides because of the pain this had unleashed. 'No. To find out the truth.'

Tramnitz grunted. 'Yes, that makes sense. Much more than your daft fan story. It would at least give a plausible explanation for why you had yourself admitted and even let yourself get beaten up. Only a father can resort to such desperate measures.'

'Where's Max?'

Till had no desire to beat about the bush any longer, but Tramnitz didn't care. Clearly he preferred asking questions to answering them.

'But it doesn't explain why Kasov wants to have you killed. Are you simply trying to save your skin? I mean no sooner do I tell you how Kasov smuggles in perfectly sane patients than you're another person who's done the same.'

Tramnitz got off the mattress and forced Till into the corner of the room, merely by moving closer to him.

'I'm telling the truth.'

'That's what you said five minutes ago and it was a lie.'

'I need to see him, to say goodbye,' Till heard himself say.

'I understand,' Tramnitz nodded. His white teeth glinted in his blood-smeared face. 'I really do. In fact I understand very well. It's just that your plan...'

He touched his nose and looked at the red on his fingertips.

'Do you think that beating up the guy with the secret at the first available opportunity was well thought-out?'

No, it was a mistake. A lack of self-control.

'I fear you need to show a little more persuasiveness. All the rest of the diary entries are in here,' he said, tapping his head. 'I don't think a little nudge to the head is going to be enough to make me open up to you any further. Here, have a go with this.'

To his astonishment, Tramnitz passed Till the razor blade that he'd taken from the secret compartment along with the diary.

'What am I meant to do with this?'

'Well, if I were you, and fortunately I'm not, I would slam that elbow of yours in my face again, then grab my hand and push the razor blade right under my fingernail, like this.'

Tramnitz then put his words into action by grabbing Till's hand with brute force.

'Lever it off.'

'What?'

'The nail. You heard me. From the side if possible – it's slower and much more painful.'

Till's hand felt as if it were cast in concrete. He couldn't move it or the razor blade in it at all.

'Oh, don't be like that,' Tramnitz said, then did the unimaginable. He removed the nail off himself.

He slid the blade beneath his fingernail, pushing the tip deep into his flesh and used it like a lever.

'Jesus Christ!'

'You see?' he said, nonplussed. 'Well, that didn't hurt one bit.'

With his bloody finger Tramnitz pointed at the prised-out fingernail on the floor.

'Actually, I'm lying,' he said with a smile. 'There was a slight twinge. I mean, I'm not completely insensitive. My sense of pain is just very much reduced.'

You can say that again.

Till stared at him in disbelief, searching for a scientific explanation of how this madman hadn't even whimpered under such extreme torture. Tramnitz himself provided the explanation.

'My first psychiatrist told my mother that it's typical for people with borderline personality disorder. Later it transpired that there's something wrong with the thalamus in my brain, but I bet I'm boring you with the medical details.'

He grabbed Till by the chin and with his bloody fist now held it in the same vice-like grip he had his hand.

'You just have to understand one important thing. I need extreme stimuli to feel anything at all.'

Is that why you torture little children to death?

'Unlike you, Till Berkhoff. All it takes is a little shove and you fall to pieces, isn't that right?'

With these words Tramnitz thrust his fist into Till's brow and Till's head exploded.

47

When he regained consciousness, he almost wished Tramnitz could deal another blow to his head, preferably with a sledgehammer, so hard that he'd never wake up again. That he'd never have to feel this pain again.

There was nothing to compare to this degree of agony apart from perhaps the notion that his entire brain was one giant incisor that a crazy dentist had tried to pull out with pliers without any anaesthetic, but it had snapped mid-extraction and now the nerve endings were exposed and being washed with acidic thoughts.

Where is Max?

What did the bastard do to him?

Tramnitz hadn't gone; on the contrary, his presence, like Till's pain, seemed to have intensified. This was partly down to the fact that he'd made use of Till's blackout to clean the blood from his face and hands in the bathroom. He now looked refreshed and somehow taller, stronger. Standing beside the bed where Till was lying again, he bent over, moving ever closer until their mouths were almost touching.

'Okay, shorty, you've convinced me,' he hissed. 'I'll let you live.'

'Why?' Till said, uttering his very first thought.

To torture me as well, he thought, answering his own question.

That was logical. *He's revelling in my grief.*

'Because you've piqued my curiosity.'

Then the psychopath actually kissed Till on the forehead. For a brief moment, the revulsion succeeded in surpassing Till's headache.

Curiosity about what? How much suffering a single person can take?

Tramnitz got up again and took a step backwards, his arms crossed behind his back and a frown on his face.

'We need to hurry. I've been in here far too long already. The doctor will be doing his bloody round in five minutes and I must be back in my room by then. For the time being, let's say that just for once you haven't been lying and that you really are Till Berkhoff, Max's father. The lovely little rascal who plays the lead role in my last diary.'

Till felt severe cramps in his stomach.

'If so, then you've come a long way. You've really taken on a lot to get to me. But the key question, the question whose answer makes the difference is: Will you see it through to the end?'

'I–I...' Till began stammering again and hated himself for it. 'I don't understand.'

Could anybody? Was it ever possible to comprehend the thought processes of a sick murderer?

Definitely not with a jackhammer inside your head.

'I had a – let's call it a "conversation" – with a certain Dr Frieder.'

Till had to think about this. 'The surgeon?'

'The alcoholic, yes. He asked me for a favour. He wanted me to confess my sins. Not against him.'

'Who then?'

'He asked me to tell the parents what I did with their missing children. And, let me put it this way… He had more convincing arguments than you to make me comply with his request.'

Tramnitz touched the bandage covering the operation wound on his neck and Till asked, 'Are you going to tell me what happened to Max?' *What you did to him? Where I can find his body?* 'Voluntarily?'

'Even better,' Tramnitz said, grinning again. 'Let's play a little game. I'm going to assume you really are Till Berkhoff, Max's dad. And in return I want you to ask yourself this. How far would you go? What would you do if here and now I tell you that there's just a tiny, weeny chance?'

'Of what?' Till whispered.

'Well, what do you think? That your son's still alive!'

48

Till opened his mouth – a pointless gesture, because now he was incapable of making any sound, apart from a whimper, perhaps.

Alive?

This word was no longer part of his vocabulary. Not in relation to his son or even to himself.

He fought against it, tried to stop the poisoned arrow of hope from penetrating too far into his consciousness, but the barbs had already got caught.

He's lying.

Of course he is. He wants to torture you.

'How is that possible? It's been a year since Max...'

'Went missing? Hey, I said it was improbable that he's still alive. I don't know; I've been locked up for a while. But there is a microscopically small chance that he's still breathing.'

Tramnitz, who had gone over to the window and from this top floor had a view of the world beyond the hospital perimeter, asked again, 'So, how far would you go to find out whether I'm telling the truth? But wait, before you say anything, Till Berkhoff, father of Max, let me give you a word of advice. Don't lie to me!'

He turned back to Till. All friendliness had vanished from that handsome face. 'If I realise that you've been messing with me again – and, believe you me, I'm good at reading other people – then our conversation here is over. I'll raise the alarm and show the doctors what you did to my face and fingernail for no reason whatsoever.'

Till swallowed heavily.

'You can imagine what would happen then.'

They'd separate us.

'Any chance of you ever getting even within farting distance of me again would be blown.'

For ever.

Till wasn't sure if that would signify redemption or his definitive end.

Was there any point in having this conversation?

Wasn't Skania right when he said that from the very beginning this ill-conceived plan was nothing short of a suicide mission?

'So, what would you do to find out what really happened to your son?' Tramnitz asked.

How far would you go?

'Anything,' Till said without hesitation. 'I'd give my own life.'

'Oh, that won't be necessary. There's a much simpler way to get to the truth.'

'What guarantee do I have that you're not lying?'

'None whatsoever. I mean, I don't know that you're telling the truth either, Till Berkhoff, father of Max.'

'Okay, fine. What is the way? What do I have to do for you to tell me what happened to my son?'

'No, no, I'm not going to *tell* you anything. I'll *show* you.'

'What do you mean?'

'I'll take you directly to your son. Or to what's left of him.'

Till's blood coursed through his veins at high pressure.

'What do I have to do?'

'What do you think?' Tramnitz said, putting on a diabolical grin. 'Get me out of here!'

49

RICARDA

'How did you know?'

'What?'

'That I was planning to sell the details of my visit to you to the press?'

Ricarda had waited for Gedeon in her car outside the burger restaurant until the purportedly clairvoyant fast food worker's shift was over.

When he stepped out into the rain from the staff entrance, she almost failed to recognise him as he'd pulled his baseball cap far down over his head. On his way to the street, Gedeon had to pass the illuminated drive-in menu, where hungry drivers stopped to choose between chips, chicken wings, burgers and other cardiac killers. Ricarda had intercepted him here.

'I could tell you something about my inexplicable talent, but the truth is rather more mundane.'

Gedeon, who was still wearing his staff uniform beneath his raincoat, smiled bashfully.

He didn't seem in the least surprised to see her again here in the pouring rain. He pointed to the parking spaces to his right.

'On the day we met, a van with a Cologne number plate was parked over there. On the windscreen were stickers giving him access to the RTL and WDR studios. So the vehicle had to belong to a production company.'

Ricarda stroked a damp strand of hair from her brow. The rain pounded her umbrella.

'It's not what you think. I'm not a publicity seeker.'

'You don't know what I think,' Gedeon objected. 'Unlike me. I can read you like an open book.'

'Oh, really?' Ricarda said, following him and taking care not to step in one of the many puddles.

'Any empathetic person with basic psychology training can do it.'

'What do you read when you look at me, then?'

Gedeon glanced over his shoulder. 'You're not just emotionally finished, but financially too, Frau Berkhoff. You've spent a fortune looking for Max. Private detectives, classified ads on the internet. And now you're on your own because your husband has gone.'

All that was in the papers, Ricarda thought, but she contradicted him. 'My husband hasn't... gone.'

'No? So where is he at the moment?' Gedeon asked, sounding curious but without any hint of mockery.

'I...' She faltered, then became evasive. 'I needed my space. I don't know where he is at the moment.'

Gedeon looked at her as the rain drenched his trousers. They were the only people here in the driveway to the fast food chain.

'And your daughter's being looked after by a girlfriend?'

'It's a man,' Ricarda replied truthfully. 'But it's not what you think either.' They'd reached the exit. 'I don't have a new partner, he's really just a good friend.'

'You're missing two people in your life, then,' Gedeon stated without picking up on her comment. 'Your husband and your son. But you want only one of them back, don't you?'

'What are you getting at?'

'You absolutely have to find your boy or the insurance won't pay out.'

It took a while for Ricarda to grasp just how outrageous this insinuation was. By then Gedeon was already a few steps ahead of her again and she had to hurry to catch him up.

'What makes you think that?'

'You took out a life insurance policy. But it won't pay out unless the body is found.'

Ricarda laughed. It was supposed to be scornful and to confirm the absurdity of this suggestion, but it just sounded hysterical. 'No, you're wrong. There is no insurance. I need money to keep looking. To pay you, for example.'

He flapped his hand dismissively. 'I'm not going to take any money from you. I can't help you.'

Gedeon stood beneath the roof of a deserted bus shelter on Clayallee and removed his baseball cap. Once again Ricarda was struck by how incongruously youthful the man looked for someone who claimed to have seen more of the world than most other people.

'Is it that you can't help me or you won't help me?' she asked, closing her umbrella.

Under the roof the rain now sounded like a barrage of pebbles.

Gedeon, who was studying the timetable, replied without turning around. 'All the things I feel don't quite add up. You, the money, your husband. Now, what you say may be right, Frau Berkhoff. But I can't check. Because something's not right.'

'What?'

He glanced at his watch, then replied, 'It's not just about you, your husband or your son. There's another person involved.'

All of a sudden Ricarda found it difficult to breathe. As if the rain had sucked all the oxygen from the air, and now she needed to inhale deeply twice to fill her lungs.

'Do you mean the kidnapper?' she asked.

He shrugged. 'Possibly. When you brought me that photo of Max last time, I saw a sick person near him.'

'Do you mean the sick monster who has him under his control?'

'I can't say. But I had the feeling that very soon this person will lead you to Max.'

Turning to the side, Gedeon looked up the street to check if the next bus was coming, and indeed in the far distance two beams of light were shining through the mizzle.

Ricarda grabbed his shoulder. 'Is Max still alive?'

He shook his head. 'I don't know. It was too brief.'

She pointed vaguely in the direction of her car and thus the handbag she'd left in it.

'I've got the photo with me today again. And other objects Max played with. Lego bricks and—'

Gedeon managed to put his baseball cap back on and shake his head at the same time. 'Not tonight. I'm not in the mood. Please, I've had a really tiring shift.'

The bus now came audibly closer; a menacing, droning diesel colossus, preparing to abduct her conversation partner.

'And last time?' Ricarda hastened to ask. 'Did you see anything else?'

'More like smelled rather than saw.'

'What?'

'Blood. A shot. I can't describe it any other way, but when I saw the photo it felt to me like a bullet going through someone's head.'

'Whose head?'

He smelled *a shot?*

The bus braked. Water sprayed over the kerb, but it didn't bother either Ricarda or Gedeon.

'I don't know. Only...' He looked her straight in the eye. 'You will see your son again.'

Her heart missed a beat.

'Is he still alive?' she asked, now for the third time.

'It's hard to say. With all the dead people. Something is still alive down there. In the basement. But not everyone. I really don't know if your son is among them.'

The bus opened its hydraulic doors and leaned slightly towards the pavement to make it easier to board. Gedeon moved away from Ricarda.

'And when I've found Max?' she asked him, trying in vain to hold him back by his hand. 'What then?'

He ran his hand nervously through his hair. 'Then I can see you quite clearly in my mind. You're crying. Behind a locked door.'

'Where? Why is the door locked? Where am I?'

She fired off these questions as he was getting on. Slowly Gedeon turned one final time towards her. His words were almost completely swallowed by the rain, but they managed to reach Ricarda's fear centre inside her brain.

'In a prison,' he said.

The doors closed again and the bus pulled away, while the ominous prophecy definitively robbed Ricarda of her breath as she remained there at the bus stop.

50

TILL

'W–What do I have to do?'

'You heard me,' Tramnitz said. 'Our deal is quite simple. If you get me out of here I'll take you to Max. And the quicker you do it, the greater the likelihood is that your boy is still warm.'

The killer's words triggered a tremor.

All of a sudden Till felt as if the entire room were swaying and he thought about grabbing on to the metal bedframe to prevent himself from falling over, even though he knew, of course, that these motor phenomena were merely in his imagination. But his conversation with the psychopath was similarly surreal.

Was he really in the process of striking a deal with a murderer?

Whenever he brought his first meeting with Tramnitz to mind, his thoughts had the consistency of a fever dream. Unconnected images, overlaid with uncontrollably strong emotions. But even if he'd been able to prepare level-headedly and analytically for the encounter, Till could never have even begun to predict *this* development.

'That's absurd,' he gasped.

'Why?'

'Because, because…' There were so many reasons why that Till didn't know where to start. Eventually he began with something that must be apparent even to a psychopath. 'We are prisoners on a high-security wing. How am I going to arrange for us to get out?'

Tramnitz pushed forwards his lower lip and shrugged. 'You smuggled yourself in here. But not on your own. The people who helped you clearly have contacts. Convince them to use these contacts for me and I'll take you to Max.'

Till heard every single word.

Smuggled. Not on your own. Helped. Contacts.

He understood their meaning. The words were like drawing pins fixing an imaginary note to the noticeboard of his mind. And on this board was the only part of Tramnitz's proposition that ultimately remained in his consciousness. The only part that counted. '… *and I'll take you to Max.*'

That was why he was here. That was why he'd been prepared to undergo everything here. The injections, the beatings, the pain, the fear. Why now should he listen to the voice of reason when up to now he'd only followed the voice of despair?'

'Okay,' he said in a strangely flat voice.

He felt as if the voice didn't belong to his body at all.

Even worse than that, he felt as if his mind was separated from his body and he was watching himself make a deal with a child killer in the most futile of all hopes that he might once again hold his child in his arms.

'I'll try,' he whispered, moving over to the bedside table. His hands shaking, he picked up *Ulysses* and opened the weighty tome in the middle.

SEBASTIAN FITZEK

He felt cold and the temperature inside the room seemed to drop again when he turned to Tramnitz.

'Where is it?'

'Where's *what?*'

'My mobile?'

'Your mobile?' Tramnitz sounded surprised.

'Yes, you must have found it in the book.' Till tapped the hollowed-out tome that he'd shut again.

At first he thought he saw a dark cloud of incomprehension gather before Tramnitz's eyes, but then he heard him laugh.

The killer went over to the television set that hung on the wall, stood on tiptoe to reach the top and pulled out an object that must have got stuck between the screen and the wall.

'Do you mean this thing?'

What else?

With relief Till clutched the mobile in his fingers, which Tramnitz had given back to him. The plastic casing felt different, bulkier and rougher, as if the telephone had changed since he'd used it.

'Did you hide it?'

'I thought you wouldn't want anyone to find it in your possession.'

'Why didn't you keep it?'

'Because, unlike you, I don't know who I could call to get us out of here.'

'Me neither,' Till said.

'Hmm, that's not so good.' Coming back over to him, Tramnitz gently laid his hand on Till's shoulder and squeezed it, while asking him softly but emphatically, 'Do you really want to live with the certainty that your son died only because you weren't persuasive enough?'

Tramnitz took his hand away, but it felt as if his fingers had branded Till's skin through his nightshirt.

'Make your call! Use your chance!'

What chance? How the hell am I supposed to arrange this?

Till's fingers were sweating so profusely he thought he could feel the mobile melting in his hands.

'I'm off,' Tramnitz said. 'I've been here too long as it is.'

Till waited until the psychopath had left his room then, in desperation, he took the decision to press speed dial button number one.

Skania.

51

It rang.

Six times, seven times – and this was his third attempt.

Till had let it ring at least thirty times before the line had just gone dead.

What the hell...

'Skania, where are you?'

And why have you switched your voicemail off?

Till intended to be straight with him. He would tell Skania that a diary did exist and that Tramnitz was bragging about the hiding place where they might even find Max alive rather than a corpse. And that the only chance of discovering the truth was to arrange for the killer to escape from the hospital, but under secret surveillance.

If Skania had managed to smuggle him in here then he must be in a position to organise surveillance. The escape would in fact be an undercover investigation.

Till knew, of course, how his brother-in-law would react when he finally got hold of him. And how unlikely it was that he'd get very far outlining his plan.

Are you now completely off your trolley?

The fact alone that his brother-in-law would have to make

an official admission about smuggling Till into the Steinklinik as a sham patient made the implementation of this plan 'impossible'. The only answer he'd get would be: *'I'm getting you out of there now. You've lost your marbles for good.'* Especially as the twenty-four hour deadline that Skania had allowed him had long since expired and he had no idea what his brother-in-law was organising behind the scenes.

Right at the moment, however, Till didn't even have the opportunity to be screamed at and rebuffed. Skania simply wasn't answering his phone.

He tried the second stored number, and now things got even stranger.

That's impossible.

'The number has not been recognised. Please call directory enquiries.'

That couldn't be right.

He knew Ricarda's number off by heart. He dialled it manually, with the same result.

Number not recognised?

His wife had had this simple mobile number, a variation on her date of birth, for more than twenty years. Ever since her first phone contract she'd kept it through every change of provider. There was no way she'd voluntarily relinquish it.

And yet.

'The number has not been recognised.'

Till stared at the Nokia in disbelief and once again he thought it felt different. Now it dawned on him that...

Of course. Tramnitz must have interfered with it!

He didn't know how, but that was the only logical explanation.

The guy's trying to confuse you, unsettle you; he wants

to see you suffer. He's fuelling unrealistic hopes and, in your desperate attempt to learn the truth, you're falling into the psycho trap he's set.

Till was about to try the third and last stored number, now without any hope that he would reach his lawyer, when he heard a voice that represented a threat in every sense.

It was far too close.

It wasn't coming from the phone.

And it belonged to Professor Sänger, who'd entered his room and caught him red-handed with the phone. 'What are you doing there?' she asked suspiciously.

52

'So, your real name is Till Berkhoff?'

The two of them were sitting at a round table in the nurses' room in the infirmary; Frau Sänger had asked the staff to let her be on her own with the patient.

The director had brought Till here after it had almost come to a scuffle in his room.

Till had refused point blank to hand over the mobile, even when threatened with restraint, and Sänger had wanted to avoid having the patient immobilised by force, presumably on account of the terrible physical state he was in.

Eventually they'd come to an agreement whereby Till would hand over the mobile if Sänger took him somewhere with a landline and allowed him to make a call.

This was the only reason why he'd followed her placidly, albeit in agony, to the nurses' room on the ward, which looked a little less sterile than a treatment room or patient's bedroom. In Sänger's eyes this was probably the appropriate place for a conversation in confidence. Till, however, was not in the mood for mutual confidence-building and he also rejected the cup of coffee and piece of cake the director offered him. All he wanted was the telephone in its charging cradle on the desk right in front of him. But before Sänger would let Till have it, she understandably wanted him to answer a few questions.

'Yes. I'm not Patrick Winter. That's just a cover. In truth I'm not an actuary either, but a fireman.'

If the director was surprised by this, she didn't let it show. She was probably hiding her astonishment behind her professional psychiatrist's mask that she'd trained herself to wear for tricky patient conversations.

'Why did you assume another name?'

He avoided her gaze, looking instead at the decor of the room. The nurses had made some effort to jolly up the sober hospital atmosphere with a veritable garden of lush houseplants. On the sill by the large window stood so many palms and cactuses that you could barely see the bars behind.

'Not just another name,' Till said eventually. 'I assumed Patrick Winter's identity lock, stock and barrel.'

'Why?'

'Please, I'll tell you everything just as soon as I've spoken to my wife.'

Although he'd tried to get hold of Skania first, now he realised that was the wrong order.

Ricarda must be the first to know what he'd found out here. And that there was still a chance. If he managed to transmit the flicker of hope to her, his wife would fight like a lion beside him to discover the truth. In any case, as Max's mother she ought to be the first to find out any information about him, and to hear it from Till's mouth.

Sänger suppressed a sigh. 'If you're not Patrick Winter, then we don't have a record of your wife's contact details.'

'I know the number off by heart. Please. Try it!'

Till reeled off the digits.

To his amazement, Sänger actually did it. She took the phone from its cradle and dialled the number. Till heard it ring four times, then his heart missed a beat when the connection was made.

I knew it. Tramnitz fiddled with the mobile.

Ricarda was reachable via the hospital's landline.

'Hello? It's Professor Sänger here from the Steinklinik. Hello. I've got your husband here with me. He wants to talk to you. Yes, yes, I know. I'm sorry.'

Why was she sorry?

While he was still pondering the director's apology, she passed him the phone.

Till cleared his throat. There was a bitter taste in his mouth when he swallowed.

'Hello?'

Silence.

He closed his eyes and blocked out Sänger, the nurses' room and the entire hospital. Till focused on the most important telephone conversation of his life.

'Hello, darling, it's me.'

'I know.'

Ricarda sounded anxious, which was understandable seeing as she'd just been put through to her husband by the director of a psychiatric hospital.

'Don't worry, it's all fine, I'm alright.'

Silence again. Ricarda seemed to have lost her voice, and that was understandable too.

'I–I don't know where to begin. I know that what I'm going to tell you now sounds crazy. I can scarcely believe it myself. To be honest, I just *want* to believe it.'

'I don't understand—'

'I know, me neither,' he interrupted his wife's husky-sounding voice. 'I've no idea how to put this gently, so I'll just say it as it is. I've done it. I've made contact with Tramnitz.'

'Tramnitz? The murderer?'

'Yes, exactly. Like I promised. And he says...' Till screwed up his eyelids more tightly, but couldn't prevent individual tears from finding a way out and streaming down his cheeks. 'He says our son might still be alive.'

Ricarda groaned. 'Please...'

'I know what you think. It's unlikely... but.'

'Why?'

Just one word, but it was enough to unsettle Till. He opened his eyes again and blinked.

It wasn't what she had said, but how.

Why?

So coldly, so aggressively. Almost vitriolically.

'I'm sorry?'

'Why are you doing this?' she asked as coldly as before.

He began to stutter. 'I–I want certainty, darling. We spoke about this. You wanted it too.'

You even wanted me to make him suffer.

Another groan, this time less anguished. More annoyed. Livid.

'Listen to me. I've already told Professor Sänger that I'm not going to put up with this any more. Stop it!'

'Stop?'

'Yes. Leave me in peace. Leave *us* in peace. And never, ever call me again, Patrick.'

Then the worst thing happened. She hung up. There was a brief click, which for Till was equivalent to the sound of a cell door slamming shut. Ricarda had put the phone down on him for a reason as incomprehensible as why she'd called him 'Patrick'.

Why did she call me by my cover name?

'Is there something you want to tell me?'

Till looked up. For a moment it had slipped his mind that he was not alone and that the woman, who he saw through the veil of tears before his eyes as if through a soft-focus lens, was demanding proof of his assertions. Proof he couldn't supply her with.

'I am Till Berkhoff,' he said truculently like a little child who answers a 'why' question with 'because'.

'Your wife disputes that,' Sänger stated soberly. 'She says your name is Patrick Winter.'

'And never, ever call me again, Patrick.'

'That's my cover name. Look, I don't know what's going on here. But I'm perfectly sane. I only got myself admitted here under pretence.'

'Why would you do that?'

'Because I wanted to get closer to my son's killer.'

'What's your son's name?'

'What kind of a stupid question is that? Don't you read the papers? Max. Don't you read the papers? Max was kidnapped a year ago.'

'Max Berkhoff?'

'Exactly. Why do you say that as if I'm talking about flying saucers? You know full well why Guido Tramnitz is imprisoned here.'

'Being treated here,' she corrected him, as if that made any difference. Locked up was locked up, and there was no cure for child killers.

'He didn't just kill two children, whose murders he

confessed to. He also kidnapped, tortured and murdered my son.' *Did he?* 'But he's keeping silent about Max.'

'And you want certainty?'

'Yes, of course. Which father wouldn't?'

And never, ever call me again, Patrick.

'So you had yourself smuggled in here under false pretences?'

'Yes, the idea came about when I heard that Tramnitz was keeping a diary. And do you know what? He is. I can prove that Max is his victim.'

'With the help of the diary?'

'Exactly. You have to search his room. There's a secret compartment in the bedside table.'

Or there was. I destroyed it.

'A secret compartment?'

There it was again, the tone of voice that made Sänger's question sound as if she were talking either to a little child or someone suffering from delusions.

Oh, God, I really am sounding like a madman.

'Okay, I know you don't believe me. I can understand that. I wouldn't either. But my brother-in-law will back me up. He's a policeman. He got me Patrick Winter's identity and smuggled me in here.'

Sänger took a deep breath like someone trying to calm themselves down. 'What's his name?'

'Oliver Skania.'

'Do you know his number off by heart too?'

Till had to say no.

'But he works in section 44. Call him at the station in Tempelhof – you'll easily find the number online. Ask for Oliver Skania.'

Sänger shook her head, but said, 'You'd better do it yourself.' She passed him the telephone for the second and last time, switching it first to speakerphone.

53

'Hello. This is Till Berkhoff here. I'd like to speak to Oliver Skania, please.'

'What is this about?'

'It's a private call. Inspector Skania is my brother-in-law.'

'Please hold on.'

The sober female voice on the line was replaced by a loop of classical music until an impatient-sounding older man came on and got straight to the point without introducing himself.

'Hello? Did you say you wanted to speak to Inspector Skania?'

'Yes.'

'He doesn't work here any more.'

Oh.

Shit. Did they find out that he helped me?

It was only when the man responded with a question that Till realised he must have voiced his concern out loud.

'How did Skania help you?

'That doesn't matter,' Till said, angry that he'd opened his big mouth.

It was perfectly understandable that the officer should

sound suspicious and ask further questions such as: 'What was your name again?'

'Patrick... er, Till Berkhoff. Listen, I urgently need to speak to my brother-in-law. Did he leave a phone number?'

'Oliver's your brother-in-law?'

'Yes.'

'And you don't know?'

The officer sounded even more suspicious. In the background other telephones were ringing. Voices. Keyboards. The bustling tapestry of sound of an open-plan office.

'*What* don't I know?'

'Pass me to the doctor,' the officer demanded.

'What?'

'During our conversation I've checked the number you're calling from and it appears you're in a psychiatric hospital. Is there a doctor nearby?'

Till looked at Sänger, who took the phone from him, switched off the speaker function and introduced herself to the policeman as the director of the Steinklinik.

'I'm sorry if we've disturbed you. This conversation was necessary for therapeutic reasons. I'll call you back later and give a more detailed explanation.'

Necessary?

For therapeutic reasons?

Till looked around the nurses' room. His gaze wandered across the staff's personal items – a bulbous coffee mug, the postcards on the fridge, the shoes beneath the radiator – and alighted on the plants in front of the barred window. All of a sudden he felt very scared.

Scared about being locked up in here for ever. And never finding the truth out about Max.

He looked at Sänger again, who was rubbing her neck while still on the phone.

Oh, God, she doesn't believe me. She thinks I really am Patrick Winter.

'Okay, I understand. It won't happen again.'

Sänger hung up and got to her feet.

'Wait a moment, you have to listen to me,' Till said, getting up too.

'Of course, and I will. Tomorrow we have a long session if your condition allows.'

'No. Not tomorrow,' he said, banging his fist on the table. 'Now! You don't understand. This, this is a...'

'A conspiracy?' Sänger said, taking the words out of his mouth, which made him sound even less credible.

'I don't know what's going on here. We need to get in touch with my brother-in-law – he can explain everything.'

'I don't think so, actually, after what the policeman just told me.'

Till looked at the bars again, then at the doctor.

'What did he say?'

'Do you really want to know?'

'Of course.'

'Oliver Skania is dead.'

At a stroke his throat turned dry, as if he'd swallowed a heater.

'Dead?' he croaked.

'Yes. He was found dead in his apartment after he'd failed to turn up to work. It seems as if he took his own life.'

54

They hadn't sedated him. There was no need for an injection, straitjacket or even an orderly to get him back to his room. Till remained calm. On the outside. Internally he wanted to tear the nurses' room apart. Wrench the fridge from its fixings and upend it, hurl the noticeboard with the stupid holiday postcards at the wall opposite. He wanted to pick up one of the plants, preferably the cactus with the long spines, drag it right across that face of Sänger's showing fake concern, then run screaming into the corridor, where Simon or one of the other orderlies would no doubt be waiting for him. And it wasn't self-control, reason or an awareness of how pointless such behaviour would be that held him back, but exhaustion pure and simple. He felt sick and his head was droning like that of someone dying of thirst. His eyes streamed with tears and each step back to his room, helped by Professor Sänger, felt like an interminable burden.

Even his thoughts flowed like thick slime and basically revolved around a single question:

What is happening here?

Ricarda was disowning him. *Skania was... dead?*

None of it made any sense. He'd been on the phone to him

only yesterday. Besides, he wasn't the type of guy to take his own life.

On the other hand, was there a particular type who did that?

Doesn't everybody have a point at which they crack? Forget themselves, injure themselves, damage themselves?

Get themselves committed.

The only thing there could be no doubt about was his situation. He'd manoeuvred himself into a prison from which there was no escape. And where the more doggedly he insisted on the truth, the crazier he appeared to the staff.

The result was unequivocal. Till was in a hopeless situation. He just couldn't understand *why*.

What was the plan behind this conspiracy? Who could have an interest in breaking the bridges behind him to ensure he was locked up for ever?

In his search for answers, one question kept surfacing that almost drove him mad. Was Tramnitz telling the truth? Was Max really still alive somewhere out there, crying, breathing, suffering?

And who knew, apart from Tramnitz?

Those people who were disowning and ignoring him, and abandoning him in this self-imposed hell?

After he'd been helped back into bed by Sänger, Till voluntarily took a painkiller and sleeping pill and fell into a dreamless black hole, from which he woke with a start on several occasions. So often that he felt as if he hadn't slept for an hour at a single stretch, although it was already past lunchtime the following day when the overhead light switched on and two figures entered his room.

'Seda?' Till said with a dry throat. The first thing he'd seen was the library trolley. His eyes were sticky with sleep, as if he had severe conjunctivitis. This was also the reason why he hadn't noticed the second person, who now responded, next to Seda as she closed the bedroom door.

'We don't have much time.'

Till sat up and found his suspicion confirmed. It was Simon who'd come in with Seda.

'What do you want?' he asked in a voice that sounded alien even to him. Perhaps the after-effect of the sleeping pill was the reason why his tongue felt as if it had swollen to twice its size. But perhaps he just urgently needed something to drink.

As if Simon had read his thoughts, he said, 'I've brought you some water,' and lifted up a five-litre canister.

A bottle would have sufficed, Till thought.

Then he saw Simon glance nervously at his watch, and finally the situation became utterly surreal when Seda whispered, 'I need your help.'

I'm dreaming. I'm not awake.

But Till wasn't certain of this because his senses were unusually sharp, something he'd never experienced in dreams. He heard the grinding of the wheels when Seda pushed her library trolley closer to his bed. Smelled her subtle floral perfume. Saw the red blood vessels in the whites of her dark, sad eyes.

'Help?'

If Till hadn't been worried that his headache, currently simmering on a low flame, might boil over again, he would have burst out laughing. The situation could hardly be more absurd. Here he lay, locked up and injured, incapable of extricating himself from his predicament, and this delicate woman with her pale, almost brittle, porcelain-like face was asking *him* for help.

'Please,' Simon urged again. 'Time is running out. In a few hours they're going to begin the relocation and so—'

'Wait,' Till said, switching his gaze from Seda to Simon. 'What sort of relocation?'

The orderly pointed to the window that looked as if it were covered by a blind or curtains, although in fact it was the gloomy weather outside that made it impossible to see anything.

'Several water pipes have burst because of the flooding, restricting the supply to the infirmary.'

Hence the canister.

'We're still trying literally to keep our heads above water with our supplies. But you can't shower and the toilet cisterns need to be refilled by hand after flushing. We can't go on like this and so patients are being relocated to other hospitals.'

'Where am I going?' Till asked, while Seda took the now-useless James Joyce novel from his bedside table and put it back on the trolley.

'You?' Simon asked. 'Nowhere. Your condition isn't so critical that we can't keep looking after you on Ward III. Basically you just need a bed and painkillers. And a quick wash will have to do until the showers are working again.'

'What about Tramnitz?' Till closed his eyes briefly. He didn't want to hear the answer.

'Yes, he's being relocated.'

No, no. That can't happen. It mustn't *happen.*

'But why?' he protested. 'He's in great shape.' *Unlike me.* 'I even had a lengthy conversation with him.'

'That's precisely why I'm here, Patrick,' Seda said, and at the mention of his cover name his despair grew again.

'Don't call me that.'

She swept a jet-black strand of hair behind her ear and said, 'Okay, as you wish. But we can talk openly. I've finally scraped together all my courage and confided in Simon. I told him that you were in the room when I was with Tramnitz.'

'And?'

Seda swallowed. 'Would you testify to it?'

'What? That you're working here as a prostitute?'

'Yes, and not only that...' she said, lowering her eyes in shame. 'I'd hoped that you would confirm that I'm not doing it voluntarily.'

Seda suddenly looked completely forlorn, as if not only her clothes but the entire room around her had grown in size. Her mouse-grey jumper hung from her body like a cloak, and next to the muscular orderly she looked like a feeble doll for whom even speaking required a vast amount of strength.

Till felt as if he'd known her for much longer than the few days since his admission, during which they'd only exchanged a few words. Seized by profound sympathy, he said softly, 'I know what Kasov's doing to you.'

Seda nodded and Simon audibly did a sharp intake of breath. He clenched his jaws so tightly that his cheekbones stuck out prominently.

'You're completely sane, Seda. Kasov smuggled you in here to make you take part in a drugs test, which he gets handsomely paid for.'

He glanced at Simon, whose expression had frozen.

'I assume it creates a bit of money for this hospital too, which is why they let him get away with so much here. Yes?

They turn a blind eye when he threatens patients, locks them up with violent thugs or makes you sell your body.'

'Did Tramnitz tell you all that?' Simon asked.

'Yes. He's a key witness. You ought not to let him go. Not under any circumstances.'

'Our hands are tied. His lawyer is insisting on a relocation because of "unacceptable conditions" and she actually does have the law on her side. Especially as, for some reason, Tramnitz has sustained injuries to his head and fingers, which I don't suppose you'd be able to explain, would you?'

Till hadn't heard Simon's last words. He was far too caught up in his own thoughts.

For heaven's sake.

Not only was he locked up in here, now the only reason for what had become an involuntary stay was in danger of disappearing. And if Tramnitz ever came back, he would be housed in the high-security wing, and thus still inaccessible to Till.

Simon sighed. 'We were just with him. Seda confronted him directly with her accusations against Kasov. But, as was to be expected, Tramnitz wouldn't confirm any of these. He just laughed.'

Shit!

Till threw back the covers and wanted to get up, even if he wasn't sure what that would achieve. He did actually seem to feel a bit better.

He was nowhere near as exhausted and run-down as the previous evening, and the pain was tolerable, but there was no way he could prevent Tramnitz from being relocated.

'Please stay in bed,' Simon asked. 'And ration the water. You might have to use it to flush the loo. But don't worry, someone will be here very soon and take you back to the ward. Then, tomorrow morning perhaps, I'd ask you to repeat what you've just said to Professor Sänger. Did you hear me? Would you do that, Herr Winter?'

Till, who'd only heard these words as if in a trance, was about to protest again and shout, 'I'm not Patrick Winter,' when his eyes caught the library trolley beside his bed.

Seda had put the James Joyce back between two large illustrated books, one of which had slid forwards slightly, as if inadvertently.

Till blinked.

The book, roughly A4 size, was the only one with its pages facing him rather than the spine. And because of this he could see that another book was stuck between the covers of this atlas-like tome. A slim volume. Brown. With a black ribbon for fastening the diary shut.

Till glanced at Seda, saw the knowing, approving look in her eyes, and when she nodded he asked softly, 'May I borrow something for while I'm still here?'

55

TRAMNITZ

'What's going on?' A photograph of Kasov's face would have been perfect to accompany an article entitled 'Rabies in its early stages'. His eyes looked like they might burst from their sockets and he frothed at the mouth when he spoke. His voice was even rougher than usual. 'What the hell is all this shit?'

Tramnitz moved from his position by the window and sighed theatrically. 'Yes, the thing with the water supply is lousy, but I'm being relocated soon.'

He'd actually been expecting Frieder rather than Kasov; the former, as the doctor in charge, was responsible for transferring his patients as soon as all the formalities for the move had been completed and the transporters were ready.

'Stop taking the piss!' Kasov said, foaming with rage.

Tramnitz wouldn't have been surprised to see red smoke rising from the ears of this bird-face.

'You know I'm talking about Patrick Winter. You were supposed to take care of him. I even arranged for you to have time with him alone. But you used it to let him beat you up!'

Tramnitz touched his slightly swollen nose, which alongside

a black eye was what remained from Winter's foolish attack. Then he looked at his now-bandaged fingers. The plaster on his nail bed itched and somehow he liked this sensation.

'He does have a rather short temper. And he's definitely got a screw loose. That much is certain. Now he's claiming he's Till Berkhoff, Max's father.'

'I'm not interested. I'd rather know what you discussed with Simon.'

'Simon?'

'The black giant. I saw him coming into your room with Seda earlier. What did he want?'

Tramnitz pretended to have to think hard before the answer came to him. 'Simon brought me some water and Seda wanted to collect my books.'

'I said don't take the piss. What did the two of them want?'

'A statement.'

Kasov knitted his brow, which produced the ugly optical effect that his nose seemed to grow longer, making him look even more like a crow. 'What kind of statement?'

'You wouldn't be here if you couldn't guess that one. Seda has blown the whistle on you. And she's got a witness.'

'Who?'

'Who do you think? He hid in my room while I was having it off with the tart.'

The senior doctor instinctively held his throat and tried to cover up his unease by putting on a steady voice. 'That doesn't prove a thing.'

'That doesn't. But I'm afraid Winter listened in to our conversation.'

Tramnitz was delighted by his brainwave. Of course he wouldn't tell Kasov that he was the Judas who had revealed

SEBASTIAN FITZEK

all the doctor's intrigues to Winter. There was a much better opportunity to unnerve him.

'What conversation?'

Kasov had swallowed the bait and Tramnitz had to force himself not to grin. Oh, he loved toying with people's fears, especially when they were such arseholes like Kasov. *Although*. In truth he liked nice people's fears even more. They often ran far deeper.

'In the corridor. When you offered me free coke and whores if I eliminated Winter for you.'

'How, where... that can't be right.'

'I have no idea where he was standing. But the fact is, he heard. He told me himself. After that he slipped into my room and caught me in flagrante delicto with Seda.'

'Shit.' Kasov clenched his teeth.

'For you, yes. For me it's rather funny. Hey, what are you doing?'

The senior doctor had walked around Tramnitz's bed and abruptly hauled open the drawers. One after the other.

'Hey, what's up?'

'Where is it?' Kasov asked, tipping the contents of the bottom shelf onto the bed. But even in the secret compartment he didn't seem to find what he was looking for.

'Where is *what*?'

Kasov yanked off the duvet cover and shook it out, then he felt the pillows and finally set about the sheet.

'Have you completely lost it?' Tramnitz asked, but when the doctor undid the zip to the mattress protector, he knew what he was looking for. For that was precisely where he'd hidden the razor blade, within reach at the head of the bed.

'Do you think I'm going to let you out of here armed?'

Kasov said triumphantly, holding the silver blade between his thumb and index finger.

Shit.

'Besides, unlike you, I know how to use it.' He slipped the blade into the breast pocket of his doctor's coat and turned around.

What the hell did he mean by that?

Tramnitz didn't experience bad feelings, only confusing thoughts that gave rise to a slight, barely noticeable itchiness. Like now.

'What are you going to do?' Tramnitz said.

'What do you think? I'm going to see Winter.'

Shit. That interferes with my plans.

'Why?'

The itchiness became stronger.

Kasov held a key card to the door.

In preparation for evacuation, freedom of movement in the infirmary had been severely restricted and now the doors could only be opened manually from the outside. A digital key was needed from the inside.

As he left the room, Kasov didn't take his eyes off Tramnitz, not until he'd pulled the door securely shut behind him. As a parting shot he said, 'To do what you couldn't do.'

56

TILL

The handwriting matched its owner. Plain but not pedantic, with an energetic dash. The clear impression the biro had left on the cream paper suggested a dynamic, self-confident individual. And the writing was misleading, just like its creator.

If Till didn't know any better, he would have concluded that these flawless lines had been penned by a young, educated and intelligent man, a budding doctor, engineer or lawyer. A pillar of society. Not a sadistic serial killer with a predilection for torturing little children in homemade incubators.

I bet you didn't get anywhere or through to anyone, Till read in Tramnitz's diary. He'd skipped to the last few pages to begin with the latest entry. The one he hadn't yet read.

In the short time since yesterday Tramnitz had somehow managed to write down more filth and smuggle it into his room via Seda. So as not to be caught red-handed by Sänger again Till had locked himself in the bathroom and sat on the closed loo seat, the diary resting on his lap.

Your telephone calls have come to nothing. Your contacts have either abandoned you or they no longer exist. And now you're groping helplessly in the dark and asking, 'Why? What happened?'

Do you know what, Till, father of Max? I almost feel sorry for you. The answer to this question is so clear, so obvious, but I don't want to be the one to explain your life to you. Because once you understand, everything will get much worse. For you, I mean.

The truth you're looking for won't bring you any relief. It will be more like a cancer diagnosis without which you'd live just as long, but you'd be spared the agonising awareness of death creeping slowly around your body.

I'm not going to be the one to do it because I'm not going to benefit from your suffering. It would only be fun if I could watch you suffer, but now there are a number of high-security doors between us and perhaps several kilometres too, if they really do relocate me.

And I'm not a blabbermouth. I don't believe in passing on what I know to anyone and everyone. I'd rather you found the answers you're looking for yourself. For that – and this is my first piece of advice to you – you have to ask the right questions.

Not: Where is Max and what has happened to him?

But: Who might have an interest in keeping Max hidden?

At this point Till looked up for the first time and stared at the bathroom tiles, as if in the grey joins between them, he could find an explanation for why these lines were churning him up more than the ones in which the monster had described his encounter with Max.

Perhaps because they were... *honest?* He couldn't find another word to describe them, but he did get the impression that there was a degree of truth, albeit difficult to prove, in Tramnitz's words. Especially in the confession that now followed.

Everything in life is a question of motivation. I kill because only extreme stimuli can show me that I'm still alive. I love tears, not only in the eyes of the victims, but in those of their relatives too. That's why I confessed to these crimes. Because I wanted to sense the parents' pain when they glared at me, full of hatred, in the courtroom. Only those that were still alive, of course, because I'd already eliminated Laura's mother, Myriam. But I was pleasantly moved by the anguish and despair of the rest of them when the charges against me were read out in full. Fathers, mothers, siblings... every last one of them wanted to kill me and a furious, almost crazy pain flickered in their eyes when they realised that the insanity plea would be granted and I'd be locked away out of their grasp.

Well, you found your way to me, Till, father of Max. But could I anticipate us meeting here? Why should I have spared your pain and despair for such an unlikely meeting in the Steinklinik's infirmary?

Why wouldn't I confess?

Till shuddered. His body was covered in goose pimples, brought on by the question of all questions.

The one that Till hadn't really ever asked, even though it was so obvious.

Why hadn't Tramnitz confessed?

Everything in life is a question of motivation.

Till looked up again. Having spent the last few days crying, mostly in pain, but sometimes thinking about his son too, his eyes were now dried out – for the moment at least. Even blinking was painful. His lids moved across his shrivelled irises like graters.

Why wouldn't I confess?

Till stood up, splashed water on his face, rubbed it into his eyes and drank without feeling the slightest relief. He was still thirsty; his eyes continued to hurt, as if telling him he ought to stop reading the diary.

But of course Till had to read on, for he'd understood how Tramnitz had managed to shake him to the foundations with just a few words.

This monster knew how to stick fingers into his victim's wounds. In common with so many psychopaths, he could read the people he tortured like an open book. And possibly he understood the hopes, desires and fears of his opponents better than the psychotherapist they might end up being treated by.

I was so blind, Till thought, sitting back down. *So blinded.*

All the time he'd assumed that Tramnitz was the sole perpetrator. What had Skania said when he'd asked him how sure they were?

'*Our previous assumption was ninety-nine per cent. But in the last hour we've had one hundred per cent certainty.*'

Till hadn't for one second entertained the possibility of an accomplice.

And although he had a vague, totally absurd, preposterous, ridiculous and idiotic and yet perfectly logical idea of who the person might be, he dismissed all thoughts of the individual and continued reading, partly in the hope that his horrific suspicion might be refuted by the last few lines of the diary.

Why wouldn't I confess?
If you can't find a sensible answer to this question you're back at the starting point of my reflections.
Who is very keen that Max doesn't turn up again?

Ricarda.
The thought had been articulated and Till clapped his hand over his mouth as if he could somehow push it back or at least mitigate it.

She's disowning me. She's calling me by my cover name, which she can only have learned from Skania. Her brother, who is supposed to have committed suicide.

A bittersweet smell filled his nose: his own sweat, composed of fear, pain and despair. On top of it all now came this betrayal, even though Till couldn't imagine any cause or reason for such atrocity.

Sure, there were strains in our relationship. I mollycoddled Max too much. She wanted a second baby.

Even the newspapers had written about it. Combined with the knowledge about his irascibility, his short fuse, it made for an explosive story that the tabloid press exploited to the full: 'Which relationship could survive this?' a weekly magazine had asked on page three. Followed by: 'Was the relationship already over before Max's disappearance?'

The journalist had relished in feeding her scandal-hungry readership with the details: Ricarda wanted a second baby so that Max didn't remain an only child. The father was too fixated on his son and let him do whatever he wanted. And the two were very similar.

Too similar?

The diary slipped from Till's hands in which he now buried his face.

Did she hate Max because he reminded her of me?

The more intensely Till tried to think about his wife, the more faded the image of her became.

Yes, she wanted a second child. Yes, we had our arguments. But did she loathe me so much that she took Max away from me to drive me mad?

'No!' he croaked out loud, and this word resonated with a peculiarly muffled echo in the little bathroom with its excessively bright light that seemed to grow stronger by the second. Till was getting hotter, gradually feeling as if he were in a sauna someone had set at a temperature to boil his insides.

'This is madness!'

And it made no sense. Ricarda wasn't a criminal. And certainly not a mastermind whose criminal energy could have anticipated her husband's fake patient plan.

Or did Skania egg me on?

Till shook his head in answer to his own question.

No, his brother-in-law had vehemently advised him against it. Up until the very last moment.

Or had it been reverse psychology? A 'NO ADMITTANCE' sign that had given him the idea in the first place?

But how could Skania now be dead? He hadn't come across as depressive, rather the opposite. Someone with a suicidal mind wasn't in a position to smuggle an undercover patient into a psychiatric prison. *Or were they?*

Of course you could never see right inside someone else's head... but no, *Skania would never have abandoned me here!*

None of this added up; it didn't make any sense. In his wildest nightmare Till could just about imagine Ricarda as part of a conspiracy. But as his son's kidnapper?

Who later would eliminate a confidant, Skania? Her own brother? And manage to make it look like suicide? *No. Inconceivable.*

And pointless. Far too risky. No novice criminal would pull off such capital crimes.

Max, himself, Skania.

Too many victims. Too many chances to slip up.

It then struck Till that all he had to do was take a DNA test to prove he wasn't Patrick Winter. Sooner or later they'd believe his protestations. *Or maybe not?*

Another terrible thought got caught in the web of his hypotheses:

What if the conspiracy doesn't stop at the hospital gates?

What if there are other accomplices in here too?

This led him to wonder: *What if the conspiracy started in the Steinklinik in the first place?*

What if the person pulling the strings, who has influence over the admissions procedure, room allocation, treatment options and patient contact, is actually a member of staff?

Kasov!

This was of course the first name that came to mind. The doctor had threatened him from the outset. Psychologically and physically. He had openly admitted his hatred and made sure that Till survived his first night only by a whisker.

Till sat down again, exhausted by his speculation, which

was going round and round in circles and seemed to be leading nowhere. The diary shook in his hands as he picked it up again.

'You're becoming paranoid,' he diagnosed.

Then, partly to distract himself from his absurd ruminations, he read the final section that Tramnitz had written for him.

At this point I'm afraid I must say that I wasn't completely fair to you, Till, father of Max. Those are the right questions, indeed they are. But you'll never get the right answers just by thinking about them. That's mean, I know.

But, as you know, leopards can't change their spots.

I am, however, going to make it up to you. Our deal still stands. If you get me out of here I'll take you to the truth. And to Max's body. But without any guarantee that it's still warm.

So hurry. I'm due to be relocated at 7:30 this evening. I'll wait for you ten minutes earlier so we can discuss the details in peace.

57

Till took his eyes off the joins between the bathroom floor tiles and instinctively looked at his wrist, where of course there was no watch as this had been taken off him when he arrived. He had no idea what time it was.

Quite apart from the fact that he could no longer move around freely, it must be far too late now to heed Tramnitz's mad request. His eyes were drawn to the postscript.

> *P.S. Oh, yes, there's something else. A little detail just so you know how intimate my conversations with Max were and how much he trusted me in the end. The password is 'ice cube'.*

Before he could grasp the significance of these words, Till was startled by a noise at the door. It was soft, barely louder than a page being turned, and had he not been holding his breath at that moment he might have missed it.

The lock turned or, more accurately, the knob with which you could provisionally lock the bathroom door from the inside. From the outside, of course, it could be opened at any time with a screwdriver or coin.

The movement was slow; without any grinding or

squeaking, the well-oiled lock opened like the hand on a clock. The intruder wanted to avoid being detected too early. This presented Till with a tricky dilemma. Should he get up, thereby making more noise than the supposed assailant (for who else, apart from an assailant, would try to creep up on him so secretly?); or stay seated and wait for the door to open at least a crack, at the risk of giving his potential adversary too much of an advantage? In whatever they were planning.

Till opted for the most obvious course of action – although this hadn't occurred to him in the immediate aftermath of the shock, probably because the deliberations triggered by Tramnitz's diary had slowed his logical thought processes – he behaved normally.

He flushed the loo, whose cistern was still full, all the while keeping his gaze fixed on the lock. Then he moved closer to the door, which, as he only now realised from looking at the frame, must open outwards. Of course.

This fact made it impossible for Till to somehow block the door. But it did afford him a different opportunity – to press forwards. In the truest sense of the phrase.

The flush quietened. As suspected, the sudden silence was the signal to the assailant to hurry. The lock turned more quickly and in a flash the door was moving too. Soon it would be yanked open, but Till didn't wait. He threw himself forwards with all his might, pushing his entire weight against the aluminium-reinforced door, and hit the intruder at full whack.

Till heard a crunch, as if a piece of wood were splintering, followed by a stifled scream, then he lost his balance. Staggering through the open door, he stumbled over Kasov kneeling on the floor. As hoped, he'd hit the doctor on the head and must have broken his nose.

'What do you want from me?' Till bellowed at the doctor, giving him a kick in the stomach, which made him topple to the side.

'I'm going to kill you,' Kasov gasped, although at that moment it looked as if he could do nothing of the sort. Till was injured, his head and hand bandaged, and his mobility restricted by the strong painkillers in his blood. He was also barefoot and wearing a nightshirt. But he was currently standing over his adversary, ready to land another punch even if it meant breaking his fingers again.

'What do you want? I understand that you want to make money by enslaving women and falsifying drugs tests, but what do you want from *me*? What have I done to you?'

Although Till had no intention of spitting at the psychiatrist, he was frothing at the mouth with anger.

'What do *I* want?' Kasov panted. 'For fuck's sake, I want you to stop!'

'Stop what?'

'Don't pretend, you faker. I've warned you. How often do you plan to keep playing your game in here?'

Kasov made to get up, but Till gave him an unmistakeable sign that he should stay on the floor.

'What sort of game?' he asked him.

'Oh, you're really good. I bet I could hook you up to a lie detector and the needle wouldn't even twitch.'

'I don't understand what you're saying!'

'Just stop your bloody game!'

'*What game?*' Till shouted, even louder. He was fed up with the puzzles piling ever higher, threatening to smite him with full force if the tower of unsolved questions eventually collapsed on top of him. It was already wobbling.

'I see, okay, of course. For you it isn't a game, is it? So let me put my question differently. How many more times are you going to get yourself admitted here?'

Crash.

It was as if Till and Kasov had changed places. As if the doctor had rammed the door into *his* face. It was only a question, but the force of its impact felt just as devastating.

How often have I...

'What?'

From the corner of his eye Till could see Kasov's hand edging towards the breast pocket of his coat.

'I've been here before?' he asked in disbelief.

'More than once,' Kasov said. 'Several times.'

'But... that doesn't make any sense.'

'No, it doesn't. And that's why I've finally got to silence you, if nobody else will.'

Till registered a flash. Light reflected off the metal of a pen, or were they tweezers? Till only realised it was a razor blade that Kasov had pulled with unexpected speed from his breast pocket when the sharp edge almost sliced through his left eye, soon after the doctor had leaped up to him, like a grasshopper.

At the last moment Till wrenched his head back. He heard his cervical vertebrae crack, felt a sharp tugging in his skull, and lost his balance.

Fuck. Don't fall, don't fall over. On the floor you're an easy target.

But Till was no longer in control of his movements. And so it was pure chance rather than a result of his quick reflexes that as he fell he kicked up his right foot and rammed it between Kasov's legs.

The doctor stumbled to the ground along with Till, but didn't get up again. Kasov writhed, gasping, on the lino, saliva collecting at his mouth.

The hand that had gripped the razor blade was now clutching at his groin. The blade itself lay only a few centimetres from Till's big toe, and he had half a mind to use it to slit the throat of the guy who had just admitted openly that he wanted to kill him. But Till was not the man for this job, nor did he have the time.

It was more important, far more important, to finally get some answers. Although for the time being the issue of what Kasov meant about his having been here several times before wasn't pressing.

Nor was the question as to why his wife was betraying him and herself. Nor whether all of them were in fact being duplicitous.

Only one answer counted – the answer to the question that had brought him here in the first place:

Where is Max? What happened to him?

And now Till was sure that he was far more likely to find the answer to the riddle out there than locked up in here, where dangers were quite openly lurking that nobody with a sound mind could explain.

But maybe a sick mind?

Like Tramnitz's?

Till knew that the idea of seeking a way out of this hospital at the side of a murderer was crazy. But this whole undertaking had been crazy from the start and now the priority was to get out of here. Away from Kasov, from Armin, from cancer treatment he didn't need – to freedom.

To the truth?

The truth you're looking for won't bring you any relief.

So what? He had to get out of here. As quickly as possible.

For all these reasons he settled for aiming another blow at Kasov's already broken nose, thereby knocking him into unconsciousness.

Then, in a flash of inspiration, he stripped the doctor down to his underwear and put on his trousers, shirt and coat. Although the clothes were both too big and long, the orthopaedic shoes fitted perfectly.

Holding the razor blade that he'd picked up from the lino soaked with Kasov's blood, he went to the door.

He shook the handle and a shock shot through his body when he realised that the exit was locked. *The security regulations must have been changed!*

Till looked frantically for an input device, but couldn't find an electronic keypad on the doorframe or wall. *Thank God.*

He would never have guessed the right code before Kasov regained consciousness and would probably have set off an alarm after three wrong attempts.

Behind him the doctor groaned, but wasn't moving. Feeling the coat, Till found a mobile phone that he couldn't unlock without a PIN, but that wasn't necessary once he also found the plain white key card in the doctor's trouser pocket.

It looked like an electronic hotel key, the size of a business card, just slightly thicker and made from hard plastic.

What now?

Sweat ran down Till's brow from under the bandage.

Where do I put the card?

There was no keypad, no display, no slot.

Kasov groaned again, even gave a slight cough, and this drove Till to try everything he could. He started by the handle, then the lock and he heard a faint click.

The door opened, but then the alarm went off. Not very loudly, but it was irritating. A beeping like an alarm clock.

Or a...

mobile phone?

Till removed the source of the sound from the coat pocket and as soon as he pressed the display of Kasov's smartphone the beeping stopped.

Just an incoming call! Till almost managed a smile.

Then he noticed the current time on the screen, and his rare moment of relief gave way to the realisation that it was already too late.

19:43.

Tramnitz was being relocated. And with him the last straw Till had clutched at in the absurd hope that the killer offered not only a way out of here, but also certainty about his son's fate.

58

The corridors were empty; the evacuation of the infirmary was probably complete. As long as Kasov didn't wake up and raise the alarm, it would probably remain silent too. Right now the squeaking of Till's rubber soles on the floor was the only sound to be heard. The rain had even stopped drumming down on the skylights. The wind, however, continued to gust at irregular intervals, sending a bestial howling through the gaps in the lift shafts.

The way to Tramnitz's room seemed far shorter than on the last occasion. But this time his headache wasn't so fierce and he felt more relaxed, despite his melee with the senior doctor.

The one thing that pulled him down like a lead weight was the thought that all his efforts had been in vain.

When the corridor came to a T, he glanced briefly to the right, towards the lifts where he'd seen Tramnitz in conversation with Kasov. He then hurried left in the direction of the nurses' room. He remembered that it was the first door on the left. This time there was no book trolley outside. Seda was long gone too, with Simon.

Till felt lonely and abandoned, and he was struck by the

thought that he might have been forgotten and left all alone in this wing, from which he wouldn't find a way out, not even with the key card in his trouser pocket. Nobody would come to fetch him, and the only other soul here was that doctor who for inexplicable reasons was trying to kill him.

Till shook himself like a wet dog and this dark thought did lose some of its morbidity.

Taking a deep breath he opened the door to Tramnitz's room.

Seconds later he wanted to throw up with shame and self-loathing.

59

'Are you still here, Guido?'

There was so much that wasn't right about this question and the accompanying emotions churning inside Till. For a start, the use of his first name was wholly inappropriate, even though Till couldn't imagine calling his son's killer Herr Tramnitz. But neither could he have imagined being pleased to see him.

And yet Till was relieved that there must have been a delay and Tramnitz hadn't yet been taken away.

'You're a lucky devil,' grinned the psychopath, whose nose he couldn't have broken after all yesterday, or at least the swelling was only minor. Apart from the dressing on his neck and a slight pallor, Tramnitz looked fresh and chirpy. Even the black eye barely bothered him. He'd taken off his hospital garb and presumably was wearing the clothes he'd been admitted in: a tight, black shirt that emphasised his muscles, and blue designer jeans. On his feet he wore slip-on, calf-length leather boots which looked old-fashioned but couldn't have been used more than a couple of times. Putting on his rainproof neoprene jacket with its fur collar, Tramnitz looked as if he were getting ready for a catalogue fashion shoot rather than for a journey to a hospital where the security was tailored to mentally ill serial killers.

'You got my message, then?'

Tramnitz turned to the window, which was as dark as a submarine porthole deep in the ocean.

'There must have been problems with the water pump, but now the bridge is clear. We could be off any time now. My ambulance is already waiting.'

When he held out his hand with the bandaged index finger, Till's initial thought was that Tramnitz was saying goodbye, but then he realised he was after something else.

'My diary, please.'

'Of course.' Till reluctantly gave him the book that, needless to say, he had hidden on him.

'So you escaped from Kasov,' Tramnitz said soberly, seemingly uninterested in any further details. 'Not bad. But that fool isn't really a serious opponent, is he? Far too predictable, don't you think?'

Till watched blankly as Tramnitz slipped an envelope between a couple of pages at the front and then put the diary in the bedside table. His movements were serene, as if he had all the time in the world.

'What are you doing?' Till urged. 'Kasov will raise the alarm at any moment. And you're about to be collected.'

'And?' Tramnitz smiled.

'What do you mean, *and?* You wrote that I should come here so we could discuss the details.'

'Precisely. The details of a plan that I hope you've drawn up, Till, father of Max.'

'Me?' Till's knees turned to jelly and he was desperate to sit on the bed, which – no kidding – Tramnitz had neatly made.

'Wasn't that the deal when we last parted company? You were going to make a few phone calls, use your contacts and get us out of here.'

'You know that didn't work. You even wrote it in your diary.'

With a look of amusement on his face, Tramnitz tapped his forehead. 'Yes, of course. How stupid of me. Well, it looks as if you've come all this way for nothing. I mean, I don't have the slightest clue how I might get both of us together in an ambulance we can then leap out of while it's on the move.'

At that moment the door opened and a man came in. 'Something has cropped up. I have to...' he said, but left his words hanging in mid-air when he realised that Tramnitz wasn't alone in the room.

'What's going on here?' the man asked, and if Till wasn't mistaken a faint spark of recognition flickered in his eyes, just as in Till's. He'd been under general anaesthetic when the surgeon had operated, but he knew the face from the papers and television. Recently he'd seen the man with a fondness for pink polo shirts in reports about Tramnitz's emergency operation. And now he recalled the name too: Volker Frieder, a GP who also practised at the Steinklinik when required.

'What are you doing here?' Frieder asked, one hand on the door handle, the other taking a mobile from his trouser pocket. 'And why are you wearing Dr Kasov's coat?'

He pointed to the name badge which, in all the commotion, Till had not yet removed.

'Listen, I can explain everything,' Till hurried to say, without the slightest idea how.

Should he tell the truth?

My name is Till Berkhoff, I'm the father of the boy who this monster kidnapped and probably murdered, and I only had myself admitted here under false pretences. Not wanting to wander around in a nightshirt, I borrowed the coat after escaping from the doctor, who I beat up because he was trying to kill me.

Even someone with a fanciful imagination would have problems swallowing that. Especially from an inmate of a psychiatric unit. And even if they did, what good would it do?

His goal was to get out of here. Together with Tramnitz so he could be taken to Max. But how had the psychopath just put it so accurately?

'*... I don't have the slightest clue how I might get both of us together in an ambulance...*'

Till felt his nose running with tension, which was no surprise given the head injuries he'd sustained. Maybe it was bleeding? He looked for a tissue, but couldn't find one in Kasov's clothing.

'You leave your hands where I can see them,' Frieder said. 'I'm going to ask you one last time: What are you doing here?'

'Go on, tell him.' Tramnitz laughed. He was now standing beside the bed, watching the exchange between the other two with the flagrant curiosity of a motorway rubbernecker. 'And tell him who you really are,' he said.

I'm desperate, Till thought, his hand closing around the object he'd taken from the coat when looking for a tissue.

'I'm his hostage,' he said, throwing the razor blade at Tramnitz and standing in front of him before Frieder could make a move.

'Well, well, good plan,' he heard Tramnitz say with a smile. Taking advantage of the opportunity, the psychopath put Till in a police hold and positioned the razor blade beside his carotid artery.

60

Although Tramnitz twisted his arm back and upwards more roughly than necessary, as a willing hostage he had no intention of offering resistance. The sadist, however, seemed to take pleasure in keeping him under control. Till didn't want to move because he was worried that even that might dislocate his shoulder. And the razor blade was held so tightly to his skin as if Tramnitz really were going to slice his neck.

Will he?

'Okay, Frieder,' Till heard him say. 'I hope you've had a couple of stiff ones, because a little Dutch courage wouldn't be a bad idea for what we've got in mind.'

'What the hell are you talking about?' the doctor asked, with astonishing assertiveness seeing as he was facing an armed killer who had proven several times over that killing was – in the truest sense of the world – child's play for him. And even though the surgeon wasn't in mortal danger himself, from professional experience he must have known how dangerous slash wounds were – and could be for him too in a flash should Tramnitz decide to swap victims.

'Two orderlies with tasers and pepper spray are waiting in the lift. You won't get far, Tramnitz.'

Till wondered why the men hadn't come with Frieder into the room, but of course the surgeon couldn't have anticipated this turn of events and certainly not the prospect that his patient might be armed.

Tramnitz briefly took the blade away from Till's throat and pointed at Frieder's mobile. 'Call your guard dogs and tell them to disappear.'

'And if I don't, you'll kill him?' Frieder said, pointing at Till, now standing on tiptoes to ease the pain in his shoulder joints.

'Yup, I'll let him bleed to death. And whereas the soles of my boots have a rather good tread, you'll slide around in the red soup in your silly deck shoes. And before you can say "double gin and tonic, please", I'll open up your femoral artery.'

Tramnitz was speaking faster and more excitedly, the mental conveyor belt of his perverted fantasies clearly running at full speed. 'Yes, and then I'll play elastics with your innards while you watch. How does that sound?'

Frieder gulped. All self-assurance had vanished from his bloated, affluent face. Now he looked like a beaten dog who wanted only to crawl under a bench.

He pressed a single button on his mobile and said, 'Please let me use the lift on my own with Tramnitz.' A pause. Frieder rolled his eyes and raised his voice. 'Yes, I know it's against protocol, but' – he sighed – 'but we've got a hostage situation. No, not me. Not directly, at any rate. A fellow patient. Patrick Winter, I believe.'

Tramnitz shook his head and maybe he shot a severe glance at Frieder too – Till couldn't see – but in any case his body language sufficed to encourage the surgeon to impress the urgency of the situation on the person he was talking to.

'Tramnitz is armed. He'll kill the patient and me too if you don't go away.'

'Tell them we're coming out now,' Tramnitz bellowed. 'I don't want to see a single one of them. Not in the lift and not by the transporter down below. Otherwise there'll be a bloodbath they'll still be talking about in twenty years.'

Frieder did as he was told, while the psychopath shoved Till towards the exit. The doctor had now finished his phone call. Without being given any further orders he opened the door with his key card and stepped out into the corridor.

'Don't do anything silly,' Tramnitz whispered menacingly as he kept pushing Till forwards. In any case the 'hostage' had no choice but to leave the room with Tramnitz if he wanted to avoid breaking his elbow joint or shoulder blade.

Once in the corridor, he was turned by Tramnitz to face the lifts.

Empty.

The corridor was indeed deserted. No orderlies by the lifts. No armed reinforcements. Nobody to come to the hostage's aid.

'Chop-chop. We don't have all day.'

They got moving.

'This isn't going to work,' Frieder said as the lift door opened. It must have been already waiting at their floor.

'Oh, yes it will. We've got your eyes and your chip cards.' Tramnitz ordered Frieder to put his face in front of the camera beside the lift buttons so the iris scanner could authorise the access.

A peculiar feeling crept over Till, making him momentarily forget the pain in his twisted arm.

What am I missing?

'Where's the transporter?' Tramnitz said.

'That's exactly what I'm talking about,' the surgeon answered. 'The moment this lift door opens they'll overpower you. The ambulance is in the entranceway. To get to it we have to cross the mezzanine, which is hidden from view. Perfect for eliminating you from behind.'

Tramnitz smiled, which from the corner of his eye Till could see reflected in the lift's chrome walls, its doors now closed.

'That's why we're not going to use the transporter,' he said.

'What, then?'

'Where have you parked your Porsche, Frieder?'

61

PIA WOHLFEIL

Number withheld?

Pia didn't like taking calls from people who weren't in her address book. The risk was too great that it could be a pesky client seeking advice at an inopportune moment, having got hold of her mobile number somehow or other. Maybe from a solicitor who'd passed the number on without asking if that was okay.

But now she'd been waiting for over an hour in the Im Saatwinkel car park. It wasn't the first one over the bridge on the Spandau mainland; that would have been too obvious. But the car park wasn't far away, not even two minutes from the hospital access road, hence Pia was surprised it was taking so long.

'Hello?' she said, in the hope of hearing his voice finally.

Guido hadn't told her what he was planning, and secretly she wasn't unhappy to be ignorant of the full extent of his scheme. During their last phone conversation he hadn't been willing to say more than 'Be at the car park by the tent pitches at eight p.m.'. This was to avoid making her an accomplice. How sweet that was of him, if unnecessarily considerate. She loved him so much now that, given the choice between

293

having Tramnitz and being permitted to continue as a lawyer, she would opt for him every time. In any case, there was no realistic possibility of their being able to savour their relationship undisturbed and in freedom, assuming that her sweetheart somehow managed to escape from the institution. *Not in Germany at least.*

She smiled, lost in her thoughts.

Guido was one of the few who understood this. Perhaps he was the only one. Her family, at any rate, didn't understand, least of all her annoying sister. Throughout Pia's studies she kept claiming that the only reason Pia wanted to become a defence lawyer was because she had saviour complex. Because she was a born victim. But her sister could only talk like that because she didn't know Guido. Sure, he had his faults. But he'd never had a strong woman at his side, someone his equal, canny and intelligent enough to get involved with him. And someone who could change him with the power of love, a love she'd felt ever since setting eyes on him for the first time in the police interrogation room.

'Hey, darling,' she heard him say, taking a load off her mind.

'Where are you?'

'Turn around.'

She did as she was told and smiled.

Headlights cut through the woods, lighting up the crowns of some maples lining the entry road to the car park. Then a sports car turned the corner and veered into the entrance.

'There you are, darling. We've been waiting for you.'

With a smile, Pia stroked her belly, which of course wasn't yet showing at this early stage, and got out of her car.

A Mercedes saloon, not exactly inconspicuous either, but

better than a salmon-coloured, lowered-suspension Porsche Panamera.

'Did you bring what I asked you to?'

Instead of an answer she felt inside the pocket of her mink coat and pulled out the small-calibre pistol.

The black grip shone like oil in the beam of the headlights, in which she proudly flaunted the weapon. It had been entrusted to her by a drug dealer she'd successfully defended the previous year. Only in films did criminals toss their weapons into a lake. In real life they were much more securely hidden from the police's prying eyes in a lawyer's safe.

'You're such a sweetie, darling.'

She sent a kiss down the phone and said, 'You just have to load it, I don't know how to. But there are still a few—'

She didn't get any further.

Pia's lovestruck smile was still on her lips when the Panamera's bumper shattered both her shins. The 550 hp monster had shot towards her like a deadly arrow, knocking her out of her high heels and throwing her backwards onto her Mercedes, from which she now rolled before ending up in a puddle, her spine broken in several places.

She was still breathing. She could taste blood, but felt nothing below her sixth cervical vertebra. Her sense of hearing was still intact, however.

Her last thought was: *our baby.*

And the last sound to enter her dying head was the screeching of the Porsche's tyres as it reversed.

62

TILL

'Shit, what have you done?'

Frieder shook the locked rear door. In the underground car park Tramnitz had forced him onto the back seat and activated the child lock. During the short drive they hadn't once been stopped and checked. There were only two electronic barriers, which Tramnitz was able to negotiate using the doctor's key card.

'Let me out!'

'But of course!' Tramnitz laughed. He pressed a button on the armrest and Frieder almost fell out the door that opened abruptly.

'You too,' he ordered Till, who was staring as if hypnotised in the passenger wing mirror at the contorted human bundle lying in the car park like a burst bag of second-hand clothes.

'Out!' Tramnitz ordered again, this time brandishing the razor blade in front of Till's eyes. During the drive, he'd kept it clamped between the fingers of his balled fist, ready to lacerate the face of anyone who tried to grab the steering wheel or do anything else silly.

When Till failed to react, Tramnitz got out, hurried around the sports car and yanked the door open to pull him onto the tarmac by his coat. The wind tugged at his collar and trouser legs, and Till could smell the earth, the leaves and the lake from the direction of which the gusts of wind were gathering momentum.

'Go, go, go! We're not here for a bloody picnic!'

Tramnitz pushed him over to the Mercedes of the unknown woman the psychopath had telephoned before killing in the middle of their conversation.

'Why did you do that?' Frieder said, crouching beside the dead woman to pointlessly feel her pulse. Tramnitz bent over and picked up the pistol that the woman had been holding only seconds earlier.

For a brief moment Till was annoyed at the missed opportunity, but then he realised that the weapon would have been useless in his own hands. Tramnitz was insensitive to pain; not even a shot to his thigh would have made him talk. And he didn't want to kill him.

Not before he's led me to the truth.

Frieder would have been better off trying to escape rather than worrying about the murdered woman, Till also thought. Then Tramnitz opened the driver's door of the Mercedes.

'Come on. What are you waiting for?'

He aimed the pistol at Till and the doctor in turn, then waved them both over with his other hand.

'Get in, pronto!'

The surgeon stood up, unable to take his distraught eyes off the corpse. He walked backwards, step by step, as if in a trance, staring at her all the while. He only turned around when he was beside the Mercedes.

'Why?' he whispered, tears in his eyes.

There was a red mark on his forehead, where it had

slammed into the headrest. Although Till had been wearing his seat belt, he now had a pain in his neck where it had cut into his skin on impact.

'Jump in and I'll tell you.'

While Till had already got into the passenger seat, Frieder still seemed to be hesitating, although when Tramnitz pointed the gun at him he didn't have a choice, so he climbed into the back. Again he didn't fasten his belt.

'What a mess,' he muttered. 'What a fucking mess.' He buried his head in his hands. It was impossible to work out what was loudest at that moment: the engine's revving, the surgeon's whining or Tramnitz's belly laughter as he engaged the car into gear and put his foot on the pedal. The Mercedes leaped forwards, then Tramnitz slammed on the brakes, as if he'd forgotten something.

What am I missing? Till wondered again as he stared at the woman before him, lit up by the Mercedes' headlights like a morbid art installation.

Tramnitz turned to Frieder. 'Want to know why I killed my lawyer?'

'Yes.'

'Because I don't need her any more.' He laughed. 'And because she really got on my tits.' The psychopath assumed a thoughtful expression. 'In actual fact, I could say the same about you too,' Till heard him say.

Tramnitz nodded as if confirming his own thoughts, then shot the surgeon in the stomach.

63

SÄNGER

'He's what?'

'Escaped. Broken out. Gone.'

'That's… How could it happen?'

Sänger turned 360 degrees in Tramnitz's deserted room as if there were some nook or cranny in this small space that Simon had overlooked.

'I was supposed to fetch him and take him to the transporter, but when I got here…' The orderly left his sentence unfinished.

'Have you triggered the alarm?' Sänger asked.

The blood had completely drained from her face. *Tramnitz escaped!* The most dangerous psychopath in her institution had apparently vanished into thin air.

'Of course,' Simon replied. He looked guilty even though he seemed to have done everything absolutely correctly. Each ward in the Steinklinik had hidden panic buttons – one was right beside the fire extinguishers in the corridor – that in an emergency could be used to notify the police via a dedicated line. 'A minute ago, before I called you.'

'Good,' Sänger said.

It would only be a few minutes before the driveway was

mobbed by half a dozen police cars, their blue lights rotating around the forecourt.

But where were the officers going to start looking?

Sänger went over to the window and gazed out at the deserted, weather-battered park. In the light of the lanterns all she could see was damp grass and leaves that had been blown around. Like driftwood, branches torn down by the storm covered the paths everywhere.

'The bastard might still be here. How would he have got past the security barriers without outside help?'

In the reflection of the dark window she noticed once more the contrite face of the orderly she trusted more than anyone else here.

'What's wrong?'

'I'm sorry, but there's more bad news.'

'What?'

'Kasov!'

She spun around. 'Is he behind the escape?'

Simon sighed. 'I doubt it. Kasov is lying in Winter's room, seriously injured. He must have been overpowered and now Tramnitz and Winter are on the run together. And that's not all either.'

Good God. Two patients on one day?

She was less concerned about the scorn from the press, who would put her through the shredder tomorrow, than the safety of the public.

Simon cleared his throat.

'Don't tell me someone else is missing.'

'I can't get through to Dr Frieder. But I did find this in the bedside table.'

'A diary?'

So Winter was right?

Sänger grabbed the book from Simon's hand and untied the ribbon. As she opened the book a letter fell out. Addressed to:

Professor Sänger (if she hasn't been sacked already!)

Dear Frau Sänger, you're an inquisitive person who likes sticking your nose into other people's private records. Here is an intimate, yet humorous insight into the life of Guido Tramnitz. A diary, if you like.

As she read the words, Sänger could hear that bastard's brazenly narcissistic sing-song voice.

As you can see, the report runs to a few dozen pages. I took extra care over the description of what happened to feisty little Max, paying particular attention to his final moments in the incubator. If you're in a hurry, which I imagine you must be given that I'm getting further away by the second, let me advise you to skip the delicate bits for the time being. (You can always have a cosy read of them later, in front of the fire with a glass of wine.)

If I were you I'd simply turn this letter over to find out where I am currently.

As she turned it over, the piece of paper was shaking so vigorously in the director's hand that she had difficulty reading the paragraphs jotted on the other side. When she finally managed it and got to the end – when she'd grasped the atrociousness of what Tramnitz had meticulously planned here and carried out – the letter fell to the floor and all

Professor Sänger could do was to scream her fury and despair at full force in Simon's face.

At that moment the police sirens could be heard approaching from a distance.

64

TILL

Till had climbed into the back with a first aid bag he'd found in the glove compartment and pressed a haemostatic dressing as tightly as he could over the bullet wound, but the bleeding wouldn't stop.

Too much, it's just too much.

The gauze bandage and the cotton wool and everything else he'd been able to find dripped like a wet sponge. Even the dressing on his own fingers was soaked.

Inside the car it stank of blood, sweat and fear, and all Till could think was that this was how death must smell, even though death was in fact sitting cheerfully and freshly showered at the wheel of the Mercedes.

'Help...'

The surgeon groaned, whimpered, grunted and panted for help again. Beads of sweat as large as hailstones dripped from his brow. His right leg twitched uncontrollably and his eyeballs quivered beneath the lids as if wired to an electric current.

'Stop!' Till shouted, but Tramnitz accelerated instead. If he wasn't mistaken they were heading towards Spandau or Charlottenburg, but that was irrelevant at the moment because they certainly weren't driving anywhere that might give Frieder an outside chance of survival.

'He needs to get to a hospital.'

'Couldn't he have said that earlier?' Tramnitz scoffed. 'We've just come from one!'

'He's going to die.'

'That's what I'm hoping,' Tramnitz said, giving him a wink in the rear-view mirror. 'And I bet you've got nothing against that either.'

There it was again, the question of what was evading him as he strove to stop the doctor from falling asleep.

What am I missing?

He looked through the window. Dark trees by the side of the road rolled past, their powerful trunks towering into the sky like exclamation marks.

You! Are! Missing! Something!

The exclamation marks weren't in a hurry. They moved sedately, for Tramnitz was observing the speed limit, presumably to avoid being noticed. Nevertheless the journey, which Till had experienced as if in a total daydream, was over with astonishing rapidity. Even though Frieder had spent the whole time whimpering, gasping, howling and gabbling for help as his clammy hand got ever colder and feebler.

They stopped in a small avenue with detached houses and here, when he saw for the first time these new surroundings in the light of the antiquated street lamps, Till sensed a feeling that was vaguely comparable to déjà vu.

He felt as if he were reading the beginning of a book that on the one hand looked familiar, but that with every page made him feel less certain as to whether he had read it before.

Where am I?

Most of the houses dated from the early twentieth century, impressive period buildings with tall ceilings and beaver-tail shingles on the vast roofs.

The house in front of which Tramnitz had stopped, however, stood out from the otherwise uniform ensemble. It was a modernist new build with large, floor-to-ceiling windows and a flat roof over the studio. No lights were on anywhere; not even the house number was lit up.

'Open the garden gate!' Tramnitz barked, aiming the pistol at Till's head.

Till parried with his right hand, causing him to relinquish the pressure on Frieder's bandage, though it wasn't helping anyway. 'Put the gun away. I'm not going to try to escape.'

Tramnitz chuckled. 'No, you want to see Max, don't you?'

At the mention of this name Frieder began to groan again. He stretched his hand out to Till, as if begging him not to leave him alone in the car with his madman.

Till pressed the doctor's hands back on his stomach.

'Don't worry, I'll be back.'

He got out and opened the wrought-iron gate of the drive, which was ajar rather than locked. Particularly because the house looked uninhabited and dark, Till was surprised that the property wasn't protected by some security firm against unauthorised entry.

What am I missing?

The engine gurgled as Tramnitz pulled into the gravel drive and parked in the car port which was beside the entrance to a basement. Two outside lights were activated by motion sensors, meaning that at least you could see your hand in front of your face.

Tramnitz got out.

'Is he here?' Till asked.

He felt sick. Not because of the blood on his hands, not because of the dying man in the back seat or the dead woman in the car park who they'd run over.

He felt sick because he knew that only a few moments separated him from absolute certainty.

'Is Max here in this house?'

Nothing is worse than uncertainty.

Apart from the truth...

'Well, that's the million-dollar question, isn't it?'

As Tramnitz closed the driver's door, the rear one sprang open and Frieder fell out of the car like a wet sack.

'Oh, look, how sweet! He wants to come with us.'

The surgeon briefly struggled to his feet from all fours. He staggered forwards towards Tramnitz and the cellar steps.

The killer moved aside and gave Frieder a kick, causing the doctor to tumble down the steps to the basement entrance. Till was certain that this marked Frieder's death sentence – he would break his neck – but right at the bottom the surgeon managed to grab onto the railings with his hands before his head hit the stone floor. He wasn't able to get up again, however.

This horrific scene reminded Till of a dog of his who'd spent an hour after waking from a general anaesthetic trying to stand up again in the vet's recovery room, his paws sliding away again and again on the smooth, antiseptic floor. Frieder's fruitless efforts here were similarly hopeless and pitiful.

'Leave him alone!' Till shouted, horrified, but Tramnitz, who had followed the doctor, grabbed Frieder by the collar and dragged him through the basement door. Here too motion sensors activated the necessary light as they entered, this time in the hallway. And once again the door was ajar.

What am I missing?

'Forget him,' Tramnitz ordered. '*Forget him!*' he hissed a second time, angrily, when Till tried to check on the injured surgeon, who was now lying motionless on a light-coloured carpet that was unusually homely for a basement hallway.

Tramnitz closed the door to the outside and went ahead along the corridor to the stairs that presumably led to the ground floor of the house.

'Right this way!' he called back to Till.

The smell of damp dust and old books made Till's nose itch. Although it was several degrees warmer in here than outside, he froze with every other step he took in Tramnitz's wake.

Is this what I want? Do I want certainty?

A few days ago he would have given everything for this. No, he *had* given everything. His freedom, his autonomy.

My sanity?

An ominous inkling brewed inside Till that the path this psychopath had set out for him, and whose signpost of horror he was now following, would lead him to a truth that was worse than anything he could imagine.

'Where are we?' Till's voice rang hollow in the open built-in cupboards, where presumably shoes, winter coats and laundry used to be kept. But now they were empty. Cold.

Dead.

'One at a time.'

Tramnitz ducked as he went through a doorway to the right.

'Just look at what I've prepared for you here.'

65

The itching got worse and now Till could smell a chemical too. Something acrid was irritating his nostril hairs and he had to snuffle.

In spite of all the resistance that his body was offering and which made his legs as heavy as lead, Till kept following Tramnitz. Failing to notice a step beyond the door, he stumbled into something that looked like a bedroom, probably for the guests of this house's affluent owner, who couldn't possibly be the psychopath.

Tramnitz's property must have been confiscated and sold ages ago. But maybe not?

A light-blue bedspread covered a double bed, and the thick layer of dust on the floorboards near the darkened basement windows were testament to the fact that no one had cleaned in here for a long time.

'Along here,' he heard Tramnitz call from next door. The guest room was connected to the other basement room by a sliding door.

'Oh, come on, I dare you! Come closer!'

Till closed his eyes, but there was no chance of silencing his inner voice that was pleading with him not to do it.

Turn around! Don't go any further! Don't look!

Of course he followed the call of the killer. The devil's siren song.

His eyes still closed, he took a step forwards. Now he must be in the doorframe between the two rooms. Blind, as he used to be at Christmas when his parents told him he had to wait and wasn't allowed to open his eyes until they said so.

But down here there was no Christmas tree or presents beneath it to wonder at, only suffering, agony *and...*

'Oh, God!'

Till, who'd been unable to hold back any longer, gaped at the device in the middle of the otherwise bare room. Even the carpet, which was laid everywhere else in the basement, was missing here. All he could see was a rectangular metal table and on it the hellish apparatus that looked far more hideous in real life than in a photo in the paper.

The wooden box with the windows set into its side reminded him of an iron lung.

In the Museum of Forensic History Till had once marvelled at antediluvian negative pressure ventilators, in which people used to be artificially respirated.

The only difference was that the patient's head was free in an iron lung, whereas here the box was sealed on all sides.

'What's that?' he asked flatly.

'Trixi, or so my father called it. God knows why. I don't have a name for my incubator.'

Till moved closer and stuck his hand out to the brown compressed wood. On the long side facing him he felt the two circular holes, around twenty centimetres in diameter. They were filled with glass, while the lid had a glass recess at the head end.

'Max?' Till said anxiously. He couldn't see whether anything was moving inside the box. It was large enough to accommodate a six-year-old – no, now a seven-year-old boy. All the glass was frosted, virtually opaque. *Although…*

No, that wasn't frosted glass. *It was…*

Condensation!

They're fogged up!

Till stepped closer.

From the inside!

He bent over the closed lid and could clearly see a body lying in there.

'Is that…' he said, looking at Tramnitz, who was standing beside him, watching with amusement.

Tears shot to his eyes. 'Is that my son?'

'Don't you recognise him?'

'I–I can't see. The windows are so fogged up.'

Which is a good sign, isn't it? It means he's breathing, doesn't it?

Tramnitz gave him a paternal clap on the shoulder. 'Take a closer look.'

'But how… how is that possible?'

Till snuffled and wiped the outside of the glass with the sleeve of his coat, which was pointless, of course, because the condensation was coming from the inside.

Max couldn't have been inside this box for a year. A whole year undetected in this house?

'Do you really have no clue?' Tramnitz said beside him.

He looked at Till. 'Don't you know who you are?'

Till shook his head like a little schoolboy at the blackboard, unable to solve the problem he's been set.

'Or what really happened? To Max a year ago?'

'No!' he whispered, and felt the fear about to swallow him up from the inside.

'Okay,' Tramnitz said. 'Let me give you a bit of help.'

66

MAX

One year before

Ice cube, *Max thought, clutching the model spacecraft.*

He stepped out of the front door into a cold that perfectly suited the password he and Daddy had agreed on.

They'd practised it again and again, on their walks through the forest, in the car or while they were waiting for the bus.

'What do you do if a stranger says you should go with them?'

'Then I ask them for the password.'

'And what is our password?'

'Ice cube,' Max mumbled and went carefully down the steps into the front garden. The Lego model mustn't break or anything come loose before Anna saw it. Anna, who always smelled so good and gave him such lovely cuddles.

'Hey, little boy!'

Max looked to the right and saw a man standing beneath a street lamp.

'Yes?'

'Do you know where number 65 is?'

Max didn't want to be held up on his way to Anna's and, besides, it was getting colder by the second.

'What's the password?' The words just slipped out.

'Huh?'

The man looked at Max as if he'd been speaking the secret language he'd worked out with his best friend, Anton.

'Doesn't matter,' Max said after a while and decided to help the man. 'Number 65?'

Why not? The man hadn't suggested he come with him.

And the password rule could hardly apply to a delivery man trying to pull a trolley laden with packages through the snow.

'Thanks, mate,' the delivery man said after Max had shown him the way. *The man hadn't just got the number wrong, but the street too. Not Lärchenweg, but Lerchenweg.*

But it's confusing around here where everything's got similar names.

Max waited until the driver had got back into his yellow van and driven away. That gave him the time to work out what he was going to say to Anna.

To be honest, he was scared stiff. Anna was so beautiful and he was so little. Would she laugh if he just went and rang the bell? Did she actually like Star Wars? Of course. Anna was a great girl. She had to love Star Wars.

Max was so lost in his thoughts when he eventually crossed the road that he didn't see the sports car way over the speed limit come racing towards him.

Oh no, *he thought.* My Millennium Falcon.

The Lego spaceship flew through the air and landed, broken, in the snow.

Just like his own little body, which from one moment to the next had plunged into a sea of pain, its waves crashing above him and into him, so noisily and violently that he lost consciousness.

He didn't wake up again for several hours and could see nothing but eyes. The rest of the man's face was covered by a green mask. It would take a while before he realised that the hard surface he was strapped to was an operating table.

Back then, one year ago, Max thought he'd woken up in hell. Dragged away by an evil Halloween monster to be tortured. He'd have never been able to imagine that his actual hell was still a year in the future and that its gates would only be opened to him today.

Here and now, in the basement of this strange house, where the man had brought him just this morning. The same man who'd run him over, put his broken leg into a splint and nursed him back to health, only to kill him in the end after all.

Here, in this cramped wooden crate where he lay with his legs bound, and over which a figure was now leaning. A man, probably. He looked different from the man who'd stood watch over him until now. Slimmer, younger perhaps. But he couldn't say with any certainty. Max couldn't make out his face as the windows in this stupid box were so fogged up.

'Daddy?' Max called out, full of hope, even though after all the months of isolation any hope was practically exhausted.

67

TILL

'Max?'

Till knocked against the glass of the 'incubator'. He was sure that his son had called for him, even though he could barely hear more than a muffled murmur outside the box. The hellish device was very well insulated.

'Open it!' he bellowed at Tramnitz, whose story he had difficulty believing.

A hit-and-run accident? Tramnitz wasn't the kidnapper?

Why was Max lying in this basement then? In this incubator?

What am I missing?

'Open it! Now!'

Tramnitz sighed. 'Oh, I'm afraid I can't do that. I don't have a key.'

Till blinked, puzzled. 'Why not?'

'I didn't build this thing.'

The confusion knocked Till so far off guard that he began to stammer. 'But, but… who, who…?'

Till ran his fingers over the screw joints. Nowhere could he find a lever, a knob or a hinge he could move. Not on the side windows, which must have been earmarked as hand holes, nor on the lid with its glass at the head. Now he was gripped by another worry. 'Does any air get in?'

'Yes, so long as this valve is open.'

Tramnitz indicated a metal tube on the side, about the same size as a pen lid.

'But the moment you screw it in...'

Tramnitz stuck out his tongue and made choking noises, then giggled once he was finished with his impersonation of someone suffocating to death.

'Who's got the key if the thing doesn't belong to you?' Till asked again.

'Hang on, of course it belongs to me. It's an early prototype I stored in a garage by the Teltowkanal. But the window fixings and valve are new. I didn't make those.'

'*Who, then?*' Till yelled. 'If you didn't, then who?'

There was a crash and a hunched Frieder stumbled into the room and collapsed, groaning.

Tramnitz's eyes lit up like a teenage boy whose girlfriend has promised him sex for the first time.

'Well, what timing. Speak of the devil!'

68

Blood.

It was all over the surgeon's torso, his face and hair, the carpet and everywhere he'd touched.

Till could taste, smell and sense it on his own skin, on his head and finger bandages, on his hands. And it roared in his ears like a white-water river.

'What did you just say?' he croaked. His throat was constricted.

The truth you're looking for won't bring you any relief.

'For God's sake, Till, father of Max, are you still unable to put two and two together?' Tramnitz sought to catch his eye. 'Why was our escape so incredibly simple? Why did nobody get in our way?'

Why were the doors here open?

'We had help.'

The psychopath pointed at the surgeon cowering by the door, leaning on the wall between the two rooms.

'May I introduce you to the mastermind behind our breakout? Dr Vodka – I mean, Volker Frieder. A not especially anonymous alcoholic who almost lost everything when drunk in charge of a scalpel. And who scooped up dear little Max in his Porsche last year.'

'Shut your mouth,' Frieder gasped, his bloody hands pressed against the bullet wound.

'That's what happened,' Tramnitz said, going over to Frieder and kicking his outstretched leg.

'He came flying through the 30 kph zone as pissed as a fart. I can imagine what went through your head as you stood there in the snow beside the seriously injured child, Lego everywhere. "Shit, if this gets out, I'm buggered for good. I'll lose it all: my job, my reputation, my freedom. Everything!"'

'It was you?'

Till moved away from the incubator and took a step towards the man whose life he'd tried to save only minutes ago.

Whose hand I'd held.

'Well, he stuffed Max into his boot and drove to his holiday home in Brandenburg,' Tramnitz went on. 'To have a quiet think about what to do next.'

He looked at Till again. 'Anyway, Frieder treated him. Put his leg in a splint and so on. He always wore a mask. I assume you were going to let him go at some point, weren't you?' He sighed. 'But one day the idiot wore his coat – can you believe it? Such a pissed-up amateur. Max didn't have to see the face, which he wouldn't have recognised anyway. He just had to read: Dr Volker Frieder. Steinklinik.'

All of a sudden the killer's words sounded peculiarly muffled, which was because the incubus on Till's chest had now moved to his ears. Clearly his brain didn't want to hear the truth that Tramnitz was serving up.

'The irony of the story was that Max could barely read. I mean he was only in the first year. But he knew enough.'

'Why are you doing this?' Frieder moaned. He'd now given up holding his hand to his stomach.

'Don't get me wrong, Till. Frieder here isn't a bad person, at least not in the same category as me. He's had a real inner struggle. He doesn't want to go to prison because of child abduction, but on the other hand he can't bring himself to kill Max. So, da-daa… that's where I come into play.' Tramnitz took a step to the side like an actor making his grand entrance onto the stage.

'For him it must have been like providence. All of a sudden I land up on his operating table. Me, who everyone thinks killed Max anyway.'

But why wouldn't he have admitted it and enjoyed the suffering of those left behind?

Because Tramnitz wasn't the killer!

'Our dear surgeon friend here kept Max hidden the whole time in his holiday home. A remote fishing hut on Scharmützelsee, where nobody would disturb him.'

Tramnitz pointed at the doctor.

'So, after the operation Frieder comes into my room and proposes a deal. I'm to make everything look as if I really were Max's killer and lead the police to his body. In return he helps me escape.'

'What about the diary?' Till said. He was still unsure what to make of this revelation. Was it good news? Confirmation that Max was still alive? Or was Tramnitz merely playing a particularly gruesome game with him? Was the monster really trying to get off on his false hopes?

'The diary is part of the deal. I didn't start writing any of it until I was in the loony bin. It was supposed to be found among my documents later on. The definitive proof that I was the killer, not Frieder.'

'What do you mean killer? Isn't Max alive?'

Till turned back to the incubator.

'For the moment, yes. That's why he got me out. So I could do his dirty work.'

Good God.

In his diary Tramnitz had described his *future* atrocities.

This is the first time he's ever seen Max. He's going to kill him today. Here and now.

Then Tramnitz said, 'I gave Frieder precise instructions – where to find the incubator, how to finish building the device so that it worked. And I told him where to take the incubator to make it look as if it had been in my possession all along.'

'Where are we?' Till asked, thinking of the street lamps outside the house and the strange itching he'd felt in his nose as he'd entered the basement.

'You know where we are,' Tramnitz insisted.

Yes. In the clutches of the devil, at Hell's very core.

'Pia found out the address for me when I realised who you actually were.' Tramnitz raised both hands in a 'Hey, no reason to get worked up' gesture. 'I know, I know. That goes against our agreement,' he said to Frieder, whose lips were squeezing out a bloody saliva bubble.

Till, meanwhile, was having an almost otherworldly experience. Physically he was still present, standing in this basement room between the devil's own machine, in which his son was perhaps imprisoned, and two criminals. But his mind was freewheeling. The voices around him became ever more muted and hollow, as if far away. Till was paralysed by shock, unable to move.

'I thought it would be more amusing to have it happen here rather than at my place. Somehow I'd hoped he'd come with us.'

'Why are you telling him all this?' he heard Frieder ask, the strength having almost drained from his voice now.

With the pistol in his outstretched hand Tramnitz went over to the surgeon cowering on the floor. 'For the same reason I chose this basement here. Because it's fun. People's suffering is greater when they see the most terrible of all truths with their own eyes.'

He put the pistol to Frieder's head. The doctor groaned. Took a hand from his stomach. The blood-soaked bandage came away. More blood seeped out.

To Till's astonishment he smiled with red-stained teeth.

'Go on. Do it. It was what I planned anyway.'

Tramnitz blinked in confusion. 'You want to die today?'

'Put an end to it. I wanted to call it all off.'

The surgeon looked at Till with an expression in his eyes that were sad and seemed to say, *'I'm really sorry. I made a mistake.'*

Till couldn't help thinking of the first words that Frieder had said when he came into Tramnitz's room earlier. *'Something has cropped up, I have to...'*

'Call it all off?' Tramnitz repeated in disbelief. 'Well, well, the gentleman has discovered some scruples after all. Too late, I'm afraid.'

Frieder shook his head. 'Kill me! But leave the boy alone! I've changed my mind.'

'The way you're bleeding, I fear you're not in the best negotiating position.'

The surgeon coughed up some blood, then said again, 'Leave Max be! Time's running out anyway. They're bound to be after you.'

'And? Maybe I don't want to escape.'

'But you want to see Max suffer. And him,' Frieder said, pointing at Till. 'And you can't do that if you're interrupted.'

'I've got time.'

With the last morsel of his strength, Frieder knocked the gun away from his head, but Tramnitz put it straight back.

'No, you don't. My key cards emit a signal. They can be tracked in case they're lost. Sänger knows where I am. They'll be here soon.'

Tramnitz laughed. 'Rubbish! You're not that stupid. I bet you wiped away any trace that could lead back to you.'

'How many times?' Frieder protested as forcefully as his body would allow. 'I've changed my mind. I realised that I couldn't go through with it. I was going to turn myself in.'

Tramnitz shrugged. 'So what? Your keys are magnetic cards; they don't transmit anything. You're bluffing. But it's a pretty good bluff, I'll give you that. I also thought you weren't bad pretending to talk to the orderlies earlier.' Tramnitz mimicked Frieder by putting the pistol to his ear as if it were a mobile and quoting his words: '*Yes, I know it's against protocol, but we've got a hostage situation.*'

He put the barrel to Frieder's head once again. 'Right, that's enough mucking about.'

'No, wait, I beg you, let Max—'

The unfinished sentence literally exploded in Frieder's mouth.

Tramnitz had pulled the trigger.

With an ear-splitting bang, the bullet entered the surgeon's brain via his forehead, before exiting at the back and ending up in the plaster wall.

'But he's right, we have to hurry,' Tramnitz said, completely unfazed by the splinters of bone, the blood and the cerebral matter splattered on the wall behind the dead doctor. For Till, however, this sight broke the spell.

The pressure vanished from his ears and he was finally freed from his state of shock.

69

'What are you doing?' he asked Tramnitz, without expecting an answer.

The psychopath felt the pockets of the murdered surgeon until he found what he was looking for in Frieder's trousers.

'There we go!'

He showed Till the key he'd pulled out. A square spindle key with a long handle. 'For the valve.'

He was about to walk past Till but the latter had the courage to stand in his way.

'Stop. You don't have to do this.'

Tramnitz nodded. 'Exactly, I'm just doing it for pleasure. If I *had* to do it, it would be work, wouldn't it?'

Removing the magazine from his pistol, he checked that there was still a bullet left, showed it to Till and then pushed past him once he'd reloaded the weapon.

'What are you going to do?'

'What do you think? I'm going to look after Max.'

Tramnitz knocked the barrel of the gun against the window at the head of the incubator.

'Hello, little boy, can you hear me? Your treatment is about to begin.'

Shit, what now?

Till looked around in a frenzied search for something to use against the armed psychopath.

He put his hand to his head and untied the bandage.

'Stop, or I'm leaving.'

Tramnitz didn't even bother turning around, but put the key on the valve pin.

'What sort of ludicrous threat is that?'

'Frieder was right, wasn't he? You wanted me to come so you could watch me suffer.'

'And?'

'If I go now, you get nothing. You won't see my pain and it would all have been in vain.'

Now Tramnitz did turn around, a smile playing on his full lips. 'Oh, you're overestimating your importance. You're not here to watch the boy die.'

Why, then?

'I'll have plenty of fun with the boy on my own. You're just a bonus I'm saving for later.'

What am I missing?

'When this business with Max is finished, with a little luck you're going to experience something that will absolutely shatter you. That's why you're here. I want to watch your face and feast on your suffering.' He snuffled. 'And just for your information, you won't get very far. Pia did the research. You can't get out of here once the basement door is closed. The door up to the ground floor is locked. So for the time being there's no way out. By all means wait in the corridor until I'm done with Max. I'll show you what remains of him later, before we carry on.'

He turned the spindle key and started to restrict the air supply.

Thudthudthud.

Almost immediately someone inside started hitting the glass and wooden panels.

'It's a shame we don't have much time, because there's so much else I'd have loved to do with him. But look, you can see better now. The glass isn't so misted up; you'll get a good view of him suffocating,' he said. At that very moment Till looped the cord he'd undone from his bandage around the neck of the killer.

In vain.

The attempt was as desperate as it was pathetic.

With a single blow from his elbow, Tramnitz detonated a firework beneath Till's skull. Sparks flew and liquid pain flooded the hollows between his eyes.

'What sort of manners are those?' Tramnitz asked as the banging from within the box got louder and more frantic.

Thud... Thud...

'Oh, this is music to my ears,' Tramnitz said, bent low over the incubator, while Till had no idea how to stop the lunatic and save Max. Right now he couldn't even get back to his feet.

70

SÄNGER

Dear Frau Sänger

In your hands you have the first ever diary that describes the future rather than the past.

Everything you read here is what awaits little Max. My fantasies are still to be played out. Probably now, at this very moment.

Dr Frieder thought he was forcing me to go along with his plan, but it was obvious that his claim he'd poisoned me during the operation was a bluff.

In truth he's dancing to my tune (although as you read these lines I doubt he's capable of dancing at all).

I made him bring Trixi (you'll find out what that is) to a place of my choosing so I could begin Max's treatment. In return, he helped me escape for reasons I'll explain when we meet again.

For we will meet again. I'll soon be back in your care, assuming you survive the disciplinary proceedings and board of enquiry which are bound to follow the debacle of my escape.

You see, the only reason I'm confiding in you so openly here is that I've absolutely no intention of remaining at liberty.

I feel comfortable with the structured life of psychiatric imprisonment, where I've wanted for nothing. Food, lodging, coke, even whores, all on the house. And my life was saved too, even if Frieder's psycho games were rather irritating. Thankfully, however, that's all history now.

In addition – and this is the main reason why I want to come back – there's going to be a second trial.

I will look Max's mother in the eye and she will know that her boy lived more than another year. She'll know that there was even a real chance of setting him free. Holding him in her arms, kissing and stroking him, watching him grow up. And after sentence has been passed I will look her in the eye and see the fury, pain and despair – an image I'll store away in my mind to recall whenever I wish to savour it.

Well, then, for my wish to be fulfilled you just have to wait. I'll be in touch when it's all over.

In joyful anticipation

Yours
Guido Tramnitz

'Trixi?'

The fat inspector, whose name Sänger had forgotten yet again (*some sort of animal – Bär, Hamster, Fisch, or something like that*) had now read the letter too.

'Do you know what he means by this?' he asked with some tension in his voice. His officers had already embarked on a manhunt and a large area surrounding the Steinklinik had been cordoned off, but his nervousness was tangible. There was no trace of Tramnitz anywhere.

'I'm afraid not. What about you, Simon?'

The three of them were sitting around her small, round

conference table that was usually piled high with patient files, but which she'd removed.

The orderly, who the inspector had summoned to the interview as a witness, cleared his throat. 'I'm not sure. But I think they mentioned it in the papers. I think that's what Tramnitz called the incubator where—'

'How big is a thing like that?' Sänger interrupted him, to the amazement of the inspector, who was no doubt used to asking the questions himself.

'Quite big. About a metre and a half long and wide enough to fit a person inside. Why?'

'Yes, why's that important?' the policeman asked.

His face turned even sourer when the doctor merely ignored him and directed another question to Simon. 'Has Frieder borrowed an ambulance recently? Or another transporter? He could hardly transport the thing in his Porsche.'

While the inspector looked as if there was a sudden whistling in his ears, Simon leaped up. 'I'll check the vehicle register.'

He hurried to the door.

'Yes, do that,' Sänger called out after him. 'And if you find anything, check the satnav data.'

71

TILL

He went into the guest room, despite all the pain that not even an adrenaline boost could alleviate now, nor panic.

It was rather the muted banging of Max's fists that drove him on. The rhythm of death giving the beat.

Thud... Thud...

Till looked for something in the guest room he could use as a weapon. A sharp object, a stick, a carpet knife, perhaps. But it was totally empty. He yanked open the built-in wardrobe, finding only two bars of soap that must have once been among the laundry, but now had lost all their fragrance.

Thud...

Max's blows were getting weaker. The intervals longer.

How much longer would he have air to breathe?

With courage born of despair Till raced back into the next room and this time landed a surprisingly decent punch on Tramnitz's chin, but to little effect. Apart from an even more violent reaction from the killer. The first swing cracked Till's ribs, squeezing all the air from his lungs. This was followed by a kick in the groin.

Till collapsed into a heap. He wanted to scream but there

was no air left in his lungs and he couldn't inhale any more even though his mouth stood open with pain.

Thud... Thud...

Then he saw them. Two empty plastic bottles. Beside the guest bed, not far from a dark stain on the light carpet.

What am I missing?

The bottoms of the bottles were brown from the liquid they'd last had in them.

Till's nose was filled with the smell of petrol. And he was getting hot. He felt the irresistible urge to scratch his head.

What am I missing?

Thud... Thud...

His son's signals were getting ever feebler. Max's spirits seemed to be dwindling just as Till's were reviving.

What...

The cupboard?

Am I...

The bottles?

Missing...

The stain?

Or was it the sports bag?

THE BAG!!!

Right beneath the guest bed! Towards which Till was now crawling. Slowly, far too slowly, on all fours because there was no hope of him walking now.

The black bag!

... which loomed ever larger the closer he came. Which he finally grabbed, opened... and this time it was more than déjà vu. This time he didn't have a hunch, but *knowledge!*

Till *knew* what he'd find in the sports bag before he opened the zip. He knew what he had to do with it.

How he had to hold it.

And when he was holding it correctly, it was an almost supernatural experience.

'Tramnitz?' he bellowed, turning around. From his position by the end of the bed he could see through the sliding door into the neighbouring room.

'What the hell...' he heard the monster say, his eyes wide open with surprise. Eyes which were far too blue in this far too chiselled, handsome face.

Which was still far too well-proportioned and attractive even after Till had emptied into it the entire magazine of the gun from the sports bag under the bed.

72

'Max?'

The spindle key was still in the valve. After a quarter turn Till could hear it hiss. After two more full turns the screw came loose.

He now set about the lid fastenings. Till found more recesses and more screws, undid each one in turn and finally was able to raise the lid.

He frantically stripped it from the crate and dropped it at his feet.

Till was ready to grab the lifeless body of his son, stimulate his heart with CPR, try mouth-to-mouth resuscitation with his own breath – anything and everything he could.

But Max's waxen, deathly pale face, contorted to the point of being unrecognisable, very briefly held him back, because he... *God forgive me...* thought that it was pointless. Thought that Max was already dead, like the lawyer in the car park or Frieder here in the basement.

Or Tramnitz.

So much death, suffering, pain and horror in such a small space.

A space I know. Where I've been before. How else could I have known what was in the bag?

'Nooooooooo!' Till screamed, pressing his lips to his beloved son, whose soul must have already departed his body given how little of the boy's warmth and love he could still feel.

How often in his mind had he gone over that moment when he would finally have certainty? How often had he promised himself relief and release? Now, however, it seemed as if the worst of all possible experiences still lay ahead of him.

To lose a child he'd believed dead, but who could have been saved after all.

Who could live with that?

He looked at Tramnitz, just to make sure that the sadist hadn't got to his feet again. *Because you would have liked this, wouldn't you?*

Watching me here, now?

Crying, blubbing, *too weak to get my son's heart beating again. Too out of breath to give some of it to him.*

Suddenly he heard a cough.

And then the boy's body twitched, reared up and almost collapsed, but Till thrust his arm under Max's back and caught him.

'Max? Oh, God, Max, are you alive?'

A flood of tears as torrential as the rain of the past few days shot from his face onto the boy. Under his kisses Till heard him groan and this was the loveliest sound he'd heard in his life. Finally he uttered a word, then another, until the child had formed an entire sentence, this beautiful boy with his sad eyes and full lips: 'What... what happened?'

Till hugged him tight. Sobbed. Shook. And now all his pain

was forgotten. Now he could feel nothing but joy, happiness and confidence.

'Oh, Jesus, you're alive. Max, my little, little boy.'

Until his son's next words shattered everything inside him.

'Who are you?'

Weakly, but with determination, Max tried to free himself from the embrace.

Till blinked. Took a step backwards. With the feeling that something inside him had fragmented into a thousand shards.

He felt a hot flush.

'I–I am...'

He looked around. Saw the bottles. Smelled the petrol.

What am I missing?

'Who are you?' the boy asked again. And while, in the distance, the sound of police sirens filtered quietly through the basement windows, Max Berkhoff asked him the question that finally broke him.

'Is my daddy here anywhere?'

73

Tramnitz hadn't been lying. There really was no way out of the basement once the door had closed. Unless you knew where the spare key was, which the owner of the house had put under a loose floorboard by the stairs after moving in some years ago.

For emergencies.

And just as he'd known what was in the sports bag, so he knew how to get up onto the ground floor.

Slowly, shuffling along, he felt his way in the gloom of the hall past the open kitchen area, for up here there were no motion sensors and no light. Only the moon, its light pouring in through the huge terrace windows. But he also knew what was beneath his feet: that ugly chessboard parquet floor, which they'd never got rid of because they didn't have the money. Just like the jacuzzi, which the crazy previous owner had put in the middle of the living room and they'd had to fill with cushions.

An adventure sofa for Linda and the children.

For Frieda.

And for Jonas.

Who he'd wanted to build a treehouse for in the chestnut tree that had been struck by lightning.

Tears came to his eyes again; he thought his flesh was burning, and now he realised the cause of this phantom pain he'd so often felt in his dreams. Now that he gazed across the overgrown garden to the nursery school which bordered this property around one hundred metres away. He closed his eyes and for a moment he was back in the dream, in which he was in his twenty-second-floor office on Potsdamer Platz, staring at the car park where his vehicle was parked right in the sun.

Then he remembered what really had happened.

How Linda had called him while he was sweating over a complicated recalculation of the risk of death of premature babies. The chief lawyer of the health insurance firm was breathing down his neck, having wanted the figures since the day before.

But somewhere he'd made a miscalculation and he couldn't find the error. The problem had prevented him from sleeping all night.

For days now these complicated formulas wouldn't give him any peace, no matter whether he was shopping, gardening or in the car. He was ruminating over the solution and in truth didn't have the time to take his wife's call. But as she'd already tried several times today, he finally picked up the mobile from his desk. The conversation that followed put an end to all the happiness that had ever been present in his life.

'*Linda?*'

'*Where is he?*'

'*Who?*'

'*Jonas. You were supposed to drop him off at nursery. He isn't there.*'

★

337

It was the first time he'd contemplated suicide.

He'd got up, gone over to the window and looked down at the car park. Where his car was.

With the child seat in the back, which Linda had put in for him specially.

'Just this once. Tomorrow I'll take him in again, okay?'

'It's fine,' he'd said, turning his mind again to the problem with the recalculation.

And forgotten everything else.

Forgotten Jonas.

In the child seat.

Down below in the car park.

In a black car.

In the back seat.

In the sweltering heat on one of the hottest days of the summer.

'Hello?'

He jumped. For a moment he was still caught up in the daydream of his recollections, but the voice behind him was real. A person of flesh and blood, who he'd never personally met before. He only knew him, like his parents, from the papers and the telly: Max, who'd followed him up to the living room from the basement.

'Sorry,' said the little boy with the sad eyes and full lips, whose picture he'd seen so often in the missing person adverts. He was wearing only a T-shirt and pants, and he had a scar on his right shin.

'Am I... did you rescue me?'

'Yes,' he said in tears at the realisation that his own son was lost for ever.

As he was.

That's what Tramnitz had meant.

'When this business with Max is finished, with a little luck you're going to experience something that will absolutely shatter you. That's why you're here. I want to watch your face and feast on your suffering.'

He looked at the kindergarten, where a light was still on, just as it had been when he'd stood in this living room holding a gun, before deciding against it. Because it would have been too cowardly. Too harmless.

Which was why he'd ended up putting the pistol in the sports bag and going for the petrol option.

Because it was his fault that his son had burned to death, and he'd wanted to burn too.

'So... who, who are you?' Max asked as the screech of tyres could be heard outside.

And sirens.

The sirens must have been getting closer all the time, but he'd completely blocked them out. Until now, when Max asked, implored again with tears in his voice, 'Please. Who are you?' and he finally answered the boy.

'My name is Patrick Winter. I'm a patient at the Steinklinik. I killed my son and it made me lose my mind.'

74

SÄNGER

Ten days later

They'd made themselves look nice. Like for a dinner with the boss. Not too formal, but not too casual either, to signal that they were aware of how special this occasion was.

Till Berkhoff wore a brown jacket with a brand-new light-blue shirt, its collar chafing as often as he scratched his neck. It was evident that the sinewy fireman didn't feel especially comfortable in this outfit and would have rather swapped it for a pair of jeans, trainers and a T-shirt. Maybe he'd taken advice from his wife, Ricarda, who had gone for a simple green-brown dress with lacy sleeves, subtle earrings and ankle boots – nowhere near warm enough for the first snow of the year, which had fallen a few days earlier.

Professor Sänger didn't know how close the two of them were at the moment and whether she should believe the papers who had written about how the 'overjoyed couple' had got back together after their son Max reappeared out of the blue.

Both of them *were* wearing wedding rings and were sitting huddled together at the small conference table in Sänger's office. But they weren't holding hands.

'I don't understand,' Till said, now for the third time. He hadn't touched the water or the biscuits that Sänger had put out for her visitors.

'This Patrick Winter believed he was me?'

Sänger wanted to nod and shake her head at the same time.

'Yes and no. It's complicated.'

'You can say that again,' Till Berkhoff said, giving the director a sheepish smile. 'But perhaps you can explain it to a simple soul like me in simple words.'

Sänger took off her reading glasses and stared at the scratched plastic lenses as she battled with herself and patient confidentiality. Then she shrugged. 'Oh, what the hell.'

In any case her assumption was that very soon she'd be sacked by the board of enquiry. And so this would scarcely make a difference. Besides, everything she told them would find its way into the papers at some point and who, if not Max's parents, had a right to know the true background?

'Patrick Winter has been a patient of ours for almost two years now,' she began. 'Before that he was treated in the Karl Bonhoeffer psychiatric hospital.'

'Is he schizophrenic?' Till asked.

'No, it's got nothing to do with that disorder. Nor is it what laypeople would term multiple personality disorder.'

'What, then?'

'Patrick Winter is a fugitive. He wants to cast off his real self to temporarily assume new identities.'

'Mine?'

'The last time it was yours, yes. He thought he was you. Till Berkhoff, fireman, father of Max.'

'But why? What gave him the idea?'

She put her glasses back on. 'Oh, we can't say with absolute certainty, but we believe it was triggered by the reports in the media. Some TV report, perhaps a documentary about you, must have moved him so much that the switch occurred.'

'Switch?'

'That's what we call the phase of transition. Usually it manifests itself in a complete nervous breakdown, beginning with Winter talking to himself, isolating himself from his surroundings, even self-harm. Then we have to sedate him and take him to the intervention room. When he comes to, often he's assumed a different identity.'

'You said he's a fugitive?' Ricarda probed.

In their preliminary talk, Max's mother had told the psychiatrist that she'd never given up the search for her son. She hired private detectives, placed advertisements, and even went to a psychic. All her money was spent on the search. When it ran out after a year, she even toyed with the idea of selling a 'story' about her desperate search to the press. Fortunately, however, no article about her visit to the clairvoyant ever appeared.

'Yes, he's a fugitive from himself,' Sänger explained to the couple. 'Patrick Winter lost his own son as the result of a tragic mistake. On a boiling hot day he forgot he'd left the boy in his car while he went to work at his insurance firm.'

'That's terrible.'

'Yes. He never got over it. A few months after the tragedy, he tried to take his own life. He poured petrol over himself and set fire to it at his daughter's kindergarten, while yelling that he wanted to burn like his son.'

'For God's sake!' Ricarda exclaimed.

'They managed to save him and he was fortunate to get

away with burns to the epidermis on his head. Sadly this was probably the cause of his skin cancer, but that's the least of his problems.'

Sänger wondered whether to have a drink of water, but abstained. 'He arrived here, but even in the psychiatric hospital was unable to get over his pain and self-hatred.'

'Hatred?'

'Yes. He hates himself so much that he wants to usurp his own identity. Like a snail he's looking for a new house. And, as I said, the slightest impulse – an image, a conversation, an item on the radio – can trigger the switch.'

Till raised his hand like a schoolboy. 'So you're saying that when he comes out of this interv—'

'Intervention room, that's right. Last time he came out, he was you, Herr Berkhoff. He thought his first name was Till, he was a fireman, and his son Max had been abducted. Externally, however, he kept his real name, and that's what makes our diagnosis and treatment so difficult.' Now it was Sänger scratching her neck. She was sweating even though she'd just opened the window.

'We never know which identity he'll wake up with next, and that's why we always greet him as a new patient. Even his fellow patients have got used to it, although some, of course, create confusion when they talk to Winter about incidents and events he can't remember because he's already in a new false identity.'

She smiled sadly. 'The time before, for example, he thought he was a detective come to uncover accounting fraud. And in the course of his "investigation",' she said, making air quotes, 'he actually rumbled one of our senior doctors.'

'Dr Kasov?' Till asked.

Sänger nodded. He must have read the reports about the doctor's corrupt dealings. 'Yes, but before he could become a danger to him, Patrick Winter had another switch.'

'And became me?' The fireman scratched his neck again.

'Precisely. Because Patrick Winter cannot cope with the real reason why he's in here he looks for an explanation that his shattered mind can more readily accept. He imagines he was only admitted as Patrick Winter under false pretences, whereas in reality he's someone of perfectly sound mind who's in the hospital for a completely different reason, and of his own free will. With a secret mission.'

'And his secret mission was to find our son?'

Ricarda was the first to take a sip of water and she put the glass back down.

'Yes. On the grapevine he found out that Tramnitz was also in the Steinklinik. This probably set him on the search for an identity that would justify trying to solve the Max Berkhoff case.'

'Can we see him?' Ricarda asked. Her husband too looked at the director expectantly.

Sänger got up. 'Come with me.'

75

They left her office and walked side by side in silence until they got to the large glass double doors, behind which lay the lobby of the Steinklinik.

Gentle piano music rang from the room and Sänger got the impression she wasn't the only one moved by the sad melody. Her visitors began to whisper as if anxious not to disturb the pianist as he played.

'Is that him?'

Sänger could only see a back at the black piano, but yes, of course it was him. Nobody else in here could play Chopin with such passion. Even though two of his fingers were still out of action.

Nocturne, E-flat major. Opus 9 no. 2.

Her favourite piece of music.

'He plays piano?'

'If he can remember, yes. He's highly gifted. If he weren't, he wouldn't be able to keep up these parallel universes around him.'

'What do you mean by "parallel universes"?' Till asked.

'We're groping in the dark here too. It appears that he has a few constants. One is the telephone number of his wife, Linda, who he keeps on wanting to call, although she's forbidden it now. The last time, Winter thought he was talking to you, Ricarda, and he told his wife their son might still be alive.'

'Meaning Max.'

She nodded. 'Exactly. Another constant is his brother-in-law, Oliver Skania, who committed suicide some years ago. Despite this, he seems to be part of Winter's visions over and over again. Like *Ulysses*.'

'Who's that?'

'Not who, but what. A book by James Joyce. Winter thinks there's a mobile phone hidden in this book which allows him to keep in touch with his contacts outside – the people he claims smuggled him in here. But it's not hollowed out or modified. It's a perfectly normal book in our library.'

Sometimes in his hallucinations Winter converted everyday objects into mobile phones, like biros or spoons.

When she'd burst in on him in the infirmary eleven days ago he was trying to call with a remote control that Tramnitz had given him.

The sadist must have seen through Winter's madness and decided to play games with the poor guy. Not only did he select him as a useful hostage so he could torture the boy to death before his very eyes, the whole thing was arranged to happen in Winter's house, which had been standing empty since the tragedy.

'Can we talk to him?' Ricarda asked.

'I don't think that's a good idea.'

'But if it hadn't been for him...' Ricarda broke off, which gave Sänger the opportunity to enjoy a complicated and beautiful tremolo that Winter was playing.

'Without him Max wouldn't be alive,' Till said, agreeing

with his wife. 'He may be ill, but in his madness he saved our son's life.'

Sänger gave a sad sigh and waited until the piece was over. Then she said, 'You're right. But just look.'

She pointed towards the room.

Simon, who had stepped out from behind the Christmas tree, carefully touched Patrick's arm. He looked up inquiringly at the orderly.

'Winter was only recently released from the intervention room,' Sänger explained as her patient closed the piano lid and got up from the stool.

Lost in thought, Winter turned around, looked over at them and raised his hand as if he'd noticed the visitors behind the glass door and was going to wave to them. But he just brushed some hair out of his face.

'He looks so lost,' Ricarda said. Tears welled in her eyes and she couldn't help thinking of her conversation with the psychic at the bus stop outside the takeaway. *'And when I've found Max?'* she'd asked Gedeon. *'What then?'*

'Then I can see you quite clearly in my mind. You're crying. Behind a locked door. In a prison.'

Beside her, Sänger was breathing heavily. 'Can you imagine how terrible it must be to keep trying to escape from yourself? Only to have to realise each time that you can never flee from your own soul?' She ran a hand through her hair. 'His tortured mind is desperately looking for a way out and has probably already found a new one.'

In the lobby, Simon pointed to the passage beside the dispensary and called Winter's name. The patient looked at the door once more, then his gaze wandered up the huge Christmas tree. Finally he followed the orderly with hesitant movements and his body hunched slightly forwards. And as, step by step, he moved away from them, the director laid one hand on Ricarda's shoulder and touched Till's upper arm with the other and said, 'I fear the Patrick Winter you wish to thank has disappeared again.'

76

SEDA

The hydraulic hiss signalled the arrival of another visitor. Seda was putting the guide to Rome back in its rightful place (*Who the hell needs a travel guide in a secure psychiatric hospital?*) and when she saw him climb the steps into the bus she was delighted that her wish had come true.

It was her last day and Simon had kept his word by bringing her favourite patient to the mobile library.

'How lovely,' she said to Patrick with a laugh. He made his way slowly down the aisle towards her.

He looked tired, with swollen eyes, while the stubble growing back slowly on his ill-treated head didn't exactly improve his appearance.

Seda took a step towards Patrick, with the firm intention of embracing him, but he stopped so abruptly that she left it for the time being.

Christ, I'm nervous, she thought.

As if this were a first date.

Rather than the last goodbye.

The thought of it filled her eyes with tears, and as she didn't want to break down crying in front of Patrick, there was only one thing for it: talk! And like a waterfall – it was

349

the only tactic she knew and the best one to avoid losing your composure.

'Okay, I know you don't want to hear this, perhaps you won't understand it either, but I have to say it. You're just going to have to hang in there, okay? Right, I'd like to say thank you. Honestly. Thanks for having confided in Simon. There was an investigation, I'm sure you know. Obviously. But you really helped get Kasov suspended. They found incriminating material on his computer, stuff like that. Now he's probably going to be charged and I'm free.'

She laughed like an excited teenager, while Patrick looked as if he'd had a stroke. His face had totally frozen.

Alright, keep talking. Don't stop. Otherwise he'll turn around and go before you've got it off your chest.

'I'm sorry for what he did to you, Patrick. You have to know that everything about you in the written record of your interrogation, about the fact that you deliberately wanted to kill Jonas, your son – all of it was a lie. It was a misfortune. Kasov made up the story about the sauna. He just wanted to turn Armin against you, make the psycho silence you, because Armin hates people who torture children. I tried to warn you in the canteen, do you remember?'

She laughed again; this time it was more forced. 'But that doesn't matter now. The only thing that counts is that because of you Kasov is history and I'm being released. And I have to thank you for that.'

She went up to him and threw her arms around his body, which had become too thin.

Patrick did what he had done throughout her waterfall monologue. He stood there, unmoved, even stiffening more in her embrace.

Eventually, when she realised he wasn't going to show the slightest emotion, Seda unclasped him and took a step back. Only now did Winter say his first words.

'I think you must have got the wrong person.'

And Seda, no longer able to hold back her tears, swallowed heavily, blew a hair out of her eyes and said, 'Yes. I know.'

77

PATRICK WINTER

Strange.

This young woman with her amber skin and oriental features smelled so nice, but her behaviour was so weird.

Alright, she knew his cover name; it wasn't a secret in the Steinklinik. But what was that story about Kasov and Jonas and an accident?

He groped his way to the back of the bus. To the third bookcase, second shelf.

For God's sake.

He had to call Skania urgently, to check the cover he'd been given. His brother-in-law really could have prepared this better, even though he'd had very little time to plan for the assignment. But the story about the phantom patient couldn't wait. They were talking on the radio already about how an illicit trade in medicines was thriving in German hospitals. If he waited any longer someone else would snatch the story from under his nose. And it shouldn't be a tall order for a policeman of Skania's calibre to provide the appropriate alias for an investigative journalist like him.

Patrick Winter. He knew little more apart from the fact that the guy had worked as an actuary. And that Winter played piano – as he did, thank goodness – but that was bound to be the only thing he had in common with the mathematical genius.

He glanced at the young woman up at the front of the bus. She was no longer looking at him; he could get going.

Ulysses. *Where are you?*

His eyes scanned the spines of the books and eventually he found it, exactly where Skania said it would be.

Bookcase three, shelf two, behind the Bibles.

'I hope you've done your job properly,' he whispered to himself and opened the tome, which surely nobody apart from him had ever picked up in this psycho prison.

Bingo!

As Skania had promised, the emergency mobile was in the hollowed-out centre of the book. It would allow him to keep in touch with his contacts.

He put the book back behind the Bibles. His visit today was just an initial recce. He wouldn't make a call until he'd found out something of substance.

He wandered to the front of the bus.

'Did you find everything you wanted?' asked the woman, who was sitting behind the driver's seat with a magazine in her lap.

'Yes, thank you.'

He paused as the bizarre feeling crept up on him that he'd seen this young woman with the dark hair and even darker eyes before. It was merely the shadow of a memory. Not exactly déjà vu, more the feeling that a special connection existed between them, even though in reality they were total strangers.

Maybe it was just wishful thinking, for in normal life he probably wouldn't dare approach her.

But here he had nothing to lose, so he gave her a smile and said, 'You're being released soon?'

She nodded shyly.

'You could leave me your phone number if you like. You can jot it down in a book of your choice.'

She giggled. 'Would you look through all of them until you found it?'

He returned her smile. 'Possibly. But I doubt I'll have the time for that.'

'No?' Her bottom lip was quivering.

'No.' He smiled, surprised again at the hint of deep sadness in her face. Just now she'd almost cried before suddenly hugging him as if they were lovers bidding farewell for the final time.

Her lower lip kept quivering and now he really wanted to embrace her. Tell her the truth. Tell her that he wasn't a patient and that he'd be out of here soon once his assignment was over. Because he wasn't Patrick Winter, the actuary, but an investigative journalist. He couldn't, however, let her in on this, no matter how pretty she was. No, he mustn't jeopardise his mission.

For the time being, therefore, he made do with just shaking her hand.

The woman opened the door for Winter and he got out of the mobile library without looking back at this strange beauty who seemed so oddly familiar.

Like a book you've once read.

A long, long time ago.

In another life.

And now, instead of the usual acknowledgements, a mini-thriller.

With the imaginative title:

The Acknowledgements

The Acknowledgements

The room was white and padded like a Chesterfield sofa, which was another thing that surprised me in addition to my panicky state. This sort of time-out room (known in popular parlance as a 'padded cell') barely existed in Germany any more. And those that did were sky blue or pink rather than white – at least not such an intense white that would make you worry about becoming snow blind merely by staring at the ceiling. At that moment I, Sebastian Fitzek, wasn't capable of much more, strapped as I was to something that felt like a cold, hard operating table. With a head vice that was as tight as the shackles on my arms and legs.

Maybe I wasn't in Germany any more? Had my abductor, who was observing me via the ceiling camera, taken me abroad?

I was assuming that I'd been abducted, even if I'd slept through the entire process. The last thing I remembered was having taken my manuscript of *The Inmate* to the post office so Droemer Verlag could begin production. Even by my own Fitzek thriller standards, it seemed a bit far-fetched to suggest that I'd drugged myself immediately after coming out of the branch on Hohenzollerndamm, then sleepwalked straight to this secure cell where I'd strapped myself to the table.

It looked as if I were in for some treatment rather unusual for an author. Not that I'd pride myself that much on my professional status. The first question people with normal jobs ask me when they learn what I do is: *'Oh, you can earn a living doing that, can you?'* This, however, was not the question my abductor had asked me soon after I regained consciousness.

He'd simply said, 'Who?'

He'd now asked me this question eleven times – or, at least, eleven times that I'd counted. He talked to me via an invisible audio device of such extraordinary quality that the bass of his voice made my skull vibrate.

'Nobody,' I answered with a dry mouth. And I was sure I was right. I'd never forgotten anybody in my previous acknowledgements.

I usually begin the eulogies at the end of my books with the people who really matter. The readers, of course! If my abductor believed I had to list them all by name then I was in an even worse situation than I'd feared.

'Oh, yes, Sebastian, there is one name,' he said. 'You've written seventeen books now and this name doesn't appear in any of the acknowledgements. It's simply been withheld. Even though without his help you'd never have written a single bestseller.'

I frowned – virtually the only movement I was capable of without my skin being cut by sharp fetters – and thought hard.

Who did he mean?

My abductor had made it clear that quite a lot was dependent on the answer. Including my life. He hadn't spelled out his threats, but that was unnecessary. As soon as I woke up I noticed that a headache and parched throat (both presumably side effects of having been drugged) were not the only things causing me physical discomfort. Besides the possibility of movement, I was also lacking something quite vital for my survival: air. There was a paucity of oxygen in the cell I'd only ever experienced on the treadmill in the gym. And as the inquisition went on, I found it harder to breathe. The padded room must be hermetically sealed; it was just a matter of time before I would suffocate if I couldn't remember the name my abductor wanted to hear.

Hmm.

If I hadn't been the victim here I would have thanked the person for the excellent plot idea.

'Who have you forgotten, Sebastian?' asked the voice that sounded annoyingly familiar, but whose name eluded me. It won't come as news to those who know me well that I have an absolutely dreadful memory for names and people. I'm also often very confused. I was in a playground recently and shouted out the name of my ex (Gerlinde), when all I wanted was for my daughter Charlotte to get off the swings. It was as difficult for me to explain this to my wife – who was also there – as it was to tell my abductor which helpful individual I'd forgotten all this time in my acknowledgements. (At any rate it wasn't my ex, Gerlinde, to whom I dedicated *The Soul Breaker* in gratitude for having inspired so many psychological thrillers.)

In my mind I ran through the publishing team, beginning with Doris Janhsen, who I really hadn't mentioned before, but only because my ability to see into the future is rather limited. How could I guess that she would take over as publisher from

Hans-Peter Übleis and send the company soaring to ever-dizzier heights?

'Not Doris,' the voice said in answer to my anxious enquiry. Which also eliminated the rest of the Droemer Knaur team: Josef Röckl, Bernhard Fetsch, Katharina Ilgen, Monika Neudeck, Bettina Halstrick, Beate Riedel, Hanna Pfaffenwimmer, Antje Buhl, Katharina Scholz, Sibylle Dietzel, Ellen Heidenreich and Daniela Meyer. I'd thanked all of them. Many of them several times. And rightly so.

Apart from...

Steffen Haselbach? I mused. This time he'd even helped with the German title after I was unhappy with my own suggestion. But no, I recalled having mentioned Steffen at least once before.

'Is Helmut still angry, by any chance?' I asked the faceless voice coming from the wall.

'Henkensiefken?' the voice replied.

'Yes.' For many years I had indeed forgotten him and his Zero agency, even though he's responsible for all the fantastic covers, including that of the German edition of *The Inmate*.

'No.'

'It can hardly be my editors,' I said, trying to be funny. Carolin Graehl and Regine Weisbrod have starred in all my acknowledgements, even though I wouldn't mind seeing the two best editors in the world locked up in a cell, especially when they stick their fingers into my literary wounds and find 150 logical errors in a manuscript that I believe to be 150 per cent perfect. If anybody, then Andrea Müller might be bitter. She discovered me in 2004, then climbed the ladder of success to another publishing house. But I'd mentioned her several times too.

'Water,' I said, which wasn't a name. I was thirsty and in urgent need of a glassful. If possible one the size of North Rhine-Westphalia, but my request met with a negative response, as did my suspicion that Regina Ziegler might be behind this abduction. It's not that I could imagine Germany's most successful film producer capable of such torture – however cinematic it might be – but Regina was somebody I hadn't mentioned before, even though I'm deeply indebted to her for having believed in me and my books for almost a decade and for having brought *Cut Off* (my collaboration with Michael Tsokos) to the big screen.

I began thinking out loud.

'Christian Meyer, my tour manager, would be more likely to tie me up at a service station on one of our long car journeys across Germany than in this cell here. And my manager, best friend and so much more, Manuela Raschke, might complain that I never wash out the coffee cups in the office, but I've already dedicated two books to her (and rightly so, for she *is* the best!). She's supported by a wonderful team of crazy people who put up with me, such as her mother Barbara, Achim, Sally, Karl-Heinz (sport-mad Karl-Heinz wouldn't have dragged me here, but to his torture gym in the basement where the treadmill would explode the moment it fell below speed 16 at 12 per cent gradient), Stolli and most recently Angela Schmidt.'

'Murhhh,' the voice went, then imitated the ticking of a clock. The pressure on my ribcage seemed to be increasing.

'Sabrina Rabow isn't just the best PR agent, she's also so kind and sensitive that even the thought of me lying here in chains would give her nightmares. Wouldn't it? Wouldn't it?'

'Not Sabrina,' my abductor said curtly. 'Not your

mother-in-law Petra, nor your web designer Markus Meiser, nor Thomas Zorbach. No, you've thought of all these people. Just not me.'

Me?

Okay, I admit it should have been obvious that the voice might have personal reasons for all this. But if you were to wake up restrained in a padded cell, with your head feeling like it's spent a week at a heavy metal festival, I dare suggest that your reasoning might be somewhat hindered too.

Right, then. It was clearly a man. That much I could hear. All the same I could discount Simon Jäger and David Nathan, the audiobook gods, because this voice sounded too amateurish, without professional training, if fairly pleasant.

It was also too deep for Roman Hocke, even if he were to try to disguise it. (I don't wish to give anyone the impression that my literary agent has a squeaky voice, but it doesn't make my skull vibrate in the manner I mentioned at the beginning.) Besides, Roman would have been busily engaged in negotiations for my release because haggling is in his blood. No, Roman would be the negotiating genius who could free me from this difficult situation, although not without keeping his 15 per cent share of the ransom money. And I've also had good reason to thank Markus Michalek often enough.

On account of their female voices, Roman's colleagues at AVA were out of the reckoning too: Claudia von Hornstein, Antonia Schultes, Cornelia Petersen-Laux and Lisa Blenninger.

My favourite Bavarian in Berlin, test reader and maker of countless helpful comments, was definitely a man, but apart from the fact that I'd once written his name incorrectly, Franz Xaver Riebel couldn't really complain about a lack of recognition either. Nor could my family, first and foremost the great love of my life... er... um... oh yes, Sandra (*the oxygen is running out!*) and Sabine and Clemens. (Thanks for the medical advice, including the description of an operation. Right at this minute, however, instructions for cutting through my shackles to avoid death by suffocation would be more useful than a diagram of the *carotis communis*.)

I was slowly getting angry.

Hadn't I always made every effort not to forget anyone? Hadn't I always thanked all the booksellers, librarians? Look, other people wrote 'Hello, darling' on the last page or listed names that mean nothing to anybody, and *they're* not strapped to an operating table in a padded cell, but having a ball on the beach on the Côte d'Azur.

'Pass,' I said, and the voice laughed gleefully.

'Okay, you've only got a few seconds anyway before your eyes swell up so much that you can see the blood running down your cheeks.'

Not a bad line, I thought, trying to commit it to memory before realising that the chances of me ever being able to use it were pretty slim.

'Well, then, I'm going to use the time we have left to tell you.'

I felt even worse.

'Who?' I said, wondering at the same time whether I really wanted to know.

Who had I forgotten?

The answer was as unexpected as it was obvious.

'Your subconscious.'

You mean the unconscious, I was initially tempted to contradict him, then fortunately it occurred to me that these weren't the most auspicious circumstances in which to highlight a lack of linguistic precision to an invisible abductor prepared to resort to extreme measures.

Then I realised why the voice sounded so omnipresent. Why it increased the pressure beneath my skull. Why I believed I'd heard it often before.

'Why did you decide to use the experiences with your best friend and mentor in *Therapy*?' he asked.

Because they were my own!

'Who ensures that your mother's death keeps finding its way subliminally into your novels? Strokes, locked-in syndrome? Eh? Any ideas?'

I nodded and blacked out.

'Who do you think was responsible for highlighting a father's inability to prioritise properly in *The Eye Collector*, where he leaves his children alone far too often? Hypersensitivity in *Splinter*, repression in *The Package*, and all the separation anxieties you feel as a father? Well?'

The voice grew louder; it was shouting and I was desperate to find a switch to allow me to put an end to all this, even if the thing only went one way and all light, warmth and life would be extinguished forever the moment I pressed it.

'Have you thanked me even once? ONE SINGLE TIME?'

The voice in my head, *MY OWN VOICE*, was cracking.

'YOUR CO-AUTHOR???' my unconscious self bellowed at me.

'No,' I heard myself admit in my own mind. 'I'm sorry.'

He or it didn't seem to have heard my apology or didn't want to accept it, for he said, 'I'm taking over now. On my own. Without you.'

What?

'Taking over?' I croaked.

'Yes. The stories are going to come from me alone. You're going to keep your trap shut.'

With these words, the room, the white and the light vanished, and for the final question I used up the last remaining air in my lungs.

'Hey, what about a happy ending?' I cried.

The short story surely can't end like this!

'Happy endings are overestimated.' His voice echoed around all the chambers of my consciousness, which closed individually until only one was left open. The one I'd come through a very long time ago. And then…

About the Author

SEBASTIAN FITZEK is one of Europe's most successful authors of psychological thrillers. His books have sold 12 million copies, been translated into more than thirty-six languages and are the basis for international cinema and theatre adaptations. Sebastian Fitzek was the first German author to be awarded the European Prize for Criminal Literature. He lives with his family in Berlin.

Walk Me Home

'Fitzek's thrillers are breathtaking, full of wild twists'
Harlan Coben
'Fitzek is without question one of the crime world's most
evocative storytellers' **Karin Slaughter**

**The terrifying psychological thriller by
internationally bestselling phenomenon Sebastian Fitzek.**

The Walk Me Home telephone helpline service has proved
indispensable. Staffed by volunteers, it provides a reassuring voice
at the end of the phone, helping to protect lone women as they
walk home at night.

Jules has only been working for Walk Me Home for a short time
and has never had to deal with a truly life-threatening situation.
But that all changes one Saturday night when Klara calls.

The young woman is terrified. She thinks she is being followed
by a man. A man from her past. A man who drew a date in blood
on her bedroom wall. And that day dawns in less than two hours...

For Klara – and Jules – the stakes have never been higher.

Will either of them ever make it home again?